# GERIANTICS

# GERIANTICS
*Rezzies Revolt*

*Carlos and Crystal Acosta*

This is a work of fiction. Names, characters, businesses, places, events, locales, and incidents are either the products of the authors' imaginations or used in a fictitious manner. Any resemblance to actual persons, living or dead, or actual events is purely coincidental.

ISBN 978-1-70460-223-3

Cover design by Carlos and Crystal Acosta

Cover illustrations:
Senior citizen image by Kolotailo Lidiia / Shutterstock
Hallway image by tinkivinki / Shutterstock

Original and modified cover art by Ano Lobb and CoverDesignStudio.com

# Acknowledgments

We wish to thank the members of all the writer's groups to which we belong. Your critique of our manuscript and your helpful suggestions helped us become better writers. More importantly, your encouragement was vital to keeping this project on track.

We are also indebted to our beta readers: Blaine, Debbie, Laurel, Nancy, Parker, and Rebecca. Your candid feedback led to some serious re-writing which significantly strengthened the story.

# CHAPTER ONE

It spread among the residents of Freedom Retirement Active Independent Living—FRAIL—like weevils in a cotton field, growing more malignant, more terrifying with time. And it had to be stopped.

It was a stormy Monday afternoon. The sounds of conversation and pinball filled FRAIL's activity room. Two of the more agile residents—rezzies—were putting up Cinco de Mayo decorations, even though none of the current crop of tenants were of Mexican heritage. Four rezzies sat at a wobbly card table, engaged in a tense discussion that was delaying the start of their poker game.

Bill Armstrong swept his hand over his bald head in frustration. "Don't get carried away. I've heard many a rumor in my eighty-two years on this earth. The sky is *not* falling."

"I know what I heard," Martin Fokker insisted. "I'm not senile yet."

Helen Hackett set down the well-worn deck of playing cards she'd been shuffling. "All I can say is that I hope you're wrong. I have no idea where I would go if this place closed down. It's not as though we can choose from a long list of retirement homes. This is the only one in the county."

"*Oui*," agreed Philippe Pelletier, Bill's closest friend at

FRAIL. "And who would have the means to pay, even if there was another *maison retraite* nearby?" Despite having lived in America most of his adult life, Philippe remained distinctly French, from his diction to his pencil mustache. Sometimes he even wore a beret, although not today.

"That's right," Helen said. "Since FRAIL is funded by a big nonprofit, we don't pay near the full cost of living here. I doubt there's any place like this in the entire state, and if there is, it probably has a long waiting list."

"Yeah, and with my luck I'd die before they got down to my name," Martin grumbled.

"Always zee doom and zee gloom with you, *non?*" Philippe said, fiddling with the poker chips. "Have you not considered that perhaps the people ahead of you on the list would pass away *en premier*? You might advance more quickly than expected."

Martin blew his nose. "Maybe so, but I bet I'd kick the bucket before I could move in. Then I'd lose my nonrefundable deposit and be really angry."

Helen fell into her nervous habit of un-braiding and re-braiding her long white hair. "Bill, why aren't you worried?"

"Why should I get bent out of shape over hearsay?" he replied. "I promise to go to pieces once the movers take my couch out from under me. How's that?" He pulled his walker close and stood.

"It's not like you to be in denial," Helen said with narrowed eyes. "Aren't you afraid of losing everything you have? Don't the close friendships and endless social activities mean anything to you? Personally I would sink into depression without them. And I'd dread having to watch reruns of old sitcoms, all by myself, all day long."

*She's not going to let this go.* Bill sighed and eased himself back into his chair. "I'm not disputing the impact. Of course I would be devastated. I came here after selling my house and moving across the country so I could be near my

2

granddaughter. Once I retired from the Air Force as a full-bird, Edith and I vowed never to move again because we were tired of relocating every few months. Oh, Edith …"

Philippe put down the last of the poker chips he had been neatly stacking. "It is evident that you miss your wife very much, Colonel"—using his usual French pronunciation by pronouncing each "L" in the word.

"I certainly do," Bill whispered, then rubbed his gray mustache. *I've felt so lonely and vulnerable since she went to be with the Lord.* "It's comforting to live here where we rezzies look out for each other."

Helen flipped the page of the miniature spiral notepad she used to keep game scores. "There you go, then. We need to *do* something. Let's brainstorm."

"It's only a rumor," Bill snarled.

Martin pounded the table, knocking over Philippe's stack of poker chips. "I tell you it's *real*. I was at the reception desk, visiting with Lisa, and I overheard Roger on the phone talking about selling the building. You can't get a more authoritative source than the facility administrator's own words."

"Why were you bothering Lisa?" Helen asked, raising an eyebrow.

"I believe that Martin, he has the crush on *la belle réceptionniste*," Philippe teased.

Martin's oversize ears turned pink. "Look, I also heard him say something about tenants, vans, and deadlines. How much more proof do you need?"

Bill furrowed his brow and stared Martin in the eye. "What did Roger say when you asked him how long it would be before we had to move out?"

Martin's bushy eyebrows amplified the surprised look in his eyes. "I … I didn't ask."

"Then let's do that first." Bill retrieved his cell phone from the basket and searched for Roger's number.

# # #

3

Odia Fangmeister had been sitting alone in her analyst's waiting room for only fifteen minutes, but was already tired of staring at the framed diplomas decorating the walls. It was inconceivable that Dr. Terah P. Sessions could have earned that many degrees and certifications unless she had started medical school at age four.

Dr. Sessions stuck her head in, brushing her curly red hair out of her eyes. "Hello, Odia. Nice to see you again. Come on back."

Odia followed the psychologist into the dimly lit office and sat in a dark leather recliner with scuffed armrests. A floor-to-ceiling mural depicting an alpine valley covered in wildflowers filled her view. The room was as quiet as an empty recording studio, except for the gentle sound of water trickling down a decorative tabletop waterfall.

The doctor positioned a wingback chair to Odia's left, picked a piece of lint off the forest-green velour upholstery, and sat.

"What's on your mind today?" Dr. Sessions asked.

Odia pushed a button on the armrest to recline the chair slightly away from vertical and extend the footrest. "I've been going to shrinks since I was a teen, and I still have problems. I want to be well."

"You agreed not to refer to us as 'shrinks' anymore. Now please continue."

"I still get terribly anxious every day. Nothing seems to help."

"Do you use the calming techniques I taught you previously?" the doctor asked.

"Yes, but it's not enough. I can't function without my meds, but I'm desperate to get off of them. Using drugs got me into this mess. I feel like I've simply traded illegal drugs for prescribed ones."

"Why does that bother you?"

Odia's thoughts flashed back to the recreational drugs she used in her twenties that had forever altered her brain chemistry. "Because I feel defective. Every pill I take is a reminder that my mind is broken."

"What do you think you should do differently?"

"I'm going to start my own rehab center," Odia announced.

"Oh?"

"Soon I shall launch Paranoia Intervention Education and Drug Rehab Assistance, or PIEDRA for short. An all-in-one intensive treatment and research facility."

"Why not check in to an existing holistic recovery center?" Dr. Sessions asked.

Odia brushed aside the suggestion with a dismissive wave. "I doubt yoga and horseback riding will do the trick. I prefer to create a brand-new, breakthrough treatment that will cure me once and for all."

"That's very interesting. How will you finance such an endeavor?"

"I'll approach a nonprofit foundation. It's only a matter of time until I get the money."

"How many beds will you have?" Dr. Sessions asked.

"Beds?"

"Yes, how many clients will you accommodate at one time?"

"No clients. Just me. PIEDRA scientists will devote themselves solely to healing me. May I have some water?"

The therapist rose and fetched a bottle of water from a small refrigerator. She handed it to Odia and resumed her seat. "Are you sure it's realistic to assume that someone will fund an enterprise for the benefit of a single person? Wouldn't it be better to share your findings with others in your situation?"

Odia stopped unscrewing the bottle cap. "Why should I? Let them start their own clinic. I'm not responsible for anyone else's problems." She resumed opening the bottle and then gulped the liquid.

"Mental health research is enormously expensive. What

will you do if you don't obtain the necessary funding?"

"Oh, I'll get it," Odia said. A soft whirring sound added to the gurgling of the fountain while she retracted the footrest.

"Humor me," said the therapist. "Imagine that something completely out of your control prevents you from securing the money or attracting qualified researchers. How would you handle that?"

Odia sprang out of the chair and glared at Dr. Sessions. "Humor you? You just don't understand, do you? I don't deal in 'What if ...?' scenarios. Nothing will stop me from finding a cure for my condition. Nothing!"

"I see," the doctor said. "Please, sit down and try to relax."

Odia began pacing. "I can't relax! That's the problem, you quack. I see what you're trying to do, you know. Your profession doesn't want me to find a cure. You're sowing the seeds of doubt so I don't put you and your colleagues out of business. Well, you're wasting your breath. I'm going to be cured, or I'll die trying, literally. But not without first wreaking havoc on those who conspire to thwart my efforts."

The doctor stood. "For the record, are you threatening me?"

Odia stopped pacing. "For the record, no. Off the record, don't oppose me." She glanced at her watch. "Same time next month?"

# # #

Thunder rumbled as Bill flipped his phone shut. "Roger is coming here to explain everything."

"Aha!" Martin said, thumping the table again and knocking over another stack of chips. "So he didn't deny it. I think I'll go start packing."

Bill gave him a stern look. "You'll stay right here until this whole matter gets cleared up."

6

Philippe gathered the errant poker chips. "And no more pounding of the table, *s'il vous plaît.*"

A minute later Roger Franklin entered the activity room. "Hello, hello. May I have your attention for a second, please?"

Cards were laid down and bingo games were suspended as he made his way to the center of the room where he would be visible to everyone.

"Colonel Armstrong called me a few minutes ago," Roger went on. "Apparently some of you are under the mistaken impression that FRAIL might be closing."

Several residents nodded in confirmation. A few simply nodded off.

Roger displayed a toothy smile that would outshine that of any game-show host. "I can assure you, FRAIL is not in danger of shutting down."

The rezzies applauded.

"Hopefully that puts your minds at ease. I guarantee that your home will be safe and secure as long as I am your administrator. Remember, I'm here to serve you. Finally, let me thank the Colonel for bringing this worrisome rumor to my attention."

Martin raised his hand.

"Yes?" Roger asked.

"I won't say who, but …" Martin's eyes shifted nervously. "Well, someone said they overheard you talking about moving vans, and tenants, and selling the building. Are you saying they made it up?"

"Oh, that? People shouldn't eavesdrop, but I guess it's my fault since I left my door open. It's nothing to do with FRAIL. You see, I'm part owner of a run-down warehouse. We've sold it to a group of investors who are going to turn it into condominiums."

Emily Crankshaft raised her hand, but did not wait for Roger to acknowledge. "That doesn't make me feel any better. This place could be the run-down warehouse you're referring to. Heck, look around. Half the lights in the hallway are out, and the landscaping is nothing but sand and tumbleweeds."

Roger shook his head. "That's a result of efforts to save energy and water. We have to protect our planet. I'll say it again: FRAIL is not in danger of being shuttered."

"Roger?" Bill cleared his throat. "You qualified your statement by saying we were safe as long as you were in charge, right?"

"I certainly can't control what will happen if I'm not here, now can I?"

Bill leaned forward in his seat. "Why even bring up the possibility?"

"I didn't bring it up. You did." Roger turned red and started to fidget. "I mean, I said it, but only to be completely accurate, you know?"

"How long do you plan to stay at FRAIL, then?" Bill asked.

"I'm late for a meeting. We can discuss your concerns later. For now, please rest easy. You're not going to be turned out. Happy Cinco de Mayo." Roger waved and hurried away.

Bill turned to Martin. "Did you learn anything from this experience?" *I sure did. Roger's hiding something.*

# # #

Odia entered the lobby of The Law Offices of Cozen and Craven and approached the twiggy receptionist. *Another twenty-something tart with perfect hair and makeup. It's no wonder my sister divorced him.* "I'm sorry I'm late. I was seeing my shrink."

The woman waved her through without saying a word.

"I'll just go on in, shall I?" Odia asked without waiting for a reply.

Cozen's suite was the stereotypical successful attorney's office—expensive mahogany furnishings, pretentious art, and absolutely no indication that any work, legal or otherwise, was conducted within. The lawyer rose from his genuine-leather executive chair and gestured for her to sit in one of the visitor chairs.

Odia nudged him aside and sat in *his* chair. She opened the humidor situated atop the desk and took out a cigar. "I see you've got a new decoration in the lobby. What happened to the last one? Did she object to staying after hours with you?" Her nose wrinkled as she slid the unlit cigar beneath her nostrils and assayed its aroma.

Cozen sat in a visitor's chair. "I resent the implication."

"And my sister resented your hanky-panky with that law school intern two years ago," Odia countered.

He frowned. "Alleged hanky-panky. There was no proof."

"I distinctly recall—"

"That's all in the past. Now, can we discuss the real issue?"

Odia marveled at Cozen's silver mane, styled like that of a 1970s country singer. *He must sleep with a hairnet to keep it so tidy.* She gave him a nod.

He flicked a piece of lint off his European-tailored shirt and adjusted his imported silk tie. "I hear you're still out of work."

"No thanks to your bungling. You couldn't get an innocent nun acquitted."

"I wasn't hired to defend you. I represented Have Mercy Hospital. They had to let you go after you retaliated against that nurse."

Odia stiffened. "I did not retaliate against Maggie Providence. I fired her."

"You can't do that once an employee files a formal complaint about workplace conditions. You messed up. End of story."

"Did you call me here for a lecture, or to help me get my job back?"

"I have something better to offer: come and work for me."

"Never." She set the cigar down and started toward the wet bar.

"No, hear me out." Cozen got up and recaptured his desk chair. "I don't mean here at the law office. I have a job for you with the Kreakey Foundation. You would report to me, on paper, but in reality you would rarely see me."

Odia used the tongs to clink four ice cubes into a glass, one at a time, then poured two fingers' worth of scotch and took a sip. "Are you still the chairman there? I thought for sure they would have forced you out by now."

His countenance suggested worry. "The truth is, they will if anyone discovers what I've done with their money. But that would be the least of my troubles."

"Gee, that's tough. Can we get back to my problem? What is this job?" She set down her glass.

"Not too different from your former supervisory duties at the hospital. Only now you would be in charge of an entire nonprofit program and its facility."

"Why would I want to do that?" She opened his mini-fridge and helped herself to a bottle of mineral water.

"The position pays well and provides good medical benefits, which you need, since you're unemployed."

Odia twisted off the bottle cap and guzzled water like a college student chugging beer during spring break. Excessive thirst was an unwelcome side effect of her prescription medications.

"What's the catch?" she asked.

"I need your help to skim funds from the facility's budget so I can restore what I've *borrowed* from a different program."

"What would I have to do?"

"I've got, er, agreements with suppliers and contractors who don't mind inflating their invoices. You will pay them without asking questions," he said.

10

She dropped the empty bottle into the wastebasket and returned to the desk. "And the extra money eventually finds its way to you, eh?"

"Something like that."

Odia picked up the cigar and carelessly manipulated the hand-rolled Cuban *puro.*

"Are you gonna light that?" he asked.

"No." Odia broke the stogie in two and flung both halves across the room. "I hate smelly things. And your offer sounds stinky."

He glared at her. "So you don't want the job, I take it?"

"Who's presently running the show over there?"

"Don't worry about that. He's not working out."

"I take it that he won't fudge the numbers for you?" she asked.

"Let's just say he's insubordinate and won't be there much longer."

Odia leaned forward. "If I agree, you've got to promise to help me create PIEDRA."

He cocked his head. "Create *what?*"

"Paranoia Intervention Education and Drug Rehab Assistance," she elaborated.

He laughed. "Really? PIEDRA? You know that's the Spanish term for crack cocaine, don't you?"

"It's not funny. There's desperately needed research to be done."

Cozen crossed his arms. "Be serious. This sounds like another one of your wacko causes, like the time you wanted to stop continental drift."

"Why is nobody interested in averting imminent calamity? You'll be sorry someday when you go out to your mailbox only to find Scotland scraping the sod off your front yard."

"If I were you," Cozen advised, "I would support something more mainstream, like saving the rain forest."

"I don't associate with environmentalists. They

overreact."

Cozen swiveled his chair to face the enormous picture window behind his desk. The view of run-down, single-story stucco edifices in the foreground diminished the grandeur of the red-rocked buttes in the distance.

"I can help you organize it," he said over his shoulder, "but you'll have to come up with the capital on your own."

Odia stood and walked to the office door. "Not good enough."

"What if I help you get a grant? You know, seed money?"

She twisted the doorknob. "I'll think about it," she said, then pulled open the door and left.

# # #

Bill leaned on his walker as he plodded through the narrow corridor on his way to a meeting in the dining room. Exactly one week had passed since he had confronted Roger about the rumored closure of FRAIL.

A clot of hallway gossipers impeded Bill's progress. "Keep moving!" he ordered in his military command voice. "You can chat once you get inside." *They certainly don't dilly-dally when it's mealtime, but …*

A squeal, like a mouse scraping its claws on a tiny chalkboard, signaled the approach of Ed Cutter. Bill plugged his ears in dramatic fashion. "Ed, why are your hearing aids in your pocket again?"

Ed stopped and saluted. "Hi, General. I sure hope they have snacks. Ice cream would be great. Pistachio. But I only like straight pistachio, not the kind with pralines."

*He obviously didn't hear me. Oh well.* "We had ice cream last week. And stop calling me 'General.' I keep telling you that I was only a colonel."

Ed ran his fingers through his thick white hair, making it stand on end. "Isn't it odd to have a town hall meeting on a Monday? Do you know what it's about? When I worked as a medical examiner, unscheduled meetings were always bad news. They were either layoffs, reorgs, or sensitivity training." He grimaced. "I don't need instruction on how to coddle people. Those delicate folks who easily get their feelings hurt should spend six weeks in boot camp so that—"

Bill put his hand on Ed's shoulder. "Enough, *Mr. Sympathy*."

Upon entering the dining room, Bill steered his walker hard to port and immediately noticed the spacing between tables was unequal. *Sloppy civilians.* "Come on," he said, pointing to the table directly in front of the lectern. "Let's sit there so you can hear."

"Not for me. Too early for beer," Ed said.

Bill backed his walker into position and made a soft landing in the seat. He noted the contents of the dessert dishes already arranged at each table. "Sorry, Ed, it looks like pudding today." He looked up and smiled at the server as she filled his glass with ice water.

*SPLAT.* From the corner of his eye, Bill saw the glob of tapioca strike the front surface of the lectern and cling to it. He turned to Ed and frowned. "Ed, really. Spoons are for eating, not for use as catapults."

Ed stuck out his tongue. "I hate tapioca pudding. It looks like boogers."

Bill shook his head and looked around the room. His granddaughter, Maggie—one of the personal care assistants on staff, or PCAs—was arguing with a tall, thin woman at the back of the room. *Who is that?* He saw Maggie poke her in the chest a few times, then turn and stomp out. *I wonder what that was all about?*

The woman, sporting a surgical mask and latex gloves, made her way to the lectern. Her comical bobbing and weaving suggested she wanted to avoid contact with the residents.

Ed besieged Bill with a cannonade of queries: "Who is

the woman in the skirt suit? She's way too young to be a rezzie. Why is she wearing a surgical mask? I hope she hasn't got anything contagious. It would be just my luck to be exposed to tapioca and tetanus on the same day."

Bill made a throat-slicing gesture, signaling Ed to suspend his salvo of speculation.

As the mystery woman neared the lectern, she lowered her mask and pulled an inhaler from her pocket. She locked her lips around the mouthpiece and took two puffs. A snarfing sound accompanied each inhalation. She raised the mask.

Ed leaned in Bill's direction. "Good golly. She looks like Popeye's girlfriend Olive Oyl."

The woman adjusted the angle of the lectern-mounted microphone. "Allow me to introduce myself. I'm Odia Fangmeister."

Bill flashed a look at Ed. "Don't," he said. There was no telling what derisive utterance Ed was formulating in response to hearing the unusual surname.

Odia continued, "Roger Franklin arranged this meeting as his last official act before leaving suddenly to pursue other interests. I'm your new administrator." She waited for the assorted gasps and general murmuring to subside. "I can tell you from experience that you will not like me. That works both ways."

The woman's insolence astounded Bill. Compared to Odia, drill sergeants were courteous and cuddly.

Odia scanned the room with her beady eyes. "I am an expert at operational efficiency. Changes are coming that may inconvenience you, but so what? FRAIL is not a theme park. It's a place for old people like you to kill time until —"

A resident at an adjacent table raised her hand.

"I don't take questions," Odia snapped. "Put your hand down."

Shouts of disapproval erupted from the audience.

Odia pulled a teeny gavel from her vest pocket. She

14

rapped it against the podium until the commotion abated. "That concludes this meeting," she said, adjusting her mask as she fled the room.

Bill tapped Ed on the shoulder. "How do you like our new overlord?"

Ed shrugged. "She could use sensitivity training."

# # #

Two days later the sound of a passing fighter jet disrupted Bill's unplanned nap. The ringtone was surprisingly realistic and often fooled his fellow rezzies.

"Hello, Maggie," he said with a raspy voice.

"Oh, Grampa, were you asleep? I'm sorry. Can I stop by for a minute?"

"Come on over. I'm not going anywhere." Flipping the phone shut and returning it to his pocket, he arose from his easy chair and pointed his walker toward the door. A knock came before he had taken a step. "Is that you, Mags?"

"Yes, Grampa. May I come in?"

"As long as Ed isn't with you. If he is, leave him outside." He heard her chuckle.

Maggie slowly opened the door and peered inside. She wore her blueberry-hued scrubs.

"I'm way over here," Bill said, letting her know she wasn't about to bean him with the door.

His overprotective granddaughter escorted him to the tiny dinette.

"You don't have to fuss over me like this, but I kind of like it," he said, and smiled at her.

She sat opposite him and tucked her straight, dark-brown hair behind her ears. Tears welled up in her hazel eyes. *She looks just like her mother.*

"Oh my," Bill said. "What's wrong?"

"It's a long story and I don't know where to start."

Bill fished a tissue from the basket on his walker and handed it to Maggie.

She scanned the ceiling as if it held a clue for where to begin, then flung herself into the narrative like a bungee jumper leaping off a bridge. "I can't afford to lose my job again, but Odia's going to fire me to get even for filing the complaint and making her lose her job at the hospital —" She took two short, sudden breaths, then continued, "And there's nothing I can do about it, and I hate myself because I'm a washed-up single mom at age twenty-six ..."

He offered up the entire box of tissues as Maggie's composure deteriorated into a watery display of woe. *Well, I'm lost.* He would have to get the backstory, at the risk of further upsetting her.

A few minutes later she apologized for getting emotional. After a deep breath she calmly enumerated her troubles.

"There's a lot there that I never knew about," Bill said. *I think I understand now.* "You say you blew the whistle on Odia, and she fired you in retaliation?"

"Yup. Then I spoke with a lawyer and threatened to take the hospital to court. They ended up settling with me, and I heard from former coworkers that Odia got the boot right after that."

Bill shifted in his chair. "If that's the case, she'd be a fool to sack you again."

Maggie shook her head. "That woman's a menace — rude, demanding, insulting, vicious, and vengeful. And those are her good qualities. She'll make every workday positively miserable until I won't be able to stand it."

He stroked his gray mustache. "It sounds as though she has sharper fangs than the creature from *Alien*."

"More like the basilisk serpent from *Harry Potter*. Either way, it's worse than a nightmare. I wish I could quit."

"Well, you can't. You have a seven-year-old who depends on you, and this little town isn't exactly overflowing with decent-paying jobs." He sighed. *In my day you didn't think of running away. You stood your ground.*

"What have I done to deserve her as my boss a second time?"

Bill took her hand. "I'm sorry you've had to endure so much trouble from her." He empathized with Maggie, but he had no sympathy for her victim mentality. "Do your job. Do it well. Maybe it won't be as terrible as you imagine."

"Grampa, if only I could believe you." She glanced at her watch. "Gotta go. I love you." She hugged him and walked out, shutting the door behind her.

Bill returned to his comfy chair and stared out the window. His granddaughter could use an infusion of courage, and a good wingman to watch her back. He pondered how best to do it.

# # #

Odia peered out of her office and spoke to the receptionist's back. "Lisa, I'm off to a meeting and don't know when I'll return." She retracted her head like a threatened tortoise and shut the door. Off came the surgical mask and latex gloves. Wearing protection was a burden, but what choice did she have? Everyone knew—didn't they?—that old people were teeming with virulent geriatric germs. Once infected, her body would enter an irreversible downward spiral of decay, no doubt culminating in gout and gum disease.

She grabbed her backpack and left through her private door that led directly to the parking lot. This cut her chances of picking up any geezer microbes the lobby might be harboring.

Odia walked around her black BMW twice, on the alert for leaking brake fluid or missing lug nuts. Using a mirror attached to a telescoping rod, she looked for explosives strapped to the chassis. *You can never be too careful.* Satisfied, she got in and sped off to meet Cozen at the isolated location she had staked out earlier. It took ten minutes to get there.

*The fool.* His red Ferrari was fully visible from the highway. He had ignored her directive to stay out of sight. Odia drove a little way past the rendezvous site, parked behind a faded billboard, and walked back. She called out to Cozen as she neared the half dozen empty boxcars coupled together on the railroad siding.

"I'm in here," he replied from the open door of a graffiti-marred railcar. "Why in the world did you pick this place? This is railroad property. We could be arrested for trespassing."

Climbing into the car took every bit of strength the muscles in her wiry arms could rally. *How did hobos jump into these things while they were rolling?* "Trespassing schmesspassing. The important thing is that our conversation not be overheard," she said, patting the dust off her skirt.

"You are the most suspicious nutcase I've ever met. My office would have been private enough, and a lot more comfortable." Cozen walked to the end of the boxcar and back. "There's nowhere to sit down in here."

"Then you won't mind if I get to the point," she said. "I've looked at FRAIL's finances, and the bad news is that I don't think your scheme will work."

"Oh, so you're suddenly an accountant?" he sneered.

"It doesn't take a CPA to know that you can't rob Peter to pay Paul if Peter has no money. I'm guessing you would have to double FRAIL's budget before you could skim enough to repay what you stole from Kreakey's other programs."

Cozen frowned. "Not to worry. I did the math. My plan will work just fine."

"You're fooling yourself. But I came up with a strategy that might save your sorry carcass after all."

His eyes widened. "What is it? Tell me. Tell me."

"FRAIL has to be shut down completely."

"What? How does that help?" he asked.

18

"Just think how easily you can cover your tracks amid the chaos and expense of closing it down. After that, divert the money to something useful. Just don't open another wretched retiree refuge."

Cozen shook his head. "It's not that easy. The Bengais Trust provides dollars to Kreakey through a restricted temporary endowment. We can only use the funds to run a senior living facility."

Odia reached into her backpack and pulled out the endowment's governing documents. "Don't tell me there's not an escape clause somewhere in all this legal gobbledygook." She tossed the spiral-bound pages onto the boxcar's wood-planked floor.

"Where did you get those?" he asked.

"I found them in Roger's old files at FRAIL. Read them."

He scratched his chin. "I know what they say, and there may be something we can do, but it's a long shot. If it ever became 'unnecessary, impracticable, or impossible' to operate FRAIL, then we could exercise our variance power and deploy the money elsewhere."

Odia bounced up and down on her toes. "Well, there you go. I'll get started," she said and made for the door.

"Hold on there." Cozen scrambled to intercept her. "Even if I agreed with you — and I don't — we would need an airtight plan that guarantees success before Kreakey's books are audited three or four months from now. It can't be done."

"That kind of attitude is why you'll never accomplish anything greater than probating wills. Now get out of my way, and I'll start making it pointless to operate FRAIL."

He turned and stared at the arid landscape outside. "I don't like it. How can we show that FRAIL isn't needed?"

"Leave it to me. I'll also tackle the endowment's 'impossible' condition. Meanwhile you've got work to do too."

19

He twisted around and gave her a surprised look. "What do you want me to do?"

"Line up your ducks so that when the time comes, the board will agree to fund PIEDRA with the freshly liberated endowment funds."

# CHAPTER TWO

One day later PCA Josie Ditzski was in the FRAIL library receiving a UHL — unsolicited history lesson — from outspoken resident Helen Hackett. Popular with the residents, especially the men, Josie nevertheless could not shake the feeling that Helen disfavored her.

Helen glared at Josie over the top of her reading glasses. "How am I supposed to find a book in this chaos? Why aren't we organized under the Dewey Decimal System? When I was in school, they held us back a grade if we couldn't use it properly."

"Yes, ma'am." Josie adjusted her long blonde ponytail. *Does she think I'm an airhead?* "What if — "

"Josie to the lobby," demanded a static-distorted voice over the public address speaker. *What is it now?*

"Well?" Helen crossed her arms and scowled.

Josie silently counted to ten to contain her frustration. "Miss Helen, maybe they need the Dewey System to organize the Library of Congress, but we barely have a hundred books on our shelves."

Helen's expression softened. "Hon, the Library of Congress doesn't use Dewey. Why don't you answer your page? I'll keep searching on my own."

Josie blushed and departed. *I hate it when she corrects me.*

21

All the way to the lobby, she puzzled over why the Library of Congress would not use Dewey. She greeted the receptionist. "Hi, Lisa. Are they remodeling Fang's office?"

Lisa grimaced at the jarring sound made by a power tool grinding away at metal. She shouted, "They're installing a new door!"

The noise stopped.

"It's steel-clad and airtight," she said at normal volume. "An electronic badge reader will limit access to her alone."

"Won't you need to get in sometimes?" Josie asked.

"I tried to tell her that. She'll have a button under her desk she can press to let me in. Perhaps Ms. Fangmeister will change her mind if she has to keep buzzing me through for every little thing. Did you want something?"

Josie giggled. "You paged me, remember?"

"Oh, so I did." She ran her fingers through her blonde, feathered hair. "I can't think straight with all the commotion. Ms. Fangmeister wants to see you in the conference room."

The grinding noise resumed, and Josie traversed the short distance to the open door of the compact meeting room. Odia was assisting a short-haired Hispanic man in his thirties who was completing employment paperwork. He had tattoos on his neck and arms.

"It's about time," Odia screeched. "Did you stop to check your hair and makeup first? I'll have to remember not to hire any perky, former cheerleaders in the future."

"Sorry, Ms. Fangmeister. What did you want?"

Odia stuck a gloved finger beneath her mask and scratched her nose. "This is Manuel Escondido. He's our new building custodian. Show him where everything is."

"What happened to —"

"He didn't work out," Odia barked.

Josie suppressed a gasp. "You fired him?"

"He quit. Now stop the cross-examination and get on with your work. And take" —she pointed at Manuel— "him with you. *Adios."*

"Hello, Manuel. I'm Josie." *And I wouldn't blame you if you quit before the week was out.* "Let's go take a look around."

Immediately after exiting the room, Josie paused in the hallway. "The building is shaped like a capital T. The offices, amenities, and lobby are in the up-and-down section, and way over there," she indicated the far end of the corridor, "in the crosspiece is the residential wing."

Manuel nodded.

"When do you start?" Josie asked.

"*Que?"* he responded with a quizzical look.

"What day did Ms. Fangmeister tell you to report for work?"

He wiped his hands on his pants. "Oh. I starting now."

Josie escorted him past the activity room, coffee shop, and dining room. They encountered Maggie in front of the Gray Trader convenience store. Josie introduced Manuel to her.

"Pleased to meet you," Maggie said. "Do you like doing maintenance?"

"Where are the *viejitos?"* he asked, ignoring the question.

Maggie pursed her lips. "We don't call the residents 'old people,' Manuel. They prefer the term 'rezzies.' They'll soon be heading for breakfast."

"Are they mean?"

Josie laughed. "Not at all. In fact Maggie's grandfather, Bill, is a rezzie. You'll like him."

"Odia's staff meeting starts in ten minutes," Maggie growled, shaking her head as she walked away.

"Come on, Manuel," Josie said. "I'll show you the shed out back where all the tools and stuff are kept."

Manuel looked around suspiciously.

"Are you okay?" Josie asked. *Why is he so nervous and fidgety?*

His eyes darted up and down the corridor. "Any *viejitos* retire from *policía*?"

# # #

One week later—and exactly ten days after taking over as FRAIL's administrator—Odia dialed Lisa on the desk phone. "Bring me a copy of the activity schedule and a list of upcoming outings. Now!"

She had confidence in her ability to capitalize on the endowment's technicalities. All she had to do was execute her clever game plan. *I won't even break a sweat.*

There was a knock on the metal-sheathed door.

"Come in." Odia pressed the button beneath her desktop. A solid *clunk* from the metal doorframe confirmed the bolt had retracted. The heavy, intrusion-proof door swung open as ponderously as one of the lock gates on the Panama Canal.

Lisa entered the undecorated office and placed a folder on the gray, metal desk. "Here are the schedules you asked for, Ms. Fangmeister." On the credenza behind Odia, a police scanner emitted a bolus of garbled, nasal-toned speech.

"Which are the most popular outings?" Odia asked.

Lisa pulled a sheet from the folder and checked off three items. She showed the list to her boss.

"Cancel those for the rest of the year," Odia commanded. "And cut the frequency of the others by half. Then cancel anything in the activity room after five in the afternoon."

Lisa, wide-eyed, returned the sheet to its folder.

Odia waved her arms. "Oh, don't look at me like that. Make the changes and post notices all over the building."

"Yes, Ms. Fangmeister."

"Is Manuel working days or nights this week?" Odia asked. "I never know."

Lisa thought for a moment. "I think it's days. Shall I

24

look for him?"

"Get him on the phone and transfer the call in here."

"Yes, Ms. Fangmeister," she said, then took her leave.

Odia tried wringing her hands malevolently but the latex gloves made it too difficult. Uttering "Heh, heh, heh!" would have to do for now.

"Ms. Fangmeister," Lisa announced over the intercom. "I have Manuel on the line."

Odia depressed the Speaker button on her desk phone. "Manuel, listen. Change the locks on the activity room. Make sure it's a unique key and don't give copies to anyone. I want the room locked after five o'clock every day. *Comprende?*"

"I do it next week—ees okay?" Manuel replied.

"Do it today, you lethargic lunkhead."

"Okay, *Jefe.*"

"I'm not your chief. I'm Ms. Fangmeister."

"Okay, Meez Fongmystorss."

Odia sighed. "On second thought, call me *Jefe.*"

She hung up and grinned under her mask. *Get rid of the fun and you get rid of the geezers.*

# # #

The following day Bill and Philippe waited patiently at a tiny table in FRAIL's coffee shop. It reminded Bill of an airport eatery—a shallow recess in the corridor with insufficient seating.

Charlie Newcomb shuffled up to their table, fumbling with a blister package containing two coin cell batteries. "I just came from the Gray Trader. Six dollars for two little buttons of lithium and manganese, and they don't even last six months in my remote control. I have a mind to design the ultimate coin cell and put these guys out of business."

"But you were not a designer of zee batteries, were you?" Philippe asked.

"Heavens, no. I was a physicist. Specialized in nuclear

medicine research. I was one of the very few blacks in the field back then. Not too many women took up physics either, but the ones that did were top notch."

The barista came over. "Here's your order," she chirped. "Charlie, can I get you anything?"

"No, thank you, dear."

"Tell us how you would design this superior battery," Bill said, silently registering approval of Charlie's "regulation" haircut. *It's more salt than pepper, but it's better than being bald.*

After checking for eavesdroppers, Charlie leaned in. "I'd make it nuclear," he said in hushed tones. "A power cell based on betavoltaic technology could last for years. There was a paper by L.C. Olsen in the '70s that discussed the theory. Problem is, environmentalists get their underwear in a knot at the mere mention of radioactivity. That's why I doubt consumers will ever see atomic batteries—even though they would be perfectly safe."

"People have different comfort levels when it comes to radiation," Bill said, removing the plastic lid from his coffee cup. "If it were as harmless as you claim, my dentist wouldn't wrap me in a lead jacket and flee the room when she x-rays my incisors."

Charlie's wife, Wilma, scurried over, waggling a finger at her overdue husband. Her hair was jet black and almost as short as his. Her gray sweater was buttoned askew.

"You said you was just goin' for batteries to power the remote," she said. "I been waitin' on you so I can watch my detective show. I shoulda known you'd get distracted."

"I'm comin', Wil. But first I want to ask the Colonel what he thinks about Odia locking the activity room every evening."

Wilma put her hands on her hips and narrowed her eyes. "I don't know how that hateful Fangster woman ever got hired. She got no right keepin' us out of that room."

Philippe took a sip of coffee. "Perhaps Madame Le Fang

wishes us to stay in our rooms. Do not the statistics say old people are more likely to suffer a tumble in the night?"

"If we were in bed early, she could drop evening PCA coverage and save money," Charlie opined.

"Whose side are you on?" Bill asked. "That would put Josie out of a job."

Wilma dragged a chair over from the adjacent table and sat. "She got somethin' coming if she thinks I'm going to crawl into pajamas right after supper."

Martin approached the table.

"Shh!" Charlie said. "Here comes Martin the Morose."

"I heard that." Martin gently thumped Charlie on the back of the head. "It's like I've been saying all along. This place is gonna shut down and we'll be on the street. It's inevitable."

"How do you make the leap from activity cutbacks to homelessness?" Bill asked, finishing his drink and replacing the lid.

"I don't need a billboard to spell it out. They'll cut back a little here, a little there. Next thing you know, we'll be digging latrines when they turn off the water to the building. If we have any sense, we'll evacuate before it gets to that — no pun intended."

"Oh, go be gloomy somewhere else," Wilma said. "I'm not gonna let a locked door stop me from having fun with friends."

"Monsieur le Colonel, what action do you recommend?" Philippe asked.

"Wait and see. According to Maggie, Odia's never run a facility like this. She's bound to make mistakes. One could argue that we need to help her avoid more serious blunders — ones that actually could lead to closure."

"Like failing to renew FRAIL's license?" Martin muttered as he ambled off.

# # #

27

Josie was enjoying the usual calm of second shift since the rezzies didn't need much assistance once dinner was over. This gave her over five hours to herself. Most nights she would hide out in the PCA office and struggle with coursework for her medical assistant degree.

At 9:15 her studious concentration was disrupted by a call from resident Emily Crankshaft of suite 203.

"Hello, Miss Emily. This is Josie. How can I help?"

She listened while Emily loudly protested that the neighbors were making too much noise. Josie closed her laptop and got up from her chair. Emily moved on to a general rant about inconsiderate people. Josie feared Emily was winding up to deliver her usual diatribe about enforcing rules. "Miss Emily, it will be okay. I'll go check on it right away. I won't tell anyone you complained." *Although everyone will assume it was you.* "I'm hanging up now, Miss Emily. Good night."

She started toward the suites. The admin corridor was as quiet as a silent movie on Mute, but as she neared the residential wing, the reason for the complaint became clear. Johnny Cash music and loud laughter radiated from suite 201.

Josie knocked. "Ed, come to the door, please. It's Josie."

The music stopped. The door opened ever so slightly and Charlie peered out. "Uh, hi, Josie."

She heard someone behind him mutter, "Quiet. It's five-oh."

Charlie grinned. "I'd invite you in but, um, the place is a mess." His face looked flushed.

The din of chairs being dragged across tile and the clinking of glassware raised Josie's suspicions. "Ed! Please come out."

Charlie backed away and Ed appeared. "Good evening Josie," he said, his voice oozing with innocence. "I see you've been talking to Charlie."

Josie crossed her arms and tapped her foot like the

perpetually grouchy teacher she had in third grade. It was difficult to keep from laughing. Nevertheless Mrs. Crankshaft's complaint required investigation and a firm response. "What's going on in there?"

Ed waved his hands. "Nothing at all. Charlie and I were just enjoying a friendly game of cards." He stuck his hands in his pockets.

Josie crossed her arms. *There's more to this story.* She waited.

"Just to pass the time," he added. "It's been three days since Fangenstein locked up the activity room and threw away the key. There's nothing to do."

She wasn't satisfied, so she probed further. "I don't believe you. May I come in and see for myself?"

"Er ... if you must." Ed stepped aside.

Josie entered the apartment. Playing cards and poker chips covered every available flat surface, except for the floor. A quick tally resulted in eleven rezzies, counting Ed. *Thank goodness they're all fully clothed.* A random check of glassware turned up nothing alcoholic, but a plate of goodies caught her eye. "Ooh, are these brownies?"

Charlie thrust himself between Josie and the brownies like a defensive lineman on the last play of the Super Bowl. "Don't eat those!"

She jumped to a worrisome conclusion. "Hold on a minute. These aren't…"

"It's not what you're thinking—no illegal substances involved. They're part of the card game. We're playing Gin Runny and the loser of each hand has to eat a brownie."

"Don't you mean 'Gin Rummy'?"

"No, I mean 'Runny' because certain brownies are laced with Mega-Lax. It's a mixed blessing. You may have a slow night at the game table, but you'll be moving fast the next day. And probably the day after that too."

Josie rolled her eyes and laughed. *I didn't see that coming.* Discarding the facade of disapproving disciplinarian, she ended the raid with a friendly admonition: "If you're going to play cards, please do it quietly so the neighbors won't complain. No loud music, no loud voices, and no more purgatorial prizes—unless you want to clean commodes all week."

# # #

The same evening, Odia parked at the Buckaroo trailhead in Verde Bend Park and turned off the headlights. She climbed out and gingerly closed the door—nearly pressing the Lock button on the key fob before remembering she didn't want to trigger the *whoop-whoop* of the alarm. This one time she would sacrifice security for stealth.

Gravel crunched under her feet as she made her way to the rendezvous point by moonlight. It occurred to her that, being late spring, rattlesnakes were active. *Great.* It wouldn't do for a Fangmeister to die of snakebite.

She arrived and went inside. A foul stench instantly assaulted her nostrils. She left the door ajar and hoped the smell would escape through the gap.

The urge to pace the floor was stronger than a teenager's desire to squeeze a zit, but the confinement and darkness made pacing impractical. Standing still made her muscles tense and twitchy.

She activated her phone. *Two minutes to eleven.* The display's brightness illuminated dozens of spiderwebs. A glimpse of the silky nets was all it took to make her itch all over. She slipped the phone into her back pocket and tried to pretend the webs weren't there.

Footsteps outside commanded her attention. She held her breath. The stink became slightly more bearable. *Why didn't I think of that sooner?*

The sound of crunching gravel stopped. Seconds elapsed, but the knock she expected didn't come. More time passed. *What is he waiting for?* She strained to hear. *Did he leave?*

The door jerked open. "Ack!" Odia gasped and grabbed her chest. *Good thing I saw the cardiologist last week, but now I need to see a urologist.*

"The squeaky wheel catches the worm," she managed to say.

"But don't burn your bridges before they're hatched," whispered a male voice.

*It's him.* He had the right pass phrase. "Were you followed?"

"Who would follow me into a porta potty?" he asked.

She pulled him inside. They were pressed so close together, it was almost indecent. "Open your jacket," Odia demanded.

"Huh?"

"I wanna be sure you're not recording us."

"Lady, this ain't no spy movie. Can we get started? It reeks in here."

A cursory pat-down of her contact yielded only car keys and a small flashlight. "You can't be too careful. People are always out to get me." She returned his keys.

"You're nuts," he mumbled.

"No, just careful," Odia said, then reached into her pocket and produced a yellow sticky note. "Can you get this for me?"

The man took back his flashlight and shined it on the slip of paper. "Whoa." He aimed the light at her face. "This is dangerous stuff."

She nudged his hand to direct the light beam away from her eyes. "Only if you're careless."

He shrugged. "It's crazy hard to get something like that. Why do you want it?"

"I want to make sure something ends and stays ended."

He switched off his flashlight. "That'll do it, no doubt."

"Good. How soon can I have it?"

"It's not like buying milk at the grocery store," he grumbled. "When I have it, you'll be the first to know. Now let's get outta here before we die of asphyxiation."

"Well, get started then," she urged, and pushed him out the door.

# # #

The next morning, Odia waited impatiently for Maggie. *That girl is always putting those geezers ahead of me. I don't have all day.* She buzzed Lisa. "Page Ms. Providence again."

Lisa replied immediately, "She's right outside your office."

*Clunk.* Odia rose from her chair as soon as Maggie came into view. "Get in here and shut the door before some stray pensioner accidentally wanders in looking for their cat."

"You wanted to see me?" Maggie asked as she put her weight against the heavy door and shoved it closed.

"No, actually I'd rather not see you, but I find it necessary." Odia placed her hands on her hips. "It has come to my attention that the codgers were misbehaving last night."

"Could you be more specific?"

Odia lowered her mask. "You need to prevent them from getting into mischief. Is that specific enough for you?"

Maggie's fists clenched. "I *meant* give me details of who was involved and what they were doing."

"Don't play dumb with me. You know full well I mean the all-night gambling and the karaoke over the public address system."

"What makes you think those things happened?" Maggie asked.

"I have sources."

"Who?"

"None of your business. Those retired reprobates were having unauthorized fun. Make sure it doesn't happen again." Odia retrieved a compartmentalized pill organizer from her desk drawer, flipped open one of the lids, and dumped the contents into her palm.

Maggie crossed her arms. "How do I do that? Whatever you think happened wasn't even on my shift."

"I don't care how you do it," Odia replied. "Confiscate their playing cards or something, but get those radicals under control." She popped the handful of assorted tablets into her mouth and chased them down with bottled water.

"They're acting up because they're bored," Maggie said. "You could restore access to the activity room and give them back their scheduled outings."

"That's out of the question. I'm not running a resort."

"The residents are probably upset that you didn't consult them before making changes."

Odia replaced her mask. She walked around the desk and positioned herself just inches in front of Maggie. "I dictate the policies here—no one else. And soon there will be other cost-saving actions."

Maggie took one step back. "Would you like me to tell them that?"

"Say nothing."

"Somehow I don't think they'll put up with your dogmatic decrees for long."

Odia tossed her head back and cackled. "What can they do? Hit me with their canes? Run me over with a walker?"

Maggie's eyes narrowed. "It would serve you right if they did."

"You insolent pest. I should—"

"What? Fire me? I dare you," Maggie said, red-faced and wide-eyed.

"No," Odia said calmly. "You'll soon quit on your own, if only to ensure your grandfather continues to enjoy himself at FRAIL. Be sure to shut the door on your way out."

# CHAPTER THREE

It was nearly time for shift change. Maggie sat in her chair in the PCA office and sulked. She had spent most of the afternoon here after the argument with Odia. *I'll go crazy if I stay here any longer, but I can't quit and let Odia win. I've got to stay to be sure Grampa isn't mistreated. ... I hate my job.*

Josie bounced into the office, her ponytail swinging like a pendulum. "Hi, Maggie. Have a good day?"

"Actually, no. I'm a little miffed at you."

Josie stiffened. "At *me*? What have I done?"

Maggie stood. "Did you tell Odia about the karaoke and the card game?"

Josie looked surprised. "No. Absolutely not."

Maggie frowned. "She's upset that the rezzies are still having fun despite her clampdown. She gave me a good scolding this morning."

"I'm sorry that happened to you."

Maggie's eyes narrowed. "I don't like Odia yelling at me for stuff that happens on *your* shift. You should be the one on the carpet. They act up on your watch because they know you'll look the other way. You're a pushover."

Josie suppressed a gasp. "I try to give them the benefit of the doubt, that's all. They're not troublemakers. They're just reacting to Fang's random acts of unkindness."

"Well, her unkindness to me wasn't random at all," Maggie griped. "How did she find out?"

"I doubt the rezzies are ratting on each other," Josie said. "I wonder if Manuel's been watching us."

"And you had to let him know that Bill's my grampa. I'm sure he blabbed it to Odia, because now she's blackmailing me."

Josie shut the door to their office. "Calm down, and lower your voice. What do you mean she's blackmailing you?"

Maggie closed her eyes and exhaled slowly. *I could use one of Odia's panic pills right about now.* "She said that my grampa won't be able to enjoy living here unless I quit."

Josie reached out and placed her hand on Maggie's shoulder. "Oh, goodness. What do you think she meant by that?"

"Obviously she's going to exercise her gift for making people miserable."

"What are you going to do?" Josie asked.

"First of all, I'm not going to tell my grampa. I wouldn't want him to move out just to save my job."

"Has Odia asked him to leave?" Josie asked.

"Grampa hasn't said so," Maggie replied, "but I wouldn't put it past her. Or maybe Grampa would offer to go voluntarily in return for Odia keeping me on."

"But you're miserable here. It's not worth all of that to stay in a job you hate."

Maggie sighed. "It is if you desperately need the money. Besides, it's not the job I hate; it's the boss. In the meantime I'll look for a position somewhere else."

"I'm so sorry you're going through this. Let me know how I can help." Josie looked at the wall clock. "It's time to give the monthly safety briefing."

"Oh no," Maggie moaned. "I forgot about that."

"Why don't you go on home and let me handle it?" Josie offered.

"Nope. The rules say we've both got to be there, and I don't want to get in trouble again. Let's go."

# # #

Bill entered FRAIL's travel-sized movie theater and traversed its length to sit in the first row. The venue barely accommodated four-across seating with an aisle on either side. Lengthwise it held five rows, plus an open space at the rear for wheelchairs. The ceiling was slightly taller than a typical single-story room, and the screen simply hung from the front wall. It felt like going to the cinema in a repurposed motor home.

He turned when he heard Maggie and Josie greeting rezzies behind him. "Hello, Mags. Is tonight's lecture about the perils of wheelchair races again?"

She waved to him, but said nothing

Bill frowned. *That's not like her. Something's on her mind.*

It was ten full minutes before the slow-motion ballet of seat selection and settling-in concluded.

The two girls marched up front, and Maggie began, "Thank you for coming, even if it *is* mandatory. Tonight's safety topic is emergency evacuation procedures."

A paper airplane soared over Bill's head, swooshed past Maggie, and crashed into the movie screen.

He saw the fury in Maggie's eyes and instantly rebuked the most likely culprit: "Ed! Shut down the departures."

"Who said I did it?" Ed sassed.

Maggie resumed the briefing, reminding the rezzies to *shelter in place* safely during a fire alarm, rather than rush to an exit and risk a fall or smoke inhalation. "I'm not making this up, in case you were wondering. This is in accordance with NFPA Standard 1616, and it's backed up by scientific studies."

Josie tackled the inevitable "But what if...?" questions from those who had a pathological need to debate the finer points of everything.

The discussion soon strayed onto ridiculously improbable scenarios. Martin demanded to know what to do if "an unstable megalomaniac released nuclear, biological, or chemical agents in the lobby."

Bill gestured "cut it short" to Maggie.

"We're out of time. Thank you for your attention," she announced.

Helen raised her hand. "Hon, we're not done. We've got questions for you."

Bill sagged. *Oh no. I asked her not to make waves.*

Ed stood. "Yeah, like, is the wicked witch going to rescind our bathroom privileges?"

"You wait your turn, Ed. I've got the floor." Helen waved her fist. "We used to have endless entertainment before Funheister started interfering. Now we're having less fun than a rottweiler during a postal strike. You might say we're all shook up."

"What are we supposed to do to pass the time?" Wilma asked. "People in prison have it better."

"I suppose it could be worse," Martin grumbled. "The capricious commandant might decide to stop feeding us."

Bill struggled to his feet and steadied himself with his walker. "I'd like to say something if I may." He eyed the crowd of curmudgeons. "Neither of these two angels created the problem. Let Maggie finish speaking." He maneuvered himself back into his seat.

Maggie mouthed "Thank you" at Bill and searched for words. "I guess I'll just come out and say that I'm sorry Ms. Fangmeister is causing problems for you. I'm not sure what I can do about it. She certainly doesn't listen to me."

"We appreciate your sympathy," Helen said, "but that doesn't undo the damage. We want restitution."

"I have no authority to change anything," Maggie snapped. "The best I can do is try to get Ms. Fangmeister to understand how you feel about the situation."

Bill shook his head. *That was weak. These rezzies want*

*action, not pop psych platitudes.*

Ed let out a Bronx cheer. "We don't need you to tell her how we feel. We need you to give her our demands! We want things back the way they were!"

Individual shouts of agreement and angry outbursts of "You tell her!" erupted like geysers.

Maggie, now on the verge of tears, looked at Bill and mouthed, "What do I do?"

He stood and faced the rowdy mob. "Enough. Everybody go to dinner. Meeting adjourned."

# # #

The following evening Bill looked disapprovingly at his dish of gelatin dessert. The quivering confection was an unnatural shade of blue that suggested it should be in a toilet tank rather than on the dinner table. "Does anyone want this? I refuse to eat nervous desserts."

"I don't," Helen said. "What flavor is blue, anyway? There's no blue food in nature."

"What about blueberries?" Martin asked.

"You taste it, then, and tell me if it's blueberry flavored," Helen retorted.

Martin sampled a spoonful of his own gelatin. "You're right. Tastes like cold medicine. Ech!"

Bill pushed away his clear glass dessert dish. A quick look around revealed that most of the others had also chosen to abstain from the blue goo. "I wonder if we'll ever get ice cream again. This place is deteriorating into a third-world retirement home."

"We've given Maggie our concerns," Helen said. "Let's see if things improve."

Martin was tapping his dessert bowl with his finger. He appeared to be fascinated with the gelatin. "Don't hold your breath. The girls won't say anything to Fangmeister."

Bill took exception to the remark. "For the record, Maggie *has* spoken to Odia about the activities."

Helen handed her glass to the server for a refill. "Well, that's a start. Maybe now that woman will realize she can't push us around."

"Unfortunately no," Bill said. "From what I can tell, she is unlikely to repent anytime soon."

Martin spiked his spoon into his jiggling dish of dyspepsia and left it standing like a flagpole. "My point exactly. It's time to find another retirement home."

Helen glared at him. "Try to contain your optimism."

"I don't blame him," Bill said. "It's hard to stay positive when the world is changing right under you."

"Did the führer give a reason for revoking most of our activities and outings?" asked Helen.

"Not a good one," Bill replied. "She told Maggie it was to save money, but I don't believe it. I'm pretty sure we can expect more changes soon."

"How does locking us out of the activity room save any money?" Martin asked. "We're either in there, or we're in our suites. We consume kilowatts regardless." He shook his head. "There must be another reason."

"Don't Maggie or Josie have *any* influence at all?" Helen asked. "Aren't they supposed to be advocates for us?"

Martin removed the spoon from his dessert. "This is a new regime. I imagine they've got to toe the line with this particular dictator."

Bill considered his granddaughter's predicament. Fate had been cruel when it doomed Maggie to work under Odia again. "Martin's right. The girls have to be very careful. From what I've heard, Odia doesn't think she has to answer to anyone."

"Something has to be done." Helen thumped her fist on the table. "If we're not going to push back, then we should pack up and leave."

Martin had produced toothpicks seemingly from out of nowhere. He was using them to create a blue gelatin porcupine. "Just five minutes ago you said we should wait to see if things get better."

Her eyes narrowed. "Well, I've changed my mind, okay? I doubt I've ever seen anyone as callous and hostile as Odia. I'll bet her mother used to leave lumps in her Cream of Wheat. What do you think, Bill?"

Bill ran his fingers over his chin. "I wouldn't know whether her Cream of Wheat was lumpy or not."

Helen rolled her eyes. "You know what I mean. Should we take action?"

"Like what?" asked Bill.

"Go toe to toe with Fangmeister," Martin suggested. "Intimidate her. Make her back down."

"With what leverage?" Bill asked. "Talking to her is a waste of time."

"We pay her salary," Helen said. "If you were to bring all the rezzies on board, we could withhold our rent and amenity fees. With you in charge we could get the woman's attention."

"Yes," Bill said. "And she would turn around and evict us for nonpayment. Anyway, not many of us would take that kind of risk. I say let's see how long she lasts. If she's trouble for us, she's probably trouble for her management too."

"Helen has a point. You would make a great rebel leader," Martin said.

"We need a strong organizer and battle-tested warrior to go up against that masked marauder," Helen added.

Bill sat back and crossed his arms. He didn't like the idea of letting Odia get away with bedeviling the residents. On the other hand the situation called for caution. *She's combative to the core.* Retaliation against the slightest resistance was practically assured. The collateral damage to the rezzies and to the girls could be severe.

If Bill had learned anything during his military career, it was that overwhelming force was needed to guarantee victory. He would always bring a nuke to a knife fight—

40

and win. He wondered if this particular gaggle of geriatric grumblers was capable of delivering the shock-and-awe necessary to prevail against Odia Fangmeister. *Why can't things just go back to being calm and orderly?*

Bill realized that Martin and Helen were staring straight at him. *They're waiting for an answer.* The "Cause" needed a tough and experienced leader.

"Well, Colonel," Helen said, "will you lead us?"

He uncrossed his arms. He had made up his mind. "No."

# # #

Bill took a seat at Helen's dinette table. He didn't think he would ever get used to her choice of décor. The crimson accent wall in the living room reminded him of a crime scene in a gangster movie. He halfway expected to have a run-in with Edward G. Robinson.

"I don't see why you stubbornly refuse to lead the fight against that masked miscreant," Helen said from the kitchen where she was filling her teakettle.

He sighed and passed his hand over his face. "We went over that last night at dinner."

Helen came out of the kitchen with two dainty teacups on a sterling silver tray. "I didn't like your explanation. Try again."

"Is there a certain right answer you're fishing for?" he asked.

"We want you to take charge of informing Odia in no uncertain terms that she cannot do as she pleases, or she will face consequences."

Bill raised an eyebrow. "*What* consequences?"

Helen waved her arms. "How should I know? That's why we need you, a military man, to draw a line in the sand and think up severe penalties for crossing it."

"I really don't think Odia's cost-cutting can be compared to one country threatening to invade its neighbor. Let's try to keep this in perspective."

"You've become a pacifist in retirement, I see," Helen said.

The teakettle began to whistle.

"This has nothing to do with war," he said as Helen started for the kitchen. "At worst it's a landlord-tenant dispute, and there are civil ways for dealing with such things."

The whistling stopped, and she soon returned with the steaming kettle and two tea bags. "Diplomacy only prolongs the agony and allows the enemy's fangs to grow, I always say."

"Why don't you just talk with Odia and tell her that you're unhappy with the recreation arrangements?"

"I've tried, but she doesn't return my calls." She poured water into their cups. "I even tried calling her boss at the foundation, but the person I reached told me they don't get involved with day-to-day management of the programs."

Bill lowered a tea bag into his cup. "I don't see how I would be any more successful."

She put her hands on her hips. "How did you get to be a colonel when you're so reluctant to launch an assault?"

"It's just a skirmish that merits a proportional response," he said. "The revolution you want is completely out of line."

She waggled her finger at him. "You mark my words. If we let her get away with things, she's going to escalate her capricious behavior. One day it will be too late to do anything."

Bill shook his head. "I doubt it will come to that. Look, all we need to do is work around the inconvenience. There's a town hall meeting tomorrow afternoon. You can confront her then."

# # #

Bill was counting on the rezzies to give Odia a verbal

pummeling at this afternoon's town hall meeting. This meeting would be the first since she took over the helm. Roger Franklin used to hold them in the dining room, and snacks were always provided. This one was scheduled in FRAIL's theater without so much as a bag of pretzels promised.

He claimed his usual seat in the front row. Philippe sat next to him. "A cent for your thoughts, Colonel?"

"You mean a *penny*, don't you?" Bill asked.

Philippe chuckled. "*Non*, I am French, remember, and it is a *cent* in Euros."

"If the rezzies behave anything like they did at Monday's safety briefing, Odia's gonna get a shellacking tonight." Bill checked his watch. *Five thirty. Time to start.* He looked around and saw the full complement of rezzies, but no staff or administrator. He was about to take charge and dismiss the crowd when Maggie and Josie rushed into the theater.

Maggie marched to the front, scowl on her face, clutching her laptop computer. "I'm sorry, but you'll have to be patient," she said to no one in particular.

Josie took the computer from her and went to a dark corner to connect it to the theater's projector.

"There was a last-minute change of plan," Maggie advised the audience. "Ms. Fangmeister will not be addressing you in person. Instead she created a video, which Josie is setting up to play. Let's give her some time."

"Is Odia dead?" Helen asked.

The room broke out in laughter, followed by applause.

"My mother, she would always say, '*Le mal ne meurt jamais*,'" Philippe said. "It means 'Evil never dies.'"

"Let's hope your mother was mistaken," Wilma said.

This prompted a chorus of "Amen!"

Bill waved his arm and caught Maggie's attention. "You'd better take control while you still have the chance," he quietly advised.

Maggie reached into the pocket of her scrubs and extracted a party-sized air horn. She held down the button for several seconds. The blast of noise startled the rezzies but achieved the intended effect.

"That wasn't what I had in mind," Bill muttered.

"Now that I have your attention," Maggie began, "let me be clear that I don't know what's on the video. Honestly I don't have a clue. Ms. Fangmeister gave me the DVD only minutes ago."

"Town hall meetings are supposed to be two-way affairs," Helen remarked. "Your boss needs to be here in person. Is she afraid of us?"

"Look, Miss Helen, I don't have an answer for you. Ms. Fangmeister does not explain herself to me. I'll tell her that all of you expected her to be here."

"It's ready to go," Josie said.

"Start the video," Bill commanded.

Playback began with the anachronistic black-and-white countdown that was common in 1950s educational films. The backward tally reached zero and a marketing photo of the FRAIL building filled the screen. The Beatles' 1967 hit "When I'm Sixty-Four" started up in mid-song at full volume.

*Is that the best she can do?* Bill recognized Odia's not-so-clever attempt to mock the rezzies by using the outdated film lead-in and the song about aging.

The opening shot dissolved into a plain pastel-blue background. The words "Town Hall Meeting" strained to make themselves visible. Bill shook his head. *White lettering against pale blue?* It was practically unreadable, especially by those with worn-out eyeballs.

An inset popped up, covering the lower right third of the frame. It showed a tall four-legged stool against a shiny golden-hued backdrop. The music stopped, followed by thumping and clicking sounds. Bill guessed it was someone fiddling with a microphone off-camera.

44

A slender individual, wearing a dark skirt and a light blouse, entered the picture and sat on a tall, backless stool. The shot captured her only from the neck down. Bill assumed it was Odia.

"Higher," said a voice in the video. Bill recognized Odia's nasal overtones.

"*Que?*" responded Manuel, off-screen.

"*Mas arriba,*" Odia replied.

The camera jerked upward and to the left. Odia's face, partially obscured by the surgical mask, now filled the inset, then snapped to full-screen.

"Good golly!" Ed blurted. "Nobody told us this would be a horror flick."

"Let's get this over with," said Odia, her voice muffled by the mask. "I promised to increase operational efficiency at FRAIL. Communicating by video is a great time-saver. It's the trend among capable leaders like myself."

"You're a legend in your own mind!" Ed squawked.

"I will cut right to the chase," Odia continued. "One of the most expensive amenities is our dining room service. Its operating costs are unacceptable. Yet rather than increase your meal plan prices, I have decided to implement an innovative solution for your benefit."

The needle of Bill's bovine waste detector pegged at maximum. Odia was about to unleash something so steamy and smelly that the cowardly controller couldn't risk a personal appearance.

"There will be no more weekend dining room service, effective Saturday, June twenty-first. Furthermore, Friday evening meals will be limited to cheese pizza, which will be sold on a per-slice basis. Now I know —"

Rezzie outbursts of "That witch!" and other venomous, unfiltered epithets drowned out the rest of her sentence. Josie paused the video.

Impromptu conversations sprang up among the rezzies. Bill silently mouthed "Get control" at Maggie.

Maggie gave the air horn another long blast.

"Could you stop doing that?" Ed complained. "You'll damage my hearing aids."

Bill stood and faced the audience. He raised his arms like Superman trying to stop a runaway locomotive and waited for the din to subside. "Before we come completely unglued, let's hear the rest. It may not be as bad as it sounds." *I think it's probably worse.*

Josie reversed the video a few seconds and resumed playback.

"... on a per-slice basis. Now I know you will immediately recognize the hidden benefits of this policy. I'm sure most of you were looking for reasons to spend more time in your individual kitchens. This way, you can be creative, stay active, and eat healthy. As always, my decision is final. If you think you can find a friendlier facility, I won't stop you from leaving."

Video color bars popped onto the screen, accompanied by the annoying "going off the air" tone from television's early days. Five seconds later the screen went black.

Maggie, still holding the air horn, faced the rezzies. "I ... don't know what to say."

Bill stood and started toward her as fast as his walker would allow. He reached her and put his hand on her shoulder. "It's okay," he said quietly.

He made eye contact with several of the seniors. *Good.* Their attention was on him. He was thankful that he had not lost his command presence, despite his imperfect posture. Still, he knew he had only seconds to suppress their sass.

"This was most unexpected," he said. "It will clearly have an impact on us, including me. It's not easy to get around the kitchen with a walker. On the other hand we have two weeks of grace. Let's use our heads and think through a rational course of action. Can we all agree on that?"

"After that, can we set fire to her office?" Ed asked.

Bill game him a menacing look. "You're not helping, Cutter."

# # #

"This will be our last weekend with dining room service," Helen said. Two weeks had passed since Odia announced the new policy. Helen had summoned Ed, Martin, Charlie, and Wilma to her suite. "Time has run out, and we need to brainstorm ways to compensate."

"Isn't Bill coming?" Martin asked.

"He's got some thinking to do," she replied. "I'm pressuring him to lead a rebellion against Odia — only I don't think he wants to." *But I'm going to wear him down like a glacier erodes a mountain.*

"You seem eager to raise a ruckus with the management," Wilma said. "Why don't you instigate the insurrection yourself?"

"I can plan a skirmish, but Bill is much better at war-winning strategy."

Martin cleared his throat. "I was thinking about the weekend meals. Why couldn't we get to-go plates from the dining room on Thursday nights? Each of us can eat leftovers until Monday."

"That would have to be one whopper of a doggie bag," Helen said. "Besides, would you like to eat the same thing for two days straight?"

"Did anyone read the flier that Lisa sent out?" Wilma asked. "It specifically says takeout boxes are no longer allowed."

Ed removed the hearing aid from his right ear and dropped it into his shirt pocket. "Battery died. I don't see the difficulty. We—"

"The problem," Charlie interrupted, "is that battery technology is stuck in the 1960s. If we were using atomic batteries—"

47

"That's not what I'm talking about," Ed growled. "As I was saying, we all have kitchens, and we know how to cook. It's not like we're gonna starve."

"Oh yeah?" Wilma sassed. "What about people who have trouble getting around, like Emily Crankshaft?"

"Yes," Helen added. "That's a real concern. But the main problem is even bigger than Emily."

"Nobody's bigger than Cranky," Ed muttered.

Wilma whacked him on the shoulder with a rolled-up magazine. "Mind your manners, you cantankerous clodhopper!"

"What I meant," continued Helen, "is that there's more to consider than just cooking. We would need to buy food every week. That's an extra expense — not just for the groceries but for delivery. Odia cut back on our complimentary shuttle service, and none of us drives anymore."

She noticed Charlie was staring at his shoes with a furrowed brow. "Charlie, what's bothering you?"

He stroked his chin twice and looked up at Helen. "This is a debacle. Not only will we need to shop, cook, and clean up on weekends, but our meal plans won't cost any less. I certainly hadn't figured on that."

Martin shifted in his seat. "Yeah, and who's to say Fangfurter won't take away the shuttle completely? Or she might decide to remove our kitchen appliances. If you ask me, I think it's time to move somewhere nicer."

"We're getting ahead of ourselves," Helen said. "Let's focus on one thing at a time. We can help each other cook and clean, but how do we secure enough food? Any solution has to work within our limited budgets and transportation options."

Ed raised his hands and rolled his eyes. "We're back to square one. Some plan you've got there, Einstein. You were right: you stink at strategy."

"Oh!" Charlie gently thumped himself on the forehead.

"Wait a second. I have the solution. It's so obvious, I can't believe I didn't see it sooner. Here's what we need to do ..."

# CHAPTER FOUR

Later that evening Charlie knocked on Martin's door.

Martin's muffled voice came through from the other side: "What's the password?"

Charlie had written down the password because he was afraid he would forget it. Unfortunately he neglected to bring the slip of paper with him.

"I can't remember the password."

"Charlie?" This time it was Ed Cutter's voice coming from inside the suite. "I'm slipping a hint under the door. Read it out loud."

Charlie carefully bent down to retrieve the note. He hoped that he would be able to straighten up again. He unfolded the note while slowly returning to an upright position. Without thinking, he read the contents aloud, "'Let me in. I ran out of hemorrhoid cream.'"

Embarrassment overtook him as he realized what he had said. *Hemorrhoid.* How could he forget a password like that? The sound of puerile giggling coming from behind the door only made it worse. "Ed, that's not funny. Open up!"

The door swung open. "Come inside," Ed said, laughing and wiping away tears.

"Enough horsing around," Charlie said with a scowl. "Martin, here's the list of items we need from the food pantry. You and I will go down the corridor, take some stuff, and bring it back here. I hope you had a nap today because you're gonna need your energy. It'll take us several trips to get everything."

Martin examined the list. "I don't know about this. It could take an hour just to find these things. And the more trips we make, the riskier it gets. Someone's going to catch us."

"Yeah? Like who? Josie will be busy braiding Helen's hair," Charlie said. "Manuel always buffs the floors in the admin wing at this time of night. No one else is here. Besides, Ed will be our lookout."

"Oh, great." Martin rolled his eyes. "We chose a deaf, attention-deficient comic to watch our backs. We're doomed."

Ed placed a large plastic shopping bag onto the dinette table. He reached in and pulled out two camouflage hunter's vests. "Here you are, boys. These have all the pockets you'll need for carrying the loot."

Charlie started to don a vest. "We'll take a bunch of ziplock plastic bags with us for the instant mashed potatoes. There's no way we can haul an entire bucket of powdered taters. We've gotta scoop some out and bag them. The same goes for rice and flour."

Ed reached into the shopping bag once more and withdrew two small flashlights. "Don't forget these."

"What are those for?" Martin asked.

Charlie tested his flashlight by shining it into Martin's eyes. "We can't turn on the lights in the kitchen and announce our presence, can we?"

Shielding his eyes from the glare, Martin nudged the flashlight aside. "By the way, how are we supposed to get in? Can you pick locks?" He placed his ear against an imaginary safe and twisted its phantom tumblers with his fingers.

"You won't have to. You can use this." Ed held up a key

for his co-conspirators to admire. "I got it from Roger Franklin last year when I helped with our Thanksgiving food drive. I was gonna return it, you know, but my memory is not what it used to be. Heh-heh."

Martin took the key from Ed and placed it into one of the front pockets of his vest. "All set, Charlie? Should we say a prayer before we go?"

"You mean ask God's blessing to break the eighth commandment—'You shall not steal'?" Charlie asked.

"No, I want to ask God to help me keep the sixth commandment—'You shall not murder,'" Martin replied.

"Who are you planning to kill?" Ed asked.

Martin pointed at Ed. "You, if you fail as a lookout and we get caught."

"Nothing's gonna happen," Ed said. "Besides, it's not stealing since we're paying for the food under our meal plans. Odia's stealing from us. Now get going."

Martin opened the door and carefully peeked into the corridor. "All clear," he said. "This is exciting. I've always wanted to go on a pantry raid."

# # #

Martin followed Ed and Charlie out of the suite and eased the door shut. He sent Ed toward Helen's apartment to verify that she was, indeed, distracting Josie. The main corridor to the admin wing ran almost directly into Martin's suite like a lane in a bowling alley. It wasn't a straight shot, however, because the prayer room jutted into the admin corridor, creating a dogleg. This was just enough to keep Manuel from seeing all the way up the hallway. Unfortunately it also kept them from making sure he was actually working where they expected.

Charlie had already covered half the distance to the food pantry. Martin paused and reached into his pants pocket. He produced a woolen ski mask and slipped it on. *The others should be wearing a mask too.* There was no sense in making it easy to be identified.

Martin sidled down the corridor, hugging the wall and hoping that he wouldn't be seen. He was falling farther behind Charlie. "Slow down, will ya?" he called out.

Charlie turned, flinched, and clutched at his chest.

Martin broke into an all-out geriatric shuffle to reach his stricken comrade. "What's wrong, Charlie? Is it your heart?"

"You old coot. You scared the granola out of me with that ski mask." Charlie took a few deep breaths. "Go on, unlock the door."

"Okay. Let me have the key," Martin said.

"What? Don't look at me. I saw you take it from Ed."

"I wonder where I put it," Martin mumbled. He began a slow, methodical search of his pants pockets. "Aha. Here we are."

"Nope. That's not it." Charlie waved his arms like a referee signaling an incomplete pass. "The one Ed gave you was not on a key ring."

"Oh, this must be the key to my room. I'd better not lose it." Martin searched his other pockets. "Ha. Here it is. It was in my vest pocket the whole time. Now where did I put my glasses?"

"Here, let me do it." Charlie snatched the key out of Martin's fingers. He hastily inserted it into the lock.

It didn't work.

# # #

The four co-conspirators were back in Martin's suite, dissecting the prior night's botched burglary attempt. The gang of would-be thieves was crestfallen—except for Helen, who was boiling with ire.

She directed her wrath toward Ed. "So who's the 'Einstein' now? Why didn't you think to try the key *before* we went to all the trouble and risk? It's a good thing you were a medical examiner and not a surgeon. At least the people you cut were already dead."

"Hold the phone," Ed said. He used the fingers of his left hand to enumerate his objections. "In the first place, the key I got from Roger worked last Thanksgiving, so why wouldn't it work now? Second, this was Charlie's plan. You can't pin any of it on me."

"Don't try to make me the scapegoat, you old codger." Charlie glared at Ed through narrowed eyes. "You shouldn't blame others for your own mistakes." He looked directly at Helen and pointed a finger at her. "Besides, none of this would have happened if you hadn't put us up to it."

Helen was neither surprised nor amused at the finger-pointing. "You're pathetic—all three of you. You couldn't break into an open cookie jar." She looked sternly at each of the men in turn, practically daring them to contradict her.

She held out her fist, turned the palm upward, and uncurled her fingers to reveal a key. "*This* will open the pantry door. I know because I tried it myself."

"But how...?" Martin spoke up for the first time since the meeting began.

"By using my head. You all should try that sometime. I noticed that Maggie and Josie can unlock any of our suites, yet there are only five keys on their key rings."

"That's because one of them is a master key," Ed said.

"Duh, Ed. If they had a master key, they would only need one key. So it occurred to me that there might only be five unique lock patterns. Then I wondered if the whole building shared those same patterns. So earlier today I borrowed keys from a few rezzies. Once the kitchen staff went home for the night, I tried opening the pantry."

Ed flailed his hands and shook his head. "That's absurd. They wouldn't do that."

"It's done all the time," Martin said. "You just key a bunch of locks to the same pattern. The building where I worked did it. I could open some of my coworkers' doors and some of them could open mine."

"How did you try all those keys without being seen?" Charlie asked.

"It only takes a few seconds." She looked at Martin. "Especially if you don't stop to put on a ski mask."

"Whose key was the one that fit?" Ed asked.

"Never mind. Now take this key and bring back the food." She handed the key to Charlie.

He compared the new key to the one he used last night. "Hey, Ed—you doofus. This can't be the key you got from Roger. These keys are for two different brands of lock."

Helen looked at the clock on the wall. "It's after nine. You'd better get going; only please try to get it right this time."

# # #

It was nearly 10:00 p.m. Josie was in Bill's suite, assuring him that he was in no immediate peril. "Your automatic blood pressure monitor must be faulty, because when I take your pressure the old-fashioned way, it's fine."

Bill shook his head. "No, it's high."

"Only the tiniest bit, and that's probably because you're stressing about it."

Bill took off his reading glasses and set them on the dinette table. "I guess I should get a new monitor, then—one that won't falsely indicate I'm having a stroke." He gave her a nervous smile.

"When you shop for one, look for a large readout that's easier to see. But even so, don't take readings one right after another. Wait at least ten minutes between measurements."

"Thank you, Miss Josie. Have a good night."

She stepped into the hallway and gently closed his door. On her way back to the PCA office, she encountered Martin and Charlie where the residential and admin corridors meet. "What in the world? Why are you two wandering around so late on a Friday? And why are you wearing camouflage vests?"

"Are-Are-Are you talking to us?" Martin stammered.

Josie looked up at the ceiling and placed a finger on her chin. "Hmm—let me see. Who else in the building is wearing camouflage?"

Charlie fidgeted with his waistband. "Uh, we were just out for a walk."

"A safari," interjected Martin. "Only not a real one. A virtual one."

"Yeah, that's right," Charlie said.

"We thought you'd be in your office studying," Martin said. "Otherwise we would have invited you along."

The overstuffed pockets and the blotchy green fabric of their vests reminded her of a pair of warty toads. "Where—" A muffled *pop* startled Josie. "Um, Martin, something just exploded inside your jacket. Should we be worried?"

He unzipped one of the vest pockets and pulled out a tube of ready-to-bake biscuits that had burst open. "A hunter never goes anywhere without emergency rations," he explained.

"Uh-huh. And do you also carry a toaster oven?" She giggled at the thought of big-game hunters telling stories around the glow of a small appliance.

Charlie cleared his throat. "Actually it is possible to build a solar oven out of common materials and bake bread in it, especially near the equator."

Josie noticed a small quantity of white powder spilling out of a plastic baggie that partially hung out of Charlie's waistband. It was piling up on the floor like sand at the bottom of an hourglass. "Looks like something is trickling out of *your* equator. What have you got shoved in your pants?"

"I don't know." Charlie wrestled a plastic bag out of his trousers. More powder escaped from the bag's torn seam as he surrendered it to Josie.

She inspected the bag and its contents. "Instant mashed potatoes? What are you doing with this?"

Charlie shrugged. "It's not mine."

Josie dangled the bag in Charlie's face, inadvertently adding to the mess on the floor. "The bag was in your pants."

"Uh … these are not my pants. I, uh … found them."

She smiled and shook her head. "You two are messing with me, aren't you? What else — "

"Yoo-hoo! Josie?" Helen called out

Josie turned and saw Helen only a few steps away.

"I've dropped my crossword puzzle book behind the couch," Helen said. "Would you be a dear and fish it out for me?"

"Okay, Miss Helen," Josie said. "I'm coming." She turned to the pair of huntsmen. "I'll clean up this mess. Meanwhile you two African safari hunters need to get back to your cabins before all this food attracts a hungry bear. I'd hate for one to sneak up and eat you."

"Josie dear," Helen said after the sportsmen had departed. "Sorry to be the one to break this to you, but there aren't any bears in Africa."

# # #

The next morning, Ed visited the coffee shop soon after it opened. He nodded to the barista and took a seat at one of the tiny tables. Less than one minute later his "usual" cup of joe arrived. He wondered if Charlie or Martin would show up today. After staying up late burgling the pantry, he wouldn't blame them for sleeping in, especially on a Saturday.

They would probably be sore at him. He was supposed to be the lookout during the heist, but had abandoned his post when an irresistible opportunity hijacked his attention. *Oh well.* They would get over it soon enough, especially if their mission had been successful.

He was halfway through his coffee when Charlie showed up. "Morning, Ed. Can I sit with you? You won't suddenly get up and leave me all alone, will you?"

So Charlie *was* miffed. *Time to do some damage control.* "Charlie, let me buy you a triple mocha with whipped cream, and I'll explain everything."

Charlie sat down opposite Ed. "Better add a cinnamon roll and a cherry turnover. You've got some *'splainin* to do."

"Okay okay. But first tell me how it went." Ed flagged down the barista and conveyed Charlie's sugary request to her.

Charlie grinned and quietly thumped his fist on the table. "We did it." The grin disappeared. "No thanks to you, of course."

"That's awesome. Congratulations. Did you collect everything on the list?"

Charlie's eyes darted back and forth like those of a nervous bootlegger. He leaned toward Ed. "Yes and no. Josie intercepted us at the end of our last run. She confiscated a tube of biscuits and a bag of instant taters."

Ed's eyes widened upon hearing the report. "What did she say? Are you guys in trouble?"

"Martin told her we were pretending to be on a hunting trip and had to carry rations with us."

"And she believed it?" Ed asked.

"Of course. We're talking about Josie Ditzski—cute and sweet, but far too trusting for her own good." Charlie leaned back as his coffee and pastries were delivered. "Now … where did *you* run off to? A lookout shouldn't leave his post."

"While you were unloading your first haul, I decided to help you grab stuff out of the pantry. So I went in to look for pancake mix, and what do you suppose I found instead?"

"What?" Charlie asked.

"Powdered tapioca pudding. There must have been two dozen fourteen-ounce bags of the disgusting stuff. I wasn't wearing a vest, so I stuffed every last one into a clean trash bag."

"That doesn't explain why we didn't see you anymore for the rest of the job," Charlie said.

"It took a long time to find someplace to hide it where nobody will ever find it."

"Why didn't you just throw it in the dumpster?"

"Nah," Ed said. "I grew up poor and can't bring myself to waste food."

Charlie shook his head. "I should be happy for you, but I'm not. Next time stick to the role you're assigned."

"Sorry, but when you find a stockpile of ghastly gruel, you have to take action." Ed rubbed his hands together in anticipation. "You know, breaking and entering is kind of exciting. When do we go again?"

"Sooner than we planned. Helen says we didn't gather enough for a single weekend. I think we're gonna have to come up with something better."

# CHAPTER FIVE

Bill was lost in thought. A week had elapsed since the rezzies' successful food heist. They would have to do it again and again unless Odia changed her mind. *That's just not sustainable.*

The lights in FRAIL's theater suddenly came on, causing him to shield his eyes. The credits to *Cash McCall* were still rolling. He and Philippe shared an interest in films starring Natalie Wood. Both had autographed photos of Natalie displayed in their respective suites. Philippe had actually met her in the 1960s when she came into his shop to buy a mink coat.

"James Garner sure had his hands full, didn't he?" Bill asked.

"Ah, zat is because ee was not a Frenchman. Ee treated *la femme* very poorly, *non?*" Philippe sometimes exaggerated his accent to get laughs.

Today's matinee had attracted only three other residents. One had made a beeline for the exit just before the last line of dialogue was delivered. Philippe silently nudged the other two awake.

"Nap time is over," Bill added, then returned his attention to the scrolling credits.

"It is not like you to take such interest in zee movie

crew, *mon ami*. Tell to Philippe what troubles you."

Bill waited for the recently awakened rezzies to shuffle out of the theater. "We're going to have to stand up against Odia."

"*Oui oui*. That is what everyone has been saying, except for you. Why have you had the *changement de coeur*?"

Bill shook his head. "It's not a change of heart. It's just that we can't wait any longer."

"Has something else happened?" Philippe asked.

"I got notice yesterday that my lease is up for renewal, but the cost will increase by 30 percent."

Philippe nodded.

"You don't look surprised," Bill said.

"That is because today I received *précisément* the same insulting offer. Tell me, did it promise an upgraded suite to compensate for the fortune demanded?"

"Yes, but that's as phony as a bank promising free checking for life. You and I know there are no 'upgraded' suites at FRAIL. It's a malicious, calculated attempt to force us out. Odia's hoping we can't afford to stay."

"Very few of us can bear the increase so severe. Do you think, *mon* Colonel, that everyone has received the same notice?"

Bill rubbed his knee. "No, I don't. It's got to be tied to the end of a lease. Mine is up in ninety days, and Odia saw her chance to get rid of me to spite Maggie. She also targeted you because she wants to avoid the appearance of singling me out," Bill said. "I'm sure there will be others affected as their leases expire."

"Then I agree, we must *engager directement l'ennemi*."

"Not so fast. Engaging the enemy through direct confrontation won't work. Not with Odia. We need to be clever about it."

"What do you have in mind, my friend?"

"First of all, not a word of this to anyone, especially not to Maggie. If she found out, she would probably quit her job—or worse."

Philippe shifted uncomfortably in his seat. "But this *cause célèbre*, it deserves support. May we not announce to the others that I, at least, am doomed to the eviction? It will—how do you say?—rile them up."

Bill pondered the request for a few seconds. "I guess we could. As far as I know, Maggie wouldn't know that my lease is also ending, unless Odia tells her."

"We cannot prevent that. We hope for the best, *non*?"

*Hope is not a strategy, but it's a start.* "Okay, then. But don't say anything to the other rezzies until I've had time to formulate a plan."

Philippe stood. "*Bon*. I will do as you say. I must depart now, for I am playing the chess with Charlie."

"Is he any good?"

"Oh yes, he is quite good, and he does not cheat like Ed."

"Take care," Bill said.

"Indeed, I shall," Philippe mumbled, and left the theater.

# # #

Two days later Bill and five of the rezzies went on an outing to Red Rock Pie Shop. The small but upscale pastry shop with linen tablecloths and cloth napkins was nice enough, but the conversation was not. He was beginning to wish he had stayed home.

"It will get worse if we don't do something soon," Helen said, poking Bill's shoulder with her index finger.

"Worse than sitting through another of your tedious meetings?" Ed asked.

"I declare," Wilma said. "Compared to you, Ed, Emperor Palpatine was a nice guy."

Ed draped his napkin over his head like a hood and grinned. "Release your anger and let it make you powerful."

"You can make jokes," Helen said, "but I'm sure Odia is up to something wicked. Haven't you noticed that no one new has come to FRAIL since she took over? Something must be scaring away prospective tenants."

"One of the vacant suites may be haunted, like room 237 in *The Shining*," Ed said. "Only in our case, visitors get chased by an ax-wielding woman rather than by Jack Nicholson. 'Heeeeere's Odia!'" He burst into laughter.

Charlie added sugar to his coffee. "Helen, are you suggesting Odia deliberately turns away potential renters?"

"Isn't it obvious? There's no doubt she's trying to empty out the place. Philippe is merely her first target. Mark my words. There will be others."

Bill focused his gaze on his slice of blueberry pie. *You're right about that.*

"To be precise," Martin said, "he isn't actually being evicted. He could stay if he agreed to take a better suite."

"Have any of you been in one of these upgrades?" Bill asked rhetorically. "No, because they don't exist. No sane person would pay 30 percent more for touched-up paint and a new toilet seat."

"Where *is* Philippe, anyway?" Helen asked. "He usually comes with us."

"I'm sorry to say he's looking for a new place to live," Bill said.

Wilma wiped a bit of whipped cream off of her chin. "We can't let that evil woman get away with this. I say let's march into Odia Fangmeister's office and give her a thumpin'. An' then we do the same with her boss." She stabbed an imaginary foe with her fork.

"And we should file formal complaints with regulatory bodies," added Charlie. "Does anyone know which ones those would be?"

Ed put his fork down beside his empty plate. "You won't get any help from the bureaucrats in this county. They'll fall all over themselves to ban a booster club bake

63

sale, but they won't do anything about a greedy landlord, that's for sure."

Martin shook his head. "Filing grievances against Odia would be futile. She'll just get angry. Complaining to her boss won't work, either. I'll give you odds he's behind it all."

"Why do you say that?" Helen asked.

"Because it's a conspiracy."

Bill rolled his eyes. *There he goes again.* "Okay, Martin, let's leave it at that. We can talk about the CIA and the black helicopters later." He held up the empty water pitcher to catch the waitress' attention.

Martin rushed to swallow a mouthful of apple pie. "Complaints could trigger an investigation and put the girls on the spot. Would they really testify against their own boss? In fact let me ask you this: Do *we* want to risk Odia's wrath? She might retaliate and throw us *all* out on our derrieres."

Bill looked at his watch. The debate had been going for over an hour. "I don't think we're getting anywhere, and I want to go home now."

"Bill's right," Helen said. "We can't argue about this all day. Raise your hand if you're on board with fighting back against this Colonel Parker wannabe."

"Who's that?" Martin asked.

"That was Elvis's allegedly crooked manager," Helen explained.

Wilma and Charlie raised their hands.

Helen sighed. "What about you, Martin?"

"Things at FRAIL are getting worse. Protests and complaints won't help. It's time to settle somewhere else."

"I'm with Martin," Ed said. "Don't provoke the vampire."

Helen slumped in her chair. "What about you, Bill? You could be in charge."

Bill pushed aside his empty water glass. "I need time to

think. I'm not afraid to take chances, mind you, but I prefer to have the deck stacked in my favor."

"Don't listen to the party poopers," Helen said. "It's obvious they only root for a team when it's winning. Once we score, they'll change their tune." She glared at Martin.

Bill looked into their eyes, one by one. "If I agree to take action, I will expect each of you to dutifully carry out my instructions."

"Wilma and I are with you all the way," said Charlie.

Ed scratched his head. "I'd rather have you calling the shots than Helen, that's for sure."

Helen gave him an icy stare. "Thank you for sparing my feelings."

Bill looked across the table at the remaining holdout. "Martin? … Martin?" *I never know if he's trying to make up his mind or if he's having a stroke.*

Martin snapped out of his pseudo-coma. "Anything we do is doomed to fail," he said, "but I'd hate to think we didn't try. Count me in."

Helen sat up straight and smiled. "Excellent. Now we can give Odia the what-for. What do we do first, Colonel?"

"I'll fill you in on the taxi ride home."

# # #

Early the next morning Bill steered his walker over to the coffee shop table where Helen was waiting. The barista came over as he settled into a chair. "Will you be ordering the usual, Colonel?"

"Yes, thank you," Bill said. "And one for Miss Helen, please."

Helen slid a folded sheet of paper across the table. "Take a look."

Bill put on his reading glasses and waited for the barista to return with the coffees before unfolding the document. He perused the contents. "I like the way this is organized. It lists our demands and lays out the consequences of ignoring us."

"Is it what you had in mind?" she asked.

"This is exactly what I wanted. The opening shot of the rebellion." *Perhaps a very short one.* Odia could probably outlast the rezzies in a war of attrition. Did they have the energy and persistence for a prolonged conflict? Few had the courage, he feared, to withhold payment of fees and rent, as the manifesto threatened.

"You look troubled," Helen said.

"This is very risky. Once I lay down the law, Odia is bound to try to get me to back off by threatening Maggie." He removed his spectacles and rubbed his eyes. "I didn't sleep very well just thinking about it."

Helen folded her hands together and stared at them. "I'm sorry, Bill. I feel like I've pushed you into a corner. Do you want to back out?"

"No. We've got to do this. I won't let Odia use me or my granddaughter as a lever. I'll have Lisa arrange a meeting with the Merchant of Venom in neutral territory. I want you and Maggie to be there as witnesses."

Helen took the last sip of her coffee and grabbed Bill's forearm. "I've got goose bumps now that Operation SCREAM is underway."

"What?" he asked.

"Operation SCREAM: Seniors Committed to Rapidly Ending Administrative Mismanagement."

"You've gotta be kidding me," Bill mumbled.

"A successful insurrection has to have a catchy acronym," she said.

Bill pulled out his phone and dialed. "Hello, Miss Lisa, it's Bill. I wonder, could you arrange a meeting with Ms. Fangmeister? Please include Maggie and Helen as well. Oh, and I'd like it to be somewhere neutral. Perhaps in the library."

"I can try. What shall I say it's about?" Lisa asked.

"The residents have a proposal for her to consider. Half

an hour should be enough."

"She's on a conference call right now. I can give you a ring when I get it set up. Her calendar is full for today, but tomorrow might work."

He thanked her and ended the call.

"You don't waste any time once you decide to act," Helen said.

"At our age there isn't any time to waste. In fact I've already briefed Ed about contingency plans, in case Odia tries to ignore us."

"Are we going to give her a copy of our demands prior to the meeting?" Helen asked.

Bill laughed. "Why don't we tape them to her door tonight? Now let's talk about something else, like my great-granddaughter."

He had been carrying on about Summer for ten minutes when his phone rang.

"Colonel Armstrong," he answered.

"Colonel, it's Lisa. I'm afraid Ms. Fangmeister has declined to meet with you. She says—well, I'm not comfortable repeating everything she said."

"Oh, I see. Thank you." He ended the call and immediately dialed a number.

"Ed Cutter here—it's your dime," Ed barked.

"Ed, listen. Odia refuses to meet. You know what to do."

# # #

Tuesday of the following week, on her way to FRAIL, Odia pondered legally defensible reasons to terminate more of the seniors' leases.

As she approached the facility's driveway, she noticed half a dozen people on the shoulder. They had erected a disheveled shelter built from poles, tarps, duct tape, and cardboard beside the monument sign that identified FRAIL.

Two professionally printed banners hung between

poles, clearly visible from the highway. One read, "Making Us Homeless." The other claimed, "FRAIL Evicts Helpless Seniors."

*They're protesting!*

Odia recognized only one resident among the miscreants, although she didn't know his name. The others were definitely not senior citizens. *Do the geezers have outside sympathizers?*

She had to stop this before the Kreakey Foundation board heard of it, or the directors would be furious. There was no room for bad press that could tarnish the reputation of the organization or its image-conscious donors.

She raced toward the parking lot. A crowd of residents and outsiders congregated near her private entrance. *This is worse than a bad acid trip.* She blasted the horn to clear a path. "Hot chili peppers!" she exclaimed. An enormous red-yellow-and-blue inflatable bouncy castle occupied her reserved space. Indignant, she hastily backed the car into the nearest open spot and got out.

Hand-printed placards bearing messages of "Agitation without Representation" and "Down with Fangism" assaulted her eyes. She was about to rush over and confiscate a sign when she saw the local television news info-blonde walking directly toward her. *Who called the media?* Those nutrition-shake imbibers would pay dearly for this. With the crowd hindering direct access to her office, Odia made a dash for the main entrance instead.

A rather large news cameraman stationed himself directly in her path. The reporter with the perfect hair and makeup zoomed over and spouted questions: "Why won't you meet with the residents? Is it true you evicted a tenant without cause?"

Odia stuck her hand in front of the lens. "No comment. This is private property. You have to leave. Go away!"

She pirouetted around the cameraman like a wide receiver eluding a tackle and made a break for the entrance.

Once inside, she came face-to-face with an even larger gathering in the lobby, listening to the animated oration of a senior dressed in green military fatigues and a false beard. She recognized this one—his name was Ed. The old and pale Fidel Castro impersonator was exhorting his listeners to chant "We Will Win!"

The walls were closing in. Odia had no mask to shield her from the perilous plume of pathogens emitted by the throng of uninvited busybodies. The situation was clearly out of control. *Oh no!* The news crew was coming inside. She ran straight to her office and shouted for Lisa to follow.

Lisa trailed close on Odia's heels and closed the door. "Ms. Fangmeister, I've been trying to reach you ever since I got to work. I kept getting your voice mail. They must have assembled at dawn or something. I didn't know what else to do."

Odia pulled her phone from the jacket of her suit and pressed its Power button, paused, then pressed it again. "No wonder. It shut itself off. The battery is low." She tossed the phone onto her desk. "Where's Ms. Providence?"

"In the lobby, somewhere, making sure nonresidents don't go where they're not allowed. She's asked the dining room staff to offer water to the residents who won't come in out of the heat. She tried her best to get them to call it off, but they won't listen."

Odia opened a drawer, extracted an inhaler, and snarfed from it twice. "Call the sheriff. Tell them we have dozens of trespassers, and I want them removed." She swapped the inhaler for her bottle of prescription alprazolam. "Get me some water."

"Right away, Ms. Fangmeister," Lisa said and bolted from the office.

Odia sat in her chair and tried to think. FRAIL lacked a standard procedure for dealing with picketing tenants. What should she do until the cops arrived? *Cozen.* He should hear about this from her rather than seeing it on the news.

"Arrrrgh!" she blurted after realizing she had forgotten to protect herself from geriatric germs. *Cozen can wait.* She wrestled on a pair of latex gloves and tied on a surgical mask, then hazarded a peek at the parking lot through the blinds. Two sheriff's deputies were speaking with a protester. *That was quick.* Perhaps Ms. Providence had already thought to summon law enforcement.

The deputies didn't appear to be shooing anyone away. *What are they doing?* The female officer lingered by Odia's BMW, spoke into her two-way radio, and took notes. Several minutes passed before the officer stepped away.

Odia now had a clear view of her car—parked in the handicapped space, with a bright-yellow citation tucked underneath the windshield wiper. Seconds later things got worse.

"No no no! This can't be happening," she said after seeing the tow truck.

# # #

Maggie sat in the PCA office, grateful for the tranquility following the morning's excitement and unrest. After order had been restored, Odia had questioned her, but only briefly. Perhaps the Wicked Witch of the Worst was satisfied with the way Maggie had handled the incident.

Was it possible that the rezzies' over-the-top reaction made Odia realize the folly of dismissing their concerns? Maggie felt that Odia got what she had coming, although she doubted life would get better for the feisty seniors. She knew Odia's natural response would be to strike back.

Josie appeared right on time for shift change. She was smiling and energetic, as usual. "Hi, Mags. Anything exciting happen today?"

"You didn't happen to watch the news on channel four, did you?" Maggie asked.

Josie shoved her oversize purse in her assigned locker.

70

"You know I never do. It's too depressing."

Maggie rolled her eyes. "Yeah, yeah, you don't watch the news and you don't use bad language either. I'll bet you've never, ever used the f-word, have you?"

Josie giggled. "Oh, I'm not that squeaky clean. I say 'phooey' all the time."

"Uh-huh," Maggie said under her breath. *Is she really a space cadet, or does she just act like one?* "Well, let me tell you what you missed this morning."

She recounted the details of the day, beginning with the delivery of the bouncy castle and the erection of the faux homeless encampment.

Josie laughed throughout the narrative. "I wish I had been here to see the reporter hounding Fang."

Maggie got up from the desk and checked for eavesdroppers. Finding none, she positioned herself next to Josie.

"Grampa told me last week that they were planning something, but he wouldn't say what it was," she whispered. "I didn't realize what a production it was going to be."

"Did you know the news crew would be here?" Josie asked.

"No, I didn't. The bouncy castle also surprised me. What a clever way to attract and keep a crowd."

Josie gathered her hair and fixed it in a ponytail. "Who were all the non-rezzies?"

"From what I could gather, about half were friends or acquaintances that the rezzies personally invited. Then those people apparently recruited the rest."

"It was certainly well-planned," Josie said. "Did everyone scatter when the sheriff's people showed up?"

"The deputies didn't bother anyone. They just walked around and talked with people, but the crowd had thinned out on its own by then. I think the rezzies were ready to wrap it up since it was getting hot outside."

"Too bad I missed it." Josie said. "Did it do any good? Has Fang agreed to meet with Bill?"

Maggie smiled. "Yes, it's set for Thursday. Helen and I will also be there." She took her purse from her own locker and dug for her car keys. "You should have a quiet night. Everyone's worn out."

"Oh, I almost forgot," said Josie. "Can you help me with the Fourth of July party? I'm going to set off fireworks after sunset while the rezzies watch from the patio."

The image of a runaway grass fire blazed across Maggie's mind. "I hope you don't expect me to light any. It sounds dangerous."

"My sisters and I did it every year as kids, and we still have all our fingers." Josie chuckled. "My dad taught us how to do it safely. It's tons of fun."

"Grampa's birthday is the Fourth," Maggie said. "Can I bring Summer? She would love the fireworks, but she might want to wear earplugs."

"Yeah, they're pretty loud, but bring her along, for sure. I'll show her how to set them off."

Maggie stuck her arm out in a "stop" gesture. "I don't know about that; she's only seven. Hey, wait a minute. You're not storing explosives in the building, are you?"

"Relax. I keep them in Manuel's toolshed. Now ... let's not mention a thing to Fang. You know she doesn't like us having fun with the rezzies."

# # #

Odia uttered an expletive as she parked in her reserved space at FRAIL. Cozen was standing in front of her private entrance. *What does he want?* She got out of the car and gave him an icy stare. "Well, if it isn't the pinhead lawyer in the pinstripe suit. Go away. I don't have time for you."

"We have to talk about yesterday's spectacle," he said.

An emergency vehicle raced past the facility with lights flashing and siren blaring. "Do you want to talk now?"

Odia asked. "I can wait if you need to chase that ambulance first."

"I would, if you were in it—then I'd run it off the road." He scanned the overcast sky. "Can we go inside? It's starting to drizzle."

Odia unlocked the door and entered, with Cozen in tow.

She opened a drawer in the credenza and retrieved a clean surgical mask. She turned to him as she tied it on. "I've got disposable masks for visitors to use. Want one?"

He shook his head. "You're truly neurotic, aren't you? There's no such thing as germs that cause aging, you know. You won't find any scientific evidence to support your paranoia."

"Noah lived for 950 years," she countered. "Why do you think that is? Let me tell you. That's because he didn't have contact with old people. There was just him, Mrs. Noah, and the kids."

Cozen looked puzzled. "So what? He died all the same."

Odia sat in her chair. "Yes, but that was after he started eating meat. Look it up in Genesis."

"I hardly expected you to be an authority on biblical studies," he said.

"My mother sent me to a Catholic girls' school."

He raised an eyebrow. "That is really hard to believe."

"After the first semester they told me not to come back."

"Ahh. *That* I can understand." He ran his hand through his silver hair and paced the room. "Can we get to the topic at hand? The mawkish melodrama on the evening news shocked our largest donor. She wasted no time calling me up and letting me have it. I *warned* you we couldn't tolerate negative publicity. We need to cultivate the approval of our benefactors, not their ire."

Odia leaned forward. "If you weren't such an amateur embezzler, you wouldn't be in this predicament. You have no one to blame but yourself."

He glowered. "Who shut down shuffleboard and tried to toss out two tenants? It certainly wasn't me."

"You exaggerate. Besides, that was supposed to demoralize the geezers, not embolden them," she said. "Not to worry, though, because I won't underestimate them again." She frowned. "Stop pacing—it's annoying!"

He sat in the guest chair. "Why don't you get some decent furniture? The iron maiden was more comfortable than this."

"Good. That means you won't stay long."

"Look, it's been seven weeks since you became administrator," he said. "I gave you the position so you could help me out—but I appear to be no better off. When will you give up on your failed scheme and do it my way?"

She stood. "Conspire with you and your vendor cronies? Don't you understand? You can't continue paying inflated invoices and getting kickbacks forever. Quit while you're ahead. FRAIL must be closed, and that's what I'm trying to do, you dipstick."

"I still don't see how exasperating the tenants accomplishes that."

"Because it makes them want to leave." Odia made a fist and pretended to knock on the side of her head. "Sheesh. You're thicker than Jethro Bodine. Once they move out, the endowment money is ours. Got it?"

"I get it," Cozen said, "but won't they flee quicker if you incentivize rather than agitate them? They might dig in their heels if you make them mad."

"They'll scamper like scorpions before you can say 'bug spray.' Old folks don't sit still for discomfort and insecurity. I plan to give them plenty of both." She walked over to her private entry and grasped the doorknob. "Now get out of my office and leave me to plot in peace."

74

# CHAPTER SIX

That evening Odia's shady contact was late again. *Or is he already here, hiding somewhere, watching? ... Why are people so suspicious of others?*

She peered between the metal slats of her enclosure and tried to discern shapes or movement in the moonless night. Tonight's meeting place was along an unmarked dirt road far from the highway. There was no sound other than the wind rustling the tree leaves in the adjacent apple orchard. She strained to hear footsteps or some other indication of her connection's approach.

The blackness made her wish she owned night-vision goggles. She would have to get a set before any future covert engagements. She gasped at her phone's unexpected vibration. "I'm here," read the incoming text message.

"Boo!" shouted her contact through an opening in the slats.

Odia dropped the phone and uttered unprintable oaths while her brain sorted out whether to be angry, scared, or dead from sudden cardiac arrest.

"Don't *do* that. I might have shot you." She retrieved the phone and unlatched the door of the horse trailer.

"Do we have to go through the password stuff again?" he asked as he stepped inside. "It's me, and I'm sure nobody followed me. By the way, why *are* these horse carriers sitting out in the middle of nowhere?"

"The owner is storing them for – well, don't ask."

"Okay. None of my business. Can we hurry? It smells like a barn in here."

"Let me see the item." She clicked on a tiny flashlight and shined it toward the floor.

"It's not as much as you asked for," he warned, "but it's the best I could do. Even so, you can do a world of hurt with this amount." He laid a small backpack at her feet.

Odia illuminated the bag. "Take it out."

He unzipped the main pocket, removed a box about the size of a coffee can, and handed it to her.

"This is much heavier than I expected." She moved the light over the labels that identified the box's contents and emphasized the danger they posed. It was hard to believe she finally possessed her weapon of last resort.

"Don't tell me what you're gonna do with it," the mystery man said. "And don't even think of opening it anywhere near me. Now pay up." He presented an upturned palm.

"How do I know it's the real thing? Prove it."

In the dim light she saw him shrug. "Lady, I don't carry a chemistry lab with me. The stuff is genuine. If you doubt me, open the container when you get home. If you're not dead, give me a call and I'll send you a refund."

Odia tucked the box under her arm. "Your payment is on top of this trailer. Climb up and count it, then stay up there until I'm safely in my car." She patted her coat pocket menacingly.

They exited the horse carrier, and he hoisted himself onto its roof. A phone call spooked her, causing her to drop her deadly cargo.

"Hey! Be careful with that thing," he shouted.

She rejected the call and began to put the phone away when it vibrated again. *Whatever they want will have to wait.*

76

"Are you done counting the money?"

"Tell you what, lady," yelled her contact from atop the trailer. "I'll have to trust you for now. Please just take your box and get as far away from me as possible."

# # #

It was Thursday morning. Bill looked at his watch. *Ten minutes after eight.* "Odia's tardiness is going to make us miss breakfast. That is, if she even shows up at all for our meeting."

Helen stood and headed for the door. "I'll go find that fence lizard and drag her over here."

"Don't get yourself all wound up," Bill advised. "Come back and wait patiently."

Maggie shifted uncomfortably in her chair. "Here she comes."

Odia slithered into the room and pulled the door shut. "Who is in charge of this pointless confabulation at the crack of dawn?" She adjusted her surgical mask. "Will this take long?"

"That depends on you," Bill said.

Odia slid a chair well away from Helen and Bill, plopped down in it, and crossed her arms.

Helen gripped the armrests of her own chair and leaned forward. "This confabulation, as you call it, will only be pointless if you refuse to negotiate in good faith."

Odia squirted nearly a tablespoon of hand sanitizer into her palm and rubbed her hands together. Squishing noises filled the quiet library as excess gel oozed between her fingers. Strong antiseptic vapors stung Bill's nostrils.

"Would you like a pair of latex gloves, Ms. Fangmeister?" Maggie asked.

Odia glared at her. "When I want gloves, I'll get them myself."

Bill cleared his throat. "Now that we've exchanged cordial greetings, let's get down to the matter at hand." He produced a copy of the rezzies' demands and handed it to Maggie. "Miss Providence, would you please deliver this to Ms. Fangmeister?"

Odia refused to accept the sheet. She turned sideways in her chair and looked away. "Is this the same list of demands you taped to my office door? I've already read them. They're rubbish."

Helen flailed her arms. "Then why are you here, you ogress?"

"Please, can we keep it civil?" Maggie interrupted.

"She is here because she wants no more unwelcome media attention," Bill said. "Isn't that true, Ms. Fang...meister?"

Odia snapped her head around to look directly at Bill. "You had no right to put on a circus and bring in the news crew. If you ever do that again—"

Bill stuck his arm out like a traffic cop. "Stop. You will not threaten us. You will sit quietly and listen to what we have to say, then it will be your turn to speak. That is how this meeting will go." He lowered his arm but maintained eye contact with Odia.

After glaring at him for nearly a minute, Odia broke off her gaze and sat straight in her chair. She sighed. "Okay, I'm listening."

"Helen, would you like to begin?" Bill asked.

Helen made a production of putting on her reading glasses and adjusting them so they perched at the very tip of her nose. "Yes, Colonel, I would." She looked at Odia over the top of her precariously positioned eyeglasses. "Now, Ms. Fangmeister, we want you to restore everything you've taken away from us. Our requests are neither extravagant nor unreasonable."

Odia stared off into space and presented her hand, palm up.

Maggie handed her a copy of the rezzies' demands.

Odia scanned the single-page document. "Weekend

meals, activity room, field trips. These things are not free, you know."

"They'll hardly break the bank," Bill said.

"I absolutely cannot afford to restore the full activity schedule. Transportation and insurance for outings really put a dent in the budget. The catering and clean-up costs associated with internal functions are also a burden. I don't see how you can expect me to agree to this."

"We're only asking what is fair," Bill said. "We pay rent and fees for a certain level of service, and we deserve to have it. You took things away from us without permission. We want them back. You must decide during this meeting what you'll do about our demands. We're not open to an endless series of negotiations." He sat back and crossed his arms.

Odia sat stiffly, fists clenched. Her chronically beady eyes narrowed into squinty slits.

Helen leaned forward. "It must be a very difficult job, balancing cost-saving with delivering value."

"That's right," Odia agreed. "You don't understand what I go through."

"Oh, I can guess," Helen replied in a sympathetic voice. "Still, you wouldn't want things to be any harder, would you? You don't want more media attention, do you?"

"Absolutely not," Odia answered.

Bill unfolded his arms and sat up straight. "Since time is running out, can we agree that you're okay with the small stuff, like restoring what we had? Then we can establish the rules for future interactions with the residents."

Odia fidgeted, wriggled, and twitched as if covered in stinging insects. "Are you asking about town hall meetings and voting on proposed changes?"

"You didn't answer the question," Helen said. "Let's try again. Will you agree to restore what we had *and* agree to attend regular, monthly town hall meetings with the residents?"

"Don't think too long," Bill added. "The clock is ticking."

Odia beat the arms of her chair with her fists. "Yes yes, okay."

"And will you agree that the residents can veto any proposals we don't like?" Helen glanced briefly at Bill and gave him a wink.

"That won't work," Odia said. "It would be like letting the inmates run the asylum."

"I think we already do," Bill said. "In fact we pay for the privilege. You don't want us to make a scene every time you tinker with things, do you? Tick, tick, tick."

Odia flailed her arms. "Oh, all right. I agree. But now you have to listen to my demands."

Bill leaned back in his chair, rested his hands in his lap, and interlaced his fingers. "Okay, we're all ears."

She squirted more hand sanitizer into her palm and initiated another microbial massacre. "I want every resident to sign a new lease—one that doesn't allow you to create pandemonium. A lease with terms that could get you evicted if you did."

"We would have to see the exact wording before we agreed to something like that," Bill said. "In fact we would insist that the period of the new lease be set to ten years, with no rent or fee increases. And, of course, this would include Mr. Pelletier."

She looked up at the ceiling for a moment, then directly at Bill. "I don't have the authority to accept those conditions."

"How unfortunate," Helen said. "Therefore you should waste no time in discussing it with your superiors. You never know what could happen in the meantime, do you?"

"Tick, tick, tick," Bill said.

Odia stood and pointed a finger at Bill. "You people are absolutely impossible. It's no wonder you have to languish in this dump, lonely and abandoned. You can't get along with anybody. I won't concede anything else today. I'm done." She stormed out.

Helen looked at Maggie and smiled. "And that is how you deal with a capricious tyrant."

Maggie, eyes wide, shook her head. "I can't believe she consented to all of that."

"Getting her to agree was easy," Bill said. "The question is, how do we get her to comply?"

# # #

Later that day Bill and Helen claimed their usual table in the dining room. "Oh no," muttered Bill. "Looks like Martin got his magazine today, and he's coming over. I know what he's going to talk about during lunch."

"Look at him, grinning from ear to ear," Helen said. There were still ten minutes to go before the dining staff would begin serving. "The centerfold must be something else this month."

Martin arrived and laid down the latest issue of *Bus Lover* magazine. He pulled back the empty chair next to Bill and sat. "Sad news," Martin said. "There's an article in here that says Honolulu Transit will retire their T8208s over the next few years."

"Oh, is that bad?" Helen asked.

"Don't encourage him," Bill grumbled.

Martin flipped to the page he had marked with a paper clip. "Look here." He slid the publication over to Helen. "These are classic RTS transit coaches. They're forty-footers with a Detroit Diesel 6V92TA engine. It's a shame to take them out of service since they're only ten years old."

"Why should I care about Honolulu buses?" Bill asked. "I don't live there."

"Come on, Colonel. Aren't you nostalgic about vintage aircraft, trains, planes, and buses? I've always been fascinated by powerful machines that move."

Bill raised an eyebrow.

Helen turned pages until she reached the center spread. "Oh my, oh my. I may get the vapors."

Martin chuckled. "That's the 2003 Neoplan Starliner model N516. It's a forty-eight-seat double-decker with—"

Two short blasts from Maggie's air horn interrupted him and succeeded in attracting the attention of everyone else in the room.

"No doubt you're eager to have your lunch," she said. "It will be right out, but first I have good news for you. Ms. Fangmeister asked me to tell you that she is restoring your activities—"

The rezzies cheered and twirled their cloth napkins above their heads.

Maggie waited for the ruckus to subside. "And she has also changed her mind about one other thing. The dining room will continue to serve meals on weekends."

"I knew you could do it, Colonel." Helen had to shout to be heard above the second wave of clapping and whooping. "Looks like yesterday's meeting was worth the trouble."

Maggie gave Bill a big smile and came over to him. "Nice going, Grampa. And on the day before the Fourth of July. Tomorrow we get to celebrate your birthday, the birth of our nation, and the rezzies' victory against tyranny."

She crossed her arms and looked at Martin. "I have a message for you. Josie wants to know if you need help returning all that food you and Charlie pilfered."

Martin's face became as red as a sore throat. He squirmed in his seat. "How did she find out?"

"Did you really think you could fool her? She may be young and pretty, but there's no empty space between her ears." She grinned at Martin, then spun around and walked away.

Rezzies began stopping by to thank Bill for standing up to Odia on their behalf. He was embarrassed by the recognition. It was premature. No one should believe for one minute that she had repented from wrongdoing.

He knew she wouldn't go down without a fight. She would find a new way to disrupt their lives, and would undoubtedly strike again when they least expected. And then, he feared, the rezzies would turn on him like the Israelites turned on Moses.

# # #

Independence Day was Bill's second-favorite holiday, after Christmas. He loved everything associated with it—the food, the flags, and the fireworks. Out on the patio of the facility, the desert heat lingered even though the sun had nearly set. Far to the west, thunderstorms formed but the celebration would be over long before they arrived to cool things down.

Josie rushed over with a small box. "Bill, could you hold these little American flags until Miss Wilma gets here, please? Manuel and I are going to get the fireworks out of the shed."

Maggie and Summer arrived just then. Summer's wavy, maple-wood-colored hair fluttered as she ran over to Bill, gave him a big hug, and wished him a happy birthday.

"Thank you, sweetie," Bill said, looking into her big brown eyes. "Would you like to hand out these flags? Please be sure every person gets one."

"Okay," Summer said. "Mom, when I'm done, can I help Josie light fireworks? Please? Please?"

Maggie looked worried. "Uh, I don't know …" She turned to Josie. "Will she be in the way?"

Josie smiled. "Not at all. And don't worry. I guarantee she'll be safe."

"Well, okay then. Do exactly as Josie tells you," Maggie said.

Summer leapt and twirled. "I will. I promise. Thank you. You're the greatest, Mom."

"Now, Summer, meet me over there when you've

handed out the flags." Josie pointed to the large dirt area that Manuel had cleared of brush and grass. "Oh, Maggie, I double-checked with all the rezzies, like you asked. Everyone is okay with us shooting fireworks. Miss Emily is watching from inside because it's so hot out here. I think Miss Helen is keeping her company."

It was nearly dark. The residents occupied two rows of plastic lawn chairs. Maggie confirmed that everyone had a bottle of water.

Maggie sat next to Bill after distributing the last of her homemade red-white-and-blue-frosted cupcakes. "Here we go," she said as they watched Josie light the first fuse.

*Bang-bang-bang! BOOM!* Loud explosions echoed off of the building. Manuel and Josie synchronized their activity, filling the night sky with a nearly continuous barrage of colorful starbursts and glittering comet trails.

Maggie clutched Bill's arm and held her breath each time Josie allowed Summer to light one of the pyrotechnic packages. A haze of stinky, sulfurous smoke hung over the field. She wrinkled her nose as the smelly, noxious cloud drifted away from ground zero and settled over the awestruck audience.

The ear-splitting production wound down after twenty minutes. Manuel and the "pyro-girls" came over to the patio for refreshments. They were greeted by a round of applause and shouts of appreciation. Maggie handed a bottle of water to a sweaty Josie. "Are there any more, or are you done?"

"We did almost all of them. There are two or three cakes left, but the breeze has picked up, and we probably shouldn't take a chance," said Josie. "I'll ask Manuel to put them back in the shed. They'll keep until next year."

"Cakes?" asked Maggie.

"Another word for 'repeaters.' Light one fuse and get multiple shots." Josie wiped the sweat off her brow.

Wilma came over. "This was such a treat, Josie," she

said. "Thank you for going to all the trouble and expense of setting this up every year. It means different things to each one of us. For some it's a celebration of freedom. Others are thankful to be among friends. For Charlie and me, it reminds us of July Fourth cookouts with our kids and neighbors in our younger days."

Ed joined them, wearing a huge smile. "That was great fun," he said. "I doubt any other retirement community has this much excitement. That's why I love it here."

At Josie's prompting, Summer gave Ed a hug. "Mr. Cutter, do you mind that I helped Miss Josie with the fireworks? She says you used to be her assistant."

"I've retired," Ed said. "Besides, you do a much better job than I ever did. You are carrying on a tradition I hope we never lose."

Bill stared off into the night. *I hope so too.*

# # #

Odia took advantage of the three-day Independence Day weekend to plan her next move. First thing Monday morning she buzzed Lisa. "Is Manuel here yet? I need to see him."

"No, Ms. Fangmeister, but—wait, he's just coming in the lobby. I'll send him right in."

Odia pressed the button under her desk to unlock her office door. The solid *clunk* signaled the steel bolt drawing back. The door opened and Manuel appeared, carrying his ball cap in his hands.

"It's about time," she said. "Why is it we can never find you when we need you?"

"I very busy," he protested.

"Yes, hiding from work is a full-time job for you, isn't it? Never mind. I have a problem."

"Okay, I go feex," he said.

"No, *you're* the problem. I got the results of your background investigation."

Manuel lowered his head and stared at the floor. "What name you check?"

His response puzzled Odia for a few seconds, but she recovered. "Your employment application says 'Manuel Escondido.' That's you, isn't it?"

"You don't like *resultados*? We try different name."

"Don't get ahead of me," she said. "Just tell me, are you the Escondido who has convictions for arson, burglary, and fishing without a license?"

"I not fishing. I hold stick while my brother go get a beer."

"Are you any good?" she asked.

"Fishing? No."

Odia rolled her eyes. "I mean the other things."

He cast a sidelong glance at her, but remained silent.

"Oh, relax. I'm thinking of sending you on a mission that will fully leverage your previous experience."

"*Que?*"

She looked up at the ceiling, exhaled, then looked him in the eye. "I mean I have a job for you, but this time you can't get caught. *Comprende?*"

He nodded and smiled. "Oh, *si si*. When?"

"Very soon. I'm planning a big surprise for those prune-eaters."

"You mean the *viejitos*?" he asked.

"Yes, that's exactly who I'm talking about." She got up from her chair and sidled over until she was right next to him. "I need your help, Manuel." She pulled down her mask and lowered her voice. "Here's what I want you to do ..."

When she finished giving him the instructions, she backed away and stared at him for a few seconds. "Do you think you can do that?"

"I don't know, *Jefe*. I don't want the *viejitos* to get hurt—know what I'm saying?"

"Nonsense," she said. "I would never let that happen.

Don't worry. Now go away."

Manuel started to leave but paused short of the door and turned around.

Odia tied her mask back on. "Was there something you wanted?"

"Do I get a bonus?"

# CHAPTER SEVEN

It was "Word Game Wednesday." Josie was on her way to the activity room, ready to intervene if any disputes arose over the rules of play. There were always a few players who didn't subscribe to the "It's only a game" concept.

When she got there, she found trouble brewing.

"Why not? It's a real word." Charlie was eyeballing Helen over the top of his reading glasses.

Helen held up the flimsy sheet of Scrabble rules. "It's not allowed."

Josie scanned the game board. "S-I-S-T-I-N-E. Sorry, Charlie, but Helen's got you there. You misspelled 'sixteen.' How did you expect to get away with that?"

Charlie and Helen exchanged amused glances.

Helen removed her reading glasses and let them hang from their chain. "Josie dear, are you familiar with Michelangelo?"

"Oh sure. Those were the guys who laid on their backs and painted the walls of that big church, right?"

"Not quite, hon," Helen said in a calm, measured voice. "Just one person, and he decorated the ceiling of the *Sistine* Chapel, which is the name of that particular vestry. That is why Charlie can't use that word. It says so, here in the rules." Helen waved the rule sheet under Josie's nose.

Josie felt her phone vibrate and reached into her pocket. "I've gotta take this," she said, and stepped into the corridor. "Hello, Philippe. Why aren't you at game night? What can I do for you?"

"Someone, they have broken through the emergency exit next to my suite."

Chills ran up her spine. "Are you sure?"

"*Oui.* They have smashed the glass door into tiny bits."

"Okay, stay inside and lock your door. I'll get help." She paused momentarily to think through her course of action. *Sheriff first, then notify Manuel, then secure the building.*

She dialed 9-1-1 on her cell phone, identified herself to the dispatcher, and confirmed the address. "Someone may have broken in through a locked exit door. I don't know if they're inside or not."

Because she needed to stay on the line with the dispatcher, she used the house phone in the corridor to call Manuel. That way she could keep an eye on the corridor and the doors to the activity room. She wasn't sure what she would do if a deranged criminal were to come down the hallway. She picked up the handset and dialed Manuel's number. It bounced to voice mail. "Manuel, it's Josie. The cops are on their way. Philippe says someone broke the glass outside 106 and they might be in the building."

Hands trembling and heart pounding, she hung up the house phone and wiped the perspiration from her forehead.

*What next?* She updated the dispatcher and got an ETA for the sheriff.

Josie listened. *All quiet.* She hurried into the activity room and locked both doors.

"Quiet, please! I need your attention. There's been a break-in. I don't know if anyone is inside the building, so please *stay here* and keep these doors locked. The sheriff will be here soon."

"I'll take charge in here," Bill said in a loud voice, "but

Ed and Philippe aren't at game night."

"Philippe's okay," Josie said, "and I'll check on Ed right now."

Still connected to 9-1-1 on her cell phone, Josie used the activity room house phone to dial Ed's number. She let it ring until she got his voice mail. "Ed, it's Josie. Stay in your suite until I tell you it's okay to come out." *I hope he's asleep or in the bathroom.* She considered going to Lisa's desk to use the public address system but decided against it. The trespasser might be prowling the offices in that part of the building.

*I need to call Fang.* She clicked the switch hook and dialed. The call bounced to Odia's voice mail. *Don't ignore me!* She hung up, redialed, and left a message when it went to voice mail again.

*Why can't I reach anyone tonight?* Frustration and fear lurked just below the surface, waiting to spring like sharks and devour her tenuous composure.

The 9-1-1 dispatcher interrupted, "Do you have a description of the prowler?"

"No, I don't. No one actually saw an intruder."

"Is anyone injured?" the dispatcher asked.

"Not to my knowledge, but I can't reach the custodian and I can't account for one resident."

"Units are reporting on scene now," the dispatcher said. "I need you to contact the officers outside by the main entrance. Can you get there safely?"

"Okay … yes, I hear sirens coming up the drive. I'm on my way out to meet them."

Nerves on high alert, Josie cautiously inched her way across the lobby to the main entrance. She glanced at the wall clock. How long had it taken for the cops to get here? *A desperate criminal could have kidnapped me by now.* Looking out through the glass facade, she saw sheriff's deputies and state troopers getting out of their cars. Intense blue lights strobed urgently and cast ever-changing shadows on the building's exterior walls. She unlocked the lobby doors and rushed outside.

A deputy came up to her. "Miss, I'm Sergeant Cadenas, the incident commander. Where are all the occupants?"

She explained that all but two were in the activity room. One was in suite 106, and the resident of 201 was not answering his phone. Oh, and the custodian was also missing.

Cadenas radioed for officers to make contact with Philippe and Ed. Although he was shorter than the stereotypical peace officer, his confidence and sense of urgency reassured her. The Kevlar vest, Taser, gun, and cuffs reinforced the message that he was not one to cross.

Josie waited outside while a pair of deputies entered with pistols drawn. Others were spreading out to search the grounds, and more patrol cars raced up the driveway. She ended the 9-1-1 call and dialed Bill Armstrong's cell number. "Bill, it's Josie. Tell the rezzies that the police are here now. Hold tight a little longer."

Fifteen minutes went by. An officer came out.

He looked Josie straight in the eye. "Don't worry, we've got lots of officers out here, but I'm pretty sure the subject has gone. Let's go check on the folks in the activity room."

Someone shouted, "Josie!"

She turned and recognized Maggie, making her way through the maze of haphazardly parked patrol cars. They hugged.

"Are you okay?" Maggie asked. "Grampa phoned me and said I should come over right away."

"Sergeant Cadenas," Josie said, "this is Maggie Providence. She works here. Can she stay in the activity room with the residents while we find the others?"

Cadenas's radio crackled before he could answer her. One of his deputies was reporting: "County 283, be advised 106 is code four and we're bringing him down to you. We found the occupant of 201 outside, also code four. Subject is

G-O-A."

Cadenas smiled at Josie. "Did you hear that? The two residents are okay. Doesn't sound like we've found the custodian yet."

"Did he say the suspect was dead?" Maggie asked in a whisper.

"No, ma'am, not D-O-A. He said G-O-A: gone on arrival."

"I need a pitcher of margaritas," Josie said as she realized that she was amped up on adrenaline. With the immediate danger over, shakiness and fatigue were setting in.

Maggie phoned Bill. "Grampa, it's Maggie. It's safe. We're coming over, so please unlock the doors. Odia never gave us keys to the activity room after she changed the locks."

Cadenas escorted Maggie and Josie to their destination. Bill was waiting by the open door and waved them through. The rezzies applauded, and several came over to comfort Josie.

"I need to sit down," Josie said.

A deputy arrived with Philippe in tow. A few minutes later a state trooper came in with Ed.

Bill put his hand on Josie's shoulder. "You deserve a commendation, young lady. Brilliant execution. Now just calm yourself while Maggie and I get these folks safely to their suites."

"We need 106 and 201 to stay behind, please," Cadenas said. "Also, anyone who heard or saw anything. The rest can go."

Josie thanked Maggie, Bill, and Cadenas. Then her world went dark.

# # #

"She's fainted," Maggie said, then directed Sergeant Cadenas to lay Josie on the floor. She scanned the room.

"Miss Helen — sit in this chair and hold Josie's legs up." She rushed over to the first aid kit hanging on the wall and retrieved an ampule of smelling salts.

Maggie hurried back and found Ed hovering over the patient, checking her airway and gently nudging her. "Ed, get away from her. She's gonna be okay."

"I *do* have a medical degree, you know," he said.

"Yes, but would *you* want to see a medical examiner staring at you upon regaining consciousness? She might think she's dead." Maggie activated the capsule of inhalant and waved it under Josie's nose for a second.

"Miss Providence," whispered Cadenas, "shall I call for paramedics?"

"No, thank you. She's coming around. I'm sure she'll be fine. If you're going to question Ed and Philippe, could you do it here? I'd like to listen, because I'll need some information for my internal incident report."

"Sure. Can we begin with...?" Cadenas thumbed through the pages of his pocket notebook. "Let's see ... Mr. Pelletier." He dragged two chairs next to Maggie and Josie. He sat in one and motioned for Philippe to sit in the other. "Tell me what you heard, sir."

Philippe sat. "I was in my living room, watching *Zee Great Race* with Tony Curtis and Natalie Wood — she is something, *non*? — when suddenly I hear a crash, like glass breaking. I realize it comes from outside the window of my bedchamber."

Cadenas scribbled on his notepad. "What did you do then?"

"I paused the DVD and then went to the bedroom. I listened for a minute but heard nothing more. Then I looked through the window blinds and saw the glass exit door shattered."

"What time was this?"

"Eh, nine o'clock, or perhaps later."

"It was dark outside. How could you see anything?"

"Have you not noticed? Outside of every exit, there is a light."

"Did you see anyone enter or leave?"

"*Non*, but I only looked for a few seconds. I went to find my *téléphone portable* to call Mademoiselle Josie."

"Did you leave your suite at any time after you heard the glass break?"

"*Non*."

"Thank you. You may go." Cadenas glanced at Josie, then turned to Maggie. "How's she doing?"

"Much better," Maggie said. "Let's get her into a chair. Ed, please go to the refreshment table and bring her something, would you?"

Cadenas helped Josie into a seat at the nearest table. Ed brought her some punch in a Styrofoam cup.

The sergeant turned his attention to Ed. "Mr. Cutter, please tell me why you were outside when all this happened."

Ed sat down in the chair next to Cadenas. "I was thoroughly enjoying a cigar on the patio." He glanced at Maggie.

"Ed, you're supposed to tell Josie when you go outside at night," Maggie said.

He mumbled something unintelligible, then looked her straight in the eye. "I forgot."

"I thought we talked about your cigars." She wagged her finger at him, then smiled. After all, he didn't smoke every day, or even every week. At his age why shouldn't he enjoy himself?

"How did you get outside?" Cadenas asked.

"We can unlock the patio door with a digital code. We're not prisoners."

Maggie feared Ed's minimal patience would soon run out. "Ed, the sergeant is unfamiliar with our facility. He needs to ask."

"I already explained a lot of this to the trooper who

located me," Ed griped. "Let's get on with it—I'm gonna need a potty break here shortly."

Cadenas continued, "Did you hear anything?"

"I don't hear so well, and my hearing aids are junk. But I definitely didn't hear what Jacques Cousteau claims he heard."

"You mean Mr. Pelletier?" Cadenas asked.

"Yes, of course. How many French guys do you think live here?"

Cadenas's eyes narrowed. "Mr. Cutter, the trooper says you told him somebody ran out of the patio door and right past you. Does that mean they had the code to unlock it?"

"Nah, I had the door propped open. That way if my cigar gave me a heart attack, maybe someone would hear me yell for help." Ed gave Maggie a sidelong glance.

Cadenas tried, but failed, to suppress a smile.

"Anyway, this guy with long green hair almost knocked me over," Ed said.

"Green?" asked Maggie, raising an eyebrow.

"Yeah, like the Incredible Hulk. Green hair. Torn shirt."

"What did you do then?" Cadenas asked.

"Obviously I chased after him."

Cadenas flipped the page of his notepad and wrote some more. "What were you going to do if you caught him?"

"Don't be a moron. I could never catch him, but I figured I should see where he was going."

"Why didn't you call for help?"

"Didn't have my phone. I couldn't go back in for it, or I'd lose sight of him."

Now Cadenas raised an eyebrow. "How do you know it was a male subject?"

"Don't you think I can tell the difference between men and women? Sheesh. How long have you been a cop?"

"Thank you for your time. You can go."

Ed stood and shuffled over to Josie. "Sorry I made you

95

worry." He patted her shoulder. "I'm glad you're okay."

Maggie winked at Josie. "Sergeant," she said to Cadenas, "what else do you need tonight?"

Cadenas slipped his pen into his pocket. "Nothing else. Good night."

As he left the room, Josie's phone rang. "It's Fang," she said, then answered and recounted the evening's events to Odia.

A minute went by. Josie turned progressively redder and got increasingly agitated as the conversation progressed. "I *did* call you — *twice*. And I called Manuel too, but I don't know where he was hiding tonight." Josie listened for a few more seconds, then abruptly hung up on her.

"What was that about?" Maggie asked.

"Can you believe it? Fang says she gave Manuel the night off. Why didn't anyone let me know? Here I was, all alone, risking my neck to warn him about the break-in," Josie said, and burst into tears.

# # #

Odia entered the FRAIL dining room right on time for the special town hall meeting she had called. She preferred to avoid any interaction with the residents, but couldn't pass up this chance. Rehashing and reframing last night's break-in was just the thing to scare the fussy fossils into expediting their departure plans.

She stepped behind the wobbly lectern and tried to test the microphone by blowing on it. This served only to puff out her surgical mask. She tapped on the mic with a gloved hand instead. "Listen up! I'm talking now and I won't repeat myself. There are many inaccurate rumors regarding the intrusion. I'm going to give you the truth." She reached into her suit jacket pocket and produced a numbered list of points to cover.

A sweater-clad geezer, seated at the table immediately

in front of the lectern, raised his hand. Despite being on the job for months, Odia had not made the slightest effort to learn the residents' names. There was no point. They would be leaving soon enough. "Put your hand down. I'm not taking questions yet."

The gentleman lowered his hand.

"We can't hear you from way back here," Ed shouted, evidently contemptuous of parliamentary procedure. He was one of the few whose names she did remember, mostly because he was prone to running his mouth.

Maggie, sitting at an adjacent table, intervened. "Ed, you're no more than ten steps from the loudspeaker. I'm sure if you sit quietly, you'll hear just fine."

Ed raised his hand. "Where are the refreshments? We always have refreshments at these meetings." He put down his hand.

Maggie went over to Ed and whispered something into his ear. He gave her a puzzled look. She whispered some more. He nodded.

Odia took that as her cue to proceed. "According to sheriff's deputies an unidentified male forcibly entered the facility last night just after 9:00 p.m."

She looked up from her notes and waited a few seconds. "Investigators say that one of you actually saw the person running away. Nothing was taken that we know of. Aside from a shattered glass door, nothing else was damaged."

Folding her list, she scanned the crowd, hoping to see worried faces but finding only expectant stares. She would have to address the rumors—both the genuine ones and the ones she had invented—to amplify the maleficence of the break-in.

"Now let me tackle the rumors. The only eyewitness claims that the burglar had green hair and green skin. I think that's unlikely."

"I saw him, and I didn't say anything about green skin, but he definitely had green hair." Ed punched the air with his fist. "Don't tell me what I did or didn't see."

Odia stuck her index finger underneath the mask and scratched at her nose. "That may be what you believe you saw, but remember you were outside. It was dark, and he was running away from you. Anyone could make a mistake."

Ed scooted his chair back and started to stand. Maggie rushed over and put a hand on his shoulder. He shook his head and crossed his arms, but remained seated.

"Another falsehood is that the bad guy spray-painted 'leave now' and 'unsafe' on an exterior wall of the facility. That is not true."

She paused while the audience members exchanged worried glances with each other. The contrived rumor had hit the mark.

"Someone speculated it was a burglary attempt that failed because the perpetrator could not manage to pick the locks. That's a faulty conclusion. Let's face it—it would be a piece of cake to defeat these locks with an easily made skeleton key. Come to think of it, even an amateur sneak-thief could have picked them with a paper clip." Odia smiled beneath her mask. *That should get them talking.*

"Oh, and excuse me for saying so, but I doubt any of you could run as fast as the prowler reportedly did. So unless you think one of the staff went psycho, I would say that the 'inside job' theory doesn't hold water ... although I must add that retirement community staff do commonly go postal these days."

The susurration of worried conversation among the residents validated Odia's approach. *Good.* "Now I'll take one or two questions."

A senior raised her hand. "I heard the prowler escaped through the patio door. If it was locked, can you explain how they got the unlock code?"

"That wouldn't be hard. The code is the same four digits as the facility's address. Anybody would try that code first.

I can't believe you would ask such a question."

"Why don't we change the code, then?" the senior asked.

"Too much trouble," Odia replied.

Ed turned to face the other tables. "She's not telling you the whole truth. I was on the patio with the door propped open."

"Excuse me, I have the floor," Odia growled. "But since you brought it up, we're going to make sure that can't happen anymore by designating the patio off-limits to residents."

A chorus of "Boo!" rose from the attendees.

*Uh-oh.* Bill had his hand up.

Odia dared not ignore him after all the trouble he had already caused her. "Yes, Colonel Armstrong."

Bill lowered his hand. "I understand that Josie was the only employee on the premises. She had to handle the situation alone and risk her own safety. Do you care so little about your own staff, or your paying tenants, that you think it's acceptable to understaff the facility? Is there a policy or procedure requiring a minimum number of staff per shift?"

"I will not answer that because it's an internal matter between me and my staff."

"No, it's not," Bill argued. "The residents of this facility expect a certain level of safety and security. If your staff is not safe, then we're not safe."

Odia moved out from behind the podium and stood beside it. "You of all people should know that we live in a dangerous world. Furthermore this facility is not a luxury estate with armed guards and perimeter security. We do what we can with the resources at our disposal. Bad things could happen even with twice as many people on duty. But if you want to go live somewhere safer, I won't stop you."

Numerous conversations broke out among the residents. They were clearly done listening to her. With any luck they would talk themselves into moving away. *And I'm going to make sure Agitator Armstrong goes first.*

# CHAPTER EIGHT

Something crunched as Maggie walked into her kitchen on Saturday morning. She looked down and sighed. Dry cat food was strewn across the room. *Not again.*

Two enormous green eyes peered innocently at her from the depths of an open cabinet.

"Lefty! How did you get in there?" Maggie asked.

She reached into the cabinet and pulled out a kitten that was black everywhere except for his left front paw, which was white. Holding him at eye level, she scolded, "You made a big mess." She set him down and swatted him gently on the rear. "Now go—and stay out of trouble." *Maybe that's what we should have named him.*

"Summer, come sweep up the mess your cat left."

No response.

"Summer, did you hear me?"

More silence. Irritated, Maggie went into the living room and found Summer curled up on the couch, reading. "I'm talking to you. Go clean up Lefty's handiwork. There's Kittie Krunchies all over the kitchen."

"Look—there's someone coming up the walkway," Summer announced.

"Stop stalling," Maggie ordered.

The doorbell chimed. A sharp rapping immediately

followed. *Great.* She didn't have time for this. Maybe they would go away.

The visitor knocked again, only harder.

Maggie rehearsed her "We give to Community Fund" speech in case it was someone seeking donations. A quick look through the peephole forced a change of strategy. She opened the heavy wooden door and confirmed that it was indeed a law enforcement badge she had seen.

"Maggie Providence?" asked the tall, well-dressed man on the other side of the smudged storm door.

"Who are you?" *That was dumb. He's a cop. His badge says so.*

"Detective Hunter Marshall, Sheriff's Department. May I come inside? Here's my official identification." He held up his department-issued ID card against the glass for her to examine.

Maggie scrutinized his credentials and accepted their authenticity. She unlocked the storm door and opened it.

The detective wiped his feet before entering.

Summer stared at him as though he were a movie star. "My name is Summer. Are you a real detective?"

"Yes, he's real," Maggie said. "Now do as I ask. I'll call you if we need you." She turned to Detective Marshall. "What is this about?"

He put away his badge and pulled a small, leather-bound notepad from his sport coat's inner pocket. "I'm conducting an investigation. Would you mind answering a few questions?"

"Sure, let's sit down at the kitchen table, if that's okay. This way."

He followed her into the tiny galley. A small, square table with a scratched glass top was pushed up against one wall. There was just room for three people to dine.

Maggie sat at the table with the wall to her right and leaned her head back against the refrigerator. *Try to look confident and relaxed.*

Marshall sat across from her. "I see you're busy. This won't take long. You're not under arrest, and you can stop answering questions at any time. Do you understand that?"

"Yes. Are you going to tell me what this is about?" She wasn't sure whether to be puzzled or worried. She took a deep breath. *Start with puzzled.* There was no need to panic just yet.

"I need some background information about you, and then I will go into detail about a suspicious fire. It's important for you to be completely truthful with me. Does that sound agreeable to you?"

*A fire?* Did this have something to do with Summer? Had she gotten into trouble? *Oh no.* Perhaps it had been a bad idea to introduce her to fireworks. Had Summer secretly obtained some and accidentally set a field ablaze?

"Miss Providence? Is that agreeable to you?"

"Oh ... yes, sorry. I'll honestly answer any questions you have."

Maggie fielded his inquiries about her job duties, work schedule, and marital status. She found that taking time to think before speaking eased her anxiety.

"Now, Miss Providence, tell me everything about the fire at Galactic Prophylactic." He sat back in the chair, crossed his right leg over his left, and put his hands on his knee.

A wave of relief came over her. Summer could not have caused that. GP was on Red Rooster Road, clear across town. "I didn't know they had a fire."

"But you're familiar with the business." It was more a statement than a question.

"Yes. They sell protective items like surgical masks, biohazard suits, disinfectants, and stuff," Maggie said.

"How do you know that?" he asked.

"An ex-boyfriend owns it."

"And his name would be...?"

Maggie wasn't sure where this was going. She

reminded herself she had done nothing wrong. *Simply answer the questions and don't blabber.* "His name is Angelo Venturi."

"Have you ever been inside the building?"

"Once. Years ago, before my daughter was born. Angelo is her biological father. He left me as soon as I got pregnant. He had just started the business back then."

"When was the last time you had contact with Angelo?" asked Marshall.

"The day he left. He doesn't bother me, and I don't bother him." She omitted the fact that their lawyers clashed frequently over child support.

"Did you torch his building?"

"What? … No!" The accusation stung like a soccer ball to the chest. The room suddenly felt hot and stuffy. "That would be stupid, wouldn't it? How can he pay child support with his business in ashes?"

"Who did it, then?"

"How should I know? I don't go there, nor do I speak to him." He was definitely trying to rattle her. *Stay calm. Breathe.*

The detective scribbled in his notebook. "Investigators discovered signs of forced entry and accelerant residue. The perpetrator used a delayed ignition method and was long gone before the fire took off."

"Why are you telling me this? You make it sound as though I had something to do with the crime—or that I know who was involved. Well, you're wrong. I'm innocent."

"Where were you on the night of the fire?"

"Remind me when that was." *Is he trying to trap me?* Should she stop talking? Should she call her lawyer?

Marshall raised an eyebrow and paged through his notebook. "Last Saturday, July fifth."

Maggie glanced at the calendar that hung beside her. "I worked the day shift, then I came home. Summer and I rented movies, made popcorn, and had a girls' night in. And before you ask, no one can confirm that. It was just the two of us."

The detective abruptly shut his notebook and stood. He thanked Maggie for her time and found his way to the front door. She followed closely but said nothing. He exited the house and got in his car.

She locked the storm door and watched him drive away. *What an infuriating man.* He reminded her of an annoying TV gumshoe that Wilma liked to watch. The scruffy one in the trench coat. *What is his name?*

She sat on the sofa. Whoever set the fire went to a lot of trouble and knew what they were doing. *Why would the police suspect me?*

At least she could put to rest her fears about Summer playing with fireworks. Maggie berated herself for not having faith in her daughter. The child knew better.

*Pop-pop-pop! Bang! Bang!*

Maggie jumped. The noise was coming from her backyard. *Firecrackers?* She sprang from the couch and ran to the back door. "Summer!"

# # #

Midmorning on Monday, Bill sat with Helen in FRAIL's coffee shop. "Maggie should be back at work today," he said.

"You miss her, I can tell, but she's only been off three days," Helen said.

"I'm glad she had a long weekend away from here," Bill said. "Goodness knows she deserves it. She works harder than an ant at a picnic."

Helen glanced in the direction of the shop's entrance and smiled. "Speaking of trouble ..."

"Hi, Grampa. Good morning, Miss Helen," Maggie said in an extra-cheerful voice.

She gave Bill a quick hug from behind.

Bill grinned and reflected on what a blessing his granddaughter was. "How was your time off, sweetie?"

"It was terrific. Summer practically wore out the pool at Mom's house on Saturday."

"She's a darling little girl," Helen said. "She really enjoyed shooting fireworks with Josie, didn't she?"

"A bit too much," Maggie lamented. "The day after the Fourth, she secretly took part of her allowance and bought firecrackers from the boy next door. Friday morning, when I wasn't looking, she sneaked out to the backyard and set off a whole string of them. It scared the cocoa pellets out of me."

Bill and Helen laughed. "Good thing nobody complained to the cops," Bill said.

"Funny you should say that, Grampa. Earlier that day a detective came to the house. It seems there was a fire at Angelo's warehouse, and the cops are sure it was arson."

"Who is Angelo?" Helen asked.

"That's Summer's father," Bill said.

Helen raised her eyebrows. "Oh, I see. They don't suspect you, do they?"

"Of course they don't," Bill said. "They're just being thorough and methodical."

Maggie wrung her hands. "Well, I'm worried anyway. He asked me flat out if I did it. He was very accusatory."

"I hope you had your lawyer there," Bill said.

"Uh, no, but later on I wondered if I should have."

He grimaced. "Let's hope he went away satisfied that you had nothing to do with it." *You've got enough trouble in your life already.*

Maggie glanced at her watch. "Well, Grampa, I've got a lot of work to do. Have a good day, and you too, Miss Helen."

After Maggie left, Helen leaned in toward Bill. "Why would the detective be suspicious of her? Do she and Summer's father have much to do with each other?"

"No, not at all, but their lawyers do. I hear Angelo's not too consistent with child support."

"Does he have visitation rights?" Helen asked.

"No. He never did. He has no interest in Maggie or Summer as far as I know."

"Then don't you think it's odd that she's a suspect?"

"She's *not* a suspect," Bill insisted. "It's just routine questioning. ... Are you saying you suspect her?" he growled.

"Not at all. But wouldn't you like to know who gave the detective the idea to question Maggie?"

"Well, I don't think they'll bother her anymore. I'm not going to lose sleep over it." *Thank you so much, Helen.* He would surely become preoccupied with it now.

# # #

Later that evening nearly half of the rezzies were in town attending a stage play. The rest were safe and snug in their own suites, given there were no other activities scheduled tonight.

Josie was in the PCA office, where she had been catching up on paperwork since dinner. Manuel was supposed to be on duty this evening, but she hadn't seen him. He had a scorpion-like talent for hiding.

The fire alarm annunciator panel just outside the office began chiming urgently, interrupting the mindless monotony. She hurried over to check it.

A blinking indicator warned Josie that smoke had been detected in zone 5A. That was the electrical closet where power and communication lines entered the facility. The door to the closet was outside, at the back of the edifice. She pressed the Timer Reset button. That would give her ten minutes to investigate before the system activated the building-wide evacuation signals.

She dialed 9-1-1. "This is Josie Ditzski. I have a smoke alarm indication." She gave the dispatcher the address and

106

other pertinent information. Then she went to see if she needed to start evacuating the building before help arrived.

Josie grabbed a flashlight from the assortment strewn about the administrative area. You couldn't have too many when you were always helping rezzies search for lost items under chairs and behind couches.

Heading up the admin corridor, Josie's senses were on alert for any indications of smoke, sound, or flame.

Before going outside to the electrical closet, she checked conditions along the residential corridor. Satisfied that nothing was amiss, she exited the building via the patio door. She plodded through the darkness, struggling to see. *Of all the flashlights I could have chosen, I took the one with dying batteries.*

An acrid odor assaulted her nose. She shined her light at the closet and saw wisps of smoke venting through the seams between the door and its frame. The sound of sirens grew louder. She walked around the corner of the building where she would be able to see arriving fire crews.

Brush Truck 7 raced up the driveway, its strobing red emergency lights creating a series of brief and ever-changing shadows. She recognized that specific unit because she was friends with one of its crew. Josie waved her flashlight at the approaching rig and watched it pull off the paved driveway and onto the dirt path she was on. Two much larger trucks were turning off the highway. Sirens off in the distance promised even more equipment would soon arrive.

A firefighter in full turnout gear exited the vehicle and walked up to Josie. "Have you started evacuating the building?" he asked.

"Not yet. We shelter in place except for imminent danger."

He pressed the push-to-talk button on his portable radio. "Brush 7 on scene, light smoke showing. Brush 7 assuming incident command. Ladder 241, meet with staff in lobby to assist with partial evac."

He returned his attention to Josie. "Move only the people occupying the rooms closest to the closet," he replied. "Go to the lobby and meet with the ladder company. They'll help you."

Josie came back inside and rushed to the alarm panel. The delay timer was about to expire. She pressed the Alarm Silence and System Reset buttons just in time. That was close. If the klaxons had sounded, the rezzies might have worried and started to self-evacuate, despite reminders not to at the last safety briefing.

She phoned Odia and Maggie while the fire crews dealt with the emergency. *Why does everything happen on my shift?*

Before long another firefighter entered the lobby. She explained to Josie that the small fire had been confined entirely within the electrical closet and had done practically no damage.

"People can return to their suites," said the firefighter. "I've got to tell you, this fire was deliberately set. An investigator is on his way."

A chill ran down Josie's spine. *Is this related to the break-in?* The evening shift had become a risky venture lately. She promised herself she would ask Odia about installing security cameras.

The firefighter started to leave, then stopped and turned back. "Oh, there's something else. Fire codes prohibit using electrical equipment rooms for storage. You'll probably get written up for that."

"But we never go in that room," Josie said.

"Well, someone's using it as a storehouse. We practically tripped over the bags of powder stacked just inside the door."

"Powder? What kind of powder?" Josie asked.

"Tapioca pudding mix."

# # #

Two days later Josie drove Bill to the office of Janus Realty. The owner, Anna Janus, was the only one of the six Kreakey Foundation directors to return Bill's phone call.

"When we get inside," Bill said, "you'll have to stay in the waiting room."

Josie nodded. "I understand. I know it would be a conflict of interest otherwise." She shut off the motor and removed her sunglasses. "Are you sure you don't want your walker?"

"Leave it," Bill said. "My knees are doing great. Really." *And it's about time too, after a bazillion weeks of physical therapy.*

"You're the boss," she said, then got out and waited by the door to the building.

Bill walked confidently to the entrance. "Thank you for bringing me over here on your own time."

"My pleasure. Too bad Helen had a doctor's appointment. I know she wanted to come."

Anna Janus greeted them in the waiting room. "Please come with me, Mr. Armstrong."

Bill followed Janus into her office. Two large and comfortable guest chairs faced each other in front of the desk. He took a seat in one.

Janus shut the door and sat in the other guest chair. "I should let you know up front that you're not popular with the board right now, and they would frown on this meeting. Can I persuade you to keep silent about it?"

"Ms. Janus—"

"Please, call me Anna."

"Okay, Anna. Let me just say that you—that is, the board—are equally unloved by the residents. You've installed an abusive agent at FRAIL—a bulldozer in a bowling alley—yet you appear to be looking the other way."

She chuckled. "Please, don't feel you have to be diplomatic."

"Don't worry about that. Now what's really on your mind?"

"You won't believe it," she replied.

"Try me."

"I admire your inventiveness. I'm talking about the residents, collectively. The homeless encampment was priceless. It made the TV news."

"You're right," Bill said. "I don't believe you."

Janus frowned. "All right, then. Why do *you* think I asked you here?"

"The other directors pressured you to warn us off. That would be my guess," he said.

"Are you always this cynical?"

He leaned forward and frowned. "I've been around the block a few times in eighty-two years. When you're through being cagey, I'd like to get on with things. Otherwise I'll go home and plan the next outbreak of embarrassment for Kreakey."

She crossed her arms. "What exactly do you want?"

"First, you must realize the extent of Odia Fangmeister's misconduct toward the residents. Second, several safety issues need immediate attention, including understaffing. Finally, we insist on a new lease agreement for every resident—one whose terms we help author, with explicit protections against future management nonsense."

Her eyes narrowed. "And if you don't get what you want, I suppose you'll burn the place down or something?"

"That's already been tried—but not by the residents."

Her eyes popped wide open, and she gripped the arms of her chair. "What do you mean?"

"FRAIL had a small fire two days ago," Bill said. *How could you not know?* "The fire investigator is convinced it was deliberately set."

"Was anyone hurt?"

Bill detected a hint of sincere concern from Janus. "There was very little damage, and nobody was harmed.

110

But it did knock out satellite TV service to the whole facility, which hasn't been restored yet."

"I'm glad you told me about the fire. I'll have to look into it."

Bill handed her two detailed lists. The first enumerated disruptions since Odia came into power, and the second itemized the rezzies' safety concerns.

Janus scrutinized each of the lists. "I'm not sure what I can do. These are internal operational matters. The board funds FRAIL but doesn't manage it."

Bill took a deep breath. Surely she didn't think he would accept such a weak response. "The board hired Odia to run the place. If she runs it into the ground, breaks the law, or has a health and safety incident, *you* are accountable."

She raised an eyebrow. "Are you an expert on nonprofit organizations?"

He stared. *No doubt about it. I don't like her.*

Now Janus leaned forward. "We are accountable to our donors. You did more damage in one day than Ms. Fangmeister has done since she took the helm. Certain donors—big donors—are *very* upset."

Bill smiled. "Precisely. The path to Kreakey's downfall is short. Odia angers the residents, and the board does nothing. The residents fight back and generate bad press. Your donors get perturbed and donations dry up. The board gets black eyes all around."

Blood rushed to Janus's face. "Okay, smartie, follow this logic: the residents cause trouble and get kicked out."

"Are you willing to evict all of us? I thought Kreakey was a nonprofit entity. I didn't realize you aspired to be a non-revenue outfit." He couldn't wait to hear her comeback.

Her shoulders sagged. She rose and moved to her desk chair. "I fear I have underestimated you. I apologize if I've been a bit snippy."

Bill shook his head. *When will people learn not to mess with me?* "I don't like to repeat myself, but since I have your attention now, I'll make an exception." He iterated his points.

This time she listened without interrupting, and she even took notes.

After a few clarifying questions Janus put down her pen. "I must say, Mr. Armstrong, your version of events is very different from what the board has been told. Are you suggesting that Odia Fangmeister engaged in selective — or perhaps creative — reporting?"

"Did Grizzly Adams have a beard?" Bill asked.

"Nevertheless I doubt that we would help you," she continued. "You see, many of the directors are afraid of Odia, although you did not hear that from me. It would be wise for you to tread carefully."

"What are they scared of — other than her physical appearance?" he asked.

She smiled. "Can you keep a secret?"

"Yes."

"So can I. I'm sorry, but our time is up. Stay in touch."

Bill snorted as he left her office. It seemed that the rezzies couldn't count on Janus, let alone the Kreakey board, for help.

# # #

A couple days after meeting with Janus, it was Maggie's turn to drive Bill into town for a different appointment.

"Let's see if this defense lawyer is any good," Bill said as they got out of the car.

Maggie rushed around to the passenger side and took hold of his arm. "I like her, and she says she's got good news."

They started toward the lawyer's office.

"You should have hired her the first time that detective came snooping around, but you didn't. Then he called again two more times. When will he leave you alone?"

"I know, Grampa, but I can't afford to hire lawyers for every little thing." Maggie held the office door open while Bill stepped inside.

The receptionist greeted them. "Miss Demeaner is ready for you. First door on the right."

Bill and Maggie entered Violet Demeaner's office, exchanged pleasantries, and sat at a highly polished, hardwood conference table. The lawyer brought them bottled water and took a seat at the table.

"Miss Demeaner," Maggie said, "you mentioned over the phone that you had good news."

"Yes, I do," Violet said. "You have very little to worry about."

"Nothing that a few more billable hours won't solve?" asked Bill.

"Grampa!" Maggie reached over and gently slapped his knee.

Violet chuckled. "No offense taken. It helps to have a sense of humor."

Bill twisted the cap off his water bottle. "The suspense is killing me, and you're undoubtedly charging us by the minute. Hurry and tell us what you discovered."

"Miss Providence, someone is trying to frame you for the fires at Galactic Prophylactic and at FRAIL."

"What?" Maggie's jaw dropped.

"And you consider this to be good news?" Bill asked.

"Please, let me finish," Violet said. "I had a very productive conversation with Detective Marshall earlier today. He admitted that he found no credible evidence to suggest your involvement in either incident."

Bill rubbed his chin as he processed the information. *Rats. I forgot to shave today.* "Why does Marshall think she's being framed?"

Violet glanced at him, then turned to Maggie and raised an index finger. "Ahh. That's the interesting part. He says he worked it out from your fingerprints."

"That's impossible," Maggie asserted. "I wasn't at either fire."

"Nevertheless your prints were lifted from a flashlight found at one of the incidents."

Bill leaned forward. "She told you she wasn't there, so if they found her fingerprints, they must have been planted. Did you explain that to the detective?"

"I didn't have to," Violet said. "Apparently someone unwisely urged Marshall to dust the flashlight for prints."

"I don't follow," Maggie said. "Wouldn't that be standard procedure?"

"The only people who had knowledge of the flashlight," Violet said, "were Marshall, the fire investigator, and — "

"The perpetrator," Bill said. He patted Maggie's hand. "Someone's out to get you."

Violet tapped her nose. "Precisely. Now who would that be?"

"My ex-boyfriend, probably," said Maggie.

"No. Angelo may be selfish, cowardly, inconsiderate, and irresponsible, but he's not malicious," Bill said. "Besides, where would he get a flashlight with your fingerprints? On the other hand you and I both know someone who could."

"You don't mean — "

"Yes. Don't you see? Odia wants revenge for the wrongful termination complaint. Or possibly she's putting you in harm's way to make me stop stirring up the rezzies. Maybe both — two reprisals for the price of one. I'm only speculating, but I'll bet I'm right."

"Who is Odia?" Violet asked. "And what are 'rezzies'? This sounds like much more than just a spiteful accusation. If I'm going to help you, you'll need to tell me everything."

# # #

"The call came sometime after eight o'clock last night. I

114

didn't recognize the voice at all," Bill said to Helen as they stood in line to place their order at the nearby Winter Freeze ice cream shop. The walls were covered in stylized, oversize snowflakes, and the store was air-conditioned to within a few degrees of freezing, or so it seemed.

"Was the voice male or female?" she asked.

"Don't know. It was electronically distorted. All the person said was, 'Back off or your granddaughter's problems will get worse.'"

The intensity of Helen's grimace took Bill by surprise. "There's no doubt it was Odia. She is such a *botheration*. Ed says we need to fight more viciously."

"What does he suggest?"

Helen smiled. "He wants to shoot her with a bazooka."

Bill laughed until he was in tears. "That's creative."

"Ed claims he was biblically inspired, according to Ephesians chapter six."

"Ephesians six?" Bill thought for a few seconds. "Ah. Stand your ground against evil by wearing the full armor of God. Let's see, the verses mention the sword of the Spirit and the shield of faith, but I don't recall a bazooka of righteous indignation."

They each ordered small sundaes. Bill shuffled across the dirty white floor to claim the last unoccupied table. He had overdone physical therapy this week and reverted to using a cane. At least it was less cumbersome than his walker.

Helen came to the table with ice cream in each hand. "I asked the teen behind the counter to put extra whipped topping on yours. She looked at me as though I wanted her to scrub the floor with a toothbrush. Is it too much effort to take her nose-picking finger and press the button on the can?"

Bill smiled. "Don't be so hard on her. Poor thing. She might chip a nail."

Helen rolled her eyes, then turned and glared at the girl

for a second.

They ate their ice cream in silence.

Several minutes later, after Helen had finished eating, she asked, "Are you going to take the threat seriously?"

Bill stuck his spoon in his unfinished dessert. "Yes, of course. But I—we can't back down." He had spoken with Maggie as soon as he received the call. She pleaded with him not to let Odia win through intimidation.

Helen frowned. "I don't know, Bill. Odia wouldn't think twice about making Maggie's life even more miserable."

He sighed. "Mags can take care of herself. Remember, she clashed with Odia once before."

"And got fired," Helen reminded him.

"Then filed a complaint and won a settlement."

"I hope you're not wrong about this," she said.

"We're not taking any chances. I've hired a great lawyer for Maggie. We met with her yesterday. Remember, I want the deck stacked in my favor. That goes double for my granddaughter."

"Should we rezzies get a lawyer too?" she asked.

"We may need one, but not just yet. Tomorrow Philippe and I will meet with the Tenant Advocates Union, the nonprofit that helps renters defend themselves against corrupt landlords."

Helen drew her hands to her chest and gasped. "Good heavens! Odia's sure to have a seizure when she finds out."

"I think it would serve her right," he said. "But we won't stop there."

Helen's eyes lit up. "Oooh. What else are we going to do?"

"I'm so glad you asked …"

# CHAPTER NINE

Odia's apartment was a cocoon of clinical sterility. The familiar scents of Lysol, lemon, and bleach greeted her as she entered. They were pleasant reminders that not a single stowaway microbe from FRAIL could establish itself in her home.

She laid the mail on the kitchen counter. One piece was from a charity pleading for donations. Odia never gave money to nonprofit organizations—she didn't trust them. She threw the unopened envelope into the recycle bucket.

There was a large postcard from the cable TV company urging her to upgrade to four thousand channels for an additional eighty-nine dollars per month. She hoped there was such a thing as Judgment Day. That way her cable provider would be sentenced to endure the "premium package" of end-time afflictions for its greed and abominable customer service.

The last item in the stack was a medium-sized, padded envelope. "Do Not Ignore—Urgent" was handwritten on the back using a thick, red marking pen. She flung it toward the recycle bin, but the parcel missed and landed faceup on the floor. *Drat!*

Odia did a double take, and her heart skipped a beat. The logo of the local television news show was printed on the front of the envelope. Now her heart was pounding and inserting extra beats to make up for the one it withheld earlier.

She picked up the package and tried to rip it open. Unfortunately the envelope was made from material that could survive an attack from a school of piranhas. She searched her junk drawer and found a box cutter. She slit open the recalcitrant package and extracted a DVD. Someone had written "Play Me" on it with a Sharpie. *What have the newspeople done?*

Curiosity and dread drove her to drop everything and find out what was on the disc. She rushed to the bedroom where her only television was located. It took her a few minutes to find all the necessary remote controls. Odia inserted the disc into her DVD player and sat on the edge of her bed. The TV screen displayed "Loading," and the player made grinding noises for nearly a minute.

"Just get on with it for Pete's sake!" she shouted at the machine.

*Finally.* The noises stopped and a dialog box popped up announcing, "A Software Update Is Available Y/N?" She stomped her feet and chose "N," hoping for no further delay.

The video began. Odia gasped. *Her?* It was the TV news personality who had badgered her during the residents' protest.

"I'm Faye Kanooze," said the bubbly news personality. "This is a demo for *Precarious*, an investigative report segment I'm pitching to the station. If my producer likes it, I'll get my own show, and the first episode will feature the residents of Freedom Retirement Active Independent Living."

*The old folks are behind this!* Odia was tempted to stop watching, but forced herself to continue. The geezers were exploiting the media to push their agenda. *Double drat!*

Her anxiety spiked like a bad haircut. Who else had

received copies? *Please, not the board members.* The fallout would be cataclysmic. She paused the video and ran to the kitchen to fetch her emergency stash of alprazolam.

Returning with her pills and a bottle of water, she took three tablets and resumed playback. The scene cut to Faye and Bill Armstrong in the TV studio, seated side by side in director's chairs, the TV station's logo on the wall behind them.

Faye began by providing background on FRAIL, then introduced Bill. "In your opinion, what is the biggest issue facing the residents?" she asked.

Bill leaned forward. "It's hard to communicate with management. The administrator rarely meets with us in person. The board ignores phone calls and e-mails."

"What are residents doing to encourage FRAIL management to be more responsive?" Faye asked.

Bill turned toward the camera. "We will raise the stakes if we don't see some results. You may think we're just a bunch of doddering old fools, content to knit socks all day, but we're fully capable of causing chaos."

The camera zoomed in on Faye's face. Her emerald-green eyes almost twinkled. "The residents recently secured outside help with a dispute. Earlier today we asked FRAIL resident Martin to explain."

The scene cut over to a headshot of Martin. "The Tenant Advocates Union, or TAU, is helping us organize a local chapter at FRAIL. Their people explained our legal rights and remedies in detail."

"What?" Odia shouted. *How did those senile stooges learn about TAU?* Old fogies couldn't possibly be so resourceful on their own. There had to be someone behind the scenes aiding them.

Another close-up of Faye filled the screen. "To be fair, one positive thing recently happened at FRAIL. Let's hear from another resident — Philippe."

"When my lease expires in less than two months, I shall

be relocating to an upgraded suite. I am so grateful for zee opportunity."

"No no no!" Odia beat the bed with the remote and inadvertently turned on closed captioning. "You're not supposed to take it," she squawked. "I expected you to move out." This put her in a bind since there were no upgraded suites, despite a contractor having been paid for "remodeling services." There would be *questions* once this became known.

Faye was back on the screen. "Wilma, a long-time resident, tells us how the physical condition of the facility has changed over the years."

The video showed exterior views of the building and grounds. "It was beautiful at first," Wilma said, "but now there's peeling paint all over and dead landscaping that looks bad. Our satellite TV service hasn't worked in over a week."

The scene faded to a shot of Faye and Helen sitting in the studio. "Another resident told us about some health and safety violations," Faye said.

"There are burned-out bulbs in the hallways," Helen said. "It makes it hard to walk safely at night. And on July 14 we had a fire in the building. It was terrifying."

*That was only two weeks ago.* The interviews were very recent, Odia deduced. She was surprised to be watching such a polished production, given the quick turnaround.

The scene changed to a shot of Faye standing next to FRAIL's main entrance. "So what options do these seniors have for getting management to respond to the dilapidated conditions?" Faye asked. "One resident, who declined to show their face on camera, hinted at their strategy."

The screen showed a silhouette of a person in a dimly lit room, facing away from the camera. The mystery interviewee wore a hooded sweatshirt. "We have obtained copies of the state landlord and tenant laws, as well as the county building codes. We're pretty close to filing formal complaints. Once we do that, we're protected against retaliatory rent increases and eviction."

Odia paused the DVD and ran from the room. She returned seconds later, snarfing frantically from her inhaler. Her scheme was coming apart like a pair of worn-out sneakers. *All those plague-ridden pensioners should have moved out by now.* Why hadn't they gone if conditions were as bad as they described?

It would be a disaster if the Kreakey board saw the video. It would be a catastrophe if the geezers filed official grievances. The directors would certainly launch an investigation. No amount of dirt that Odia had on the board members would prevent an inquisition—not when the shiny public image of the foundation was in danger. Her dream of PIEDRA would perish in a picosecond.

Where could she turn for help? Cozen? Did she trust him? No, she didn't. Why were people so disturbingly dishonest these days? Nevertheless he had connections in county and state government. It was possible for complaints to get hopelessly entangled in the wheels of bureaucracy. One simply greased palms rather than axles.

Her meds were starting to take effect. She had to finish watching the video before drowsiness overcame her.

Faye was back in the studio with Bill. "You heard from a few of the seniors who call FRAIL home," Faye said. "Bill, would you like to add anything before we end this segment?"

"Yes," he said, then pointed a finger at the camera. "You can utterly fail if you *frame* your problem incorrectly. Sort of like a *fire* with unknown origin. It's a challenging mystery if you look at the clues one way. But you can detect tampering with evidence when you take a different approach."

Odia hit the Stop button.

She leaned backward and lay on the bed, still clutching the remote. *Bill knows the truth about the fire.* This was getting to be too much. Each calamitous clash with the geezers ended up making life harder for her. *It was supposed to be the other way around.*

"I'll make you pay for this," she managed to say, slurring every word. Her meds were really kicking in now. Then she dropped the remote and closed her eyes.

# # #

After a good night's sleep Odia drove to the abandoned laundromat for another meeting with Cozen. Nine years ago the very spot she occupied would have been hot, humid, and detergent-scented. Today she was surrounded by a collapsing ceiling, broken floor tiles, and eerie silence.

Although the windows were boarded up, two large skylights allowed sunbeams to spotlight rows of defunct, coin-operated clothes dryers. When the nearby copper mine closed, the jobless folks left and took their laundry with them.

*I will do the same to FRAIL.* She fantasized roaming its corridors after its ungovernable inhabitants had decamped—demoralized, defeated, or dead. She imagined the overturned walkers and empty nutrition shake containers littering its unlit and uninhabited spaces.

Her phone tolled the somber notes of Chopin's "Funeral March." It was Cozen. "Where are you?" she asked.

"Right outside the back door, as you ordered."

She put her phone back in her pocket and let him in. "Were you followed?"

He furrowed his brow and stared. "Only by half a dozen feral cats. Nobody comes out here. It's a scary part of town."

"Then you should be packing a .357," she said.

He stepped back. "Are you?"

She frowned. "No, but I've got pepper spray, so don't make me angry."

"We're trespassing, you know. How did you get in? I

doubt you have a key."

She waved away his concern. "That's unimportant. I need your help."

"A thousand lawyers couldn't begin to untangle you from the web you're weaving. And that's just the stuff I know about. Who knows what else — "

"Keep your voice down," she said. "Let's talk over here." Odia led him to the end of a row of derelict clothes dryers.

"For goodness' sake, Fangmeister. What's so unspeakably secret that you couldn't ask me in my office?"

"We shouldn't be seen together. The old folks have become friends with the fluffy-haired floozie from the TV station. She wants to feature them on a news show."

Cozen put his palm against his forehead and stepped back. "What? When did this happen? What have you done?"

Odia described the *Precarious* video she had watched the previous evening.

He righted an overturned bench, sat on it, and buried his face in his hands. After a few seconds he lowered them and scowled at her, his complexion cherry-red.

"You're a menace," he said. "You fancy yourself to be a master manipulator like J.R. Ewing — but you're not. You couldn't make a sheet of tinfoil bend to your will."

His criticism stung. It took her a moment to process the unexpected attack. She rationalized his behavior as an angry outburst and nothing more. After all, Cozen's covert criminality was on the verge of exposure. He was the bungler.

"Look, it's simple," she said. "You've got friends in government. Can you get them to lose, ignore, deny, or delay any health and safety complaints those geezers might make?"

"That's easy," he said. "On the other hand I can't control the media. Our goose will be cooked if *Precarious*

123

gets on the air."

"Leave that to me," Odia said.

"No! Do not go after the newspeople. In fact don't do anything else to anybody. You've done enough damage already."

"The sooner we get that reporter out of the way, the better."

Cozen's eyes widened. "What do you mean by 'get her out of the way'?"

"Have her discredited, transferred, fired, whatever. Then those silver-haired subversives won't have any power over us."

"Or you could just stop antagonizing them," he said.

"I'm doing it for you. You told me to raise more revenue. You need the cash, you said."

He stood. "I didn't graduate from Credulous College, you know. Who do you think you're fooling? You're trying to force out the tenants so that FRAIL will collapse. Then you'll try to get your paws on the endowment funds for your self-inflicted psychosis sanitarium."

"You promised to help me if I helped you," Odia reminded him.

"You haven't even helped yourself. All you've done is get yourself on TV and turn the residents against you. That doesn't do me any good."

"Then tell me how we can legally evict them. Especially Bill. Oh, and I need a defensible way to fire Maggie. Without the two ringleaders the others will cave."

Cozen shook his head. "You don't get it, do you? If anyone should be fired, it's you."

"I keep telling you, let's just close down the place."

"I've explained dozens of times. We can't legally shut it down on a whim. Your plan might have worked if we had the luxury of time — but we don't. The only way I'll survive a financial audit is for you to do exactly as I say."

Odia put her hands on her hips. "Suppose I don't?"

He wiped his face with his palm. "Then I've got nothing to lose by personally telling the TV news crew everything you've ever done, including the fire in the closet."

Odia pulled her inhaler from a pocket and snarfed. "You know about that?"

"We can share a jail cell," he said.

Her shoulders slumped. "What do you want me to do?"

"Here's a list of improvements your facility needs, and this is the name of a contractor I know. Call him tomorrow. Hire him. Pay him whatever he asks. Don't scrutinize his methods or results. Got it?"

Odia flailed her arms. "But that's all wrong. We don't want to improve the building."

He shoved the folded-up lists into her hand. "Stop worrying. I don't expect to get our money's worth, if you know what I mean."

"No. Spell it out."

Cozen sighed. "Really? Look, some of the money you spend will find its way back to me. Then I can replace the foundation funds that might have been, shall we say, misplaced."

"What's my reward? Are you going to make good on your promise to fund PIEDRA?"

"Did you fail *Finance 101*? Fund it with what?"

He detoured around debris on his way to the door. The seat of his dark trousers bore the imprint of the dusty bench.

Odia waited inside until she heard him drive away. She grinned as she pulled the small tape recorder out of the dryer next to where they had argued.

"Looks like someone failed *Avoiding Entrapment 101* …"

# # #

The FRAIL theater never got brighter than a camping tent at sunset, even with the lights set to full intensity. Bill sat on the wooden stool that Maggie had provided and counted heads. Only nine rezzies bothered to attend today's town hall meeting.

"Before Josie gets here with Odia's latest episode of 'impudent impropriety,' I'd like to say something," Bill said. He lifted one leg and rested it on a rung. "Nearly half of us have stopped attending these bad news briefings. This is not the time to bury our heads in the sand. We have to face adversity and fight for change."

Josie entered the theater carrying a DVD.

Bill nodded at her. "I'll be done in a few minutes." He turned back to the audience. "On your behalf I've signed us up with the Tenant Advocates Union. We're about to submit formal complaints to code enforcement and health departments as soon as Helen finishes the paperwork. The *Precarious* video clearly warned Odia we would be going down that road. She should have received it a couple days ago."

"You're assuming she watched it," Charlie said. "We spent a whole week filming that news segment, but I'll bet you money she simply tossed it out."

"Let's see what she says on tonight's DVD," Bill said. "If it's full of punitive reprisals, then we can be sure she got our message."

Martin raised his hand. "I keep telling you we're wasting our time. She wants us gone, and she won't give up until we leave."

"Why are you still here, then?" Ed asked. "If you're ready to move out, I'll help you pack."

"Okay, that's enough," Bill said. "We need all the rezzies to be engaged, so do your best to convince those who aren't here. As Henry Ford once said, 'If everyone is moving forward together, then success takes care of itself.'"

He slid off the stool and returned to his front-row seat.

Odia's video began with the same intro as her previous one, then the image dissolved to a wide shot of her sitting behind her desk.

Boos and hisses emanated from the rezzies.

"Occupants of Freedom Retirement Active yada, yada, yada ..." Odia said. "I am unshaken by your spiteful and capricious attempt to intimidate me. You *amateurs*! That puerile production with Snooze Kanooze from television news made me laugh. Ha. Ha-ha. Ahhhhhhahahahahahaha!"

She lapsed into a coughing fit. The suffocating slinger of sarcasm retrieved an inhaler from a drawer. Down came the mask. She snarfed several puffs from the device.

"Santa Maria!" Ed exclaimed. "Quick, pull up your mask!"

"*Quelle horreur!*" Philippe added. "What a horror. Why does she not edit away the spooky scenes?"

Odia wiped her eyes with a tissue and tugged the mask back into position. "Why should I be afraid of a bunch of debilitated denizens like you?" Her hand waved away an imaginary foe. "I'm not the least bit worried about your tenants union. Let me warn you about TAU. It's run by a crew of lawyer-wannabes who washed out of law school. They'll tell you what you want to hear, get your hopes up, and then steer you to a real attorney in return for a kickback. You'll end up with legal bills, but no results. Trust me on this."

Bill clenched his fists. *She's lying like a wet rug.* Speaking from a video in order to avoid being challenged was a cowardly way to fight. He worried that her false narrative might turn the more gullible rezzies against him.

"You'd better heed one other piece of advice," Odia added. "Don't embarrass yourselves by lodging complaints with regulators. You know there are no legitimate safety violations. You're wasting your time. The inspectors will throw out your case without a second thought."

The video abruptly cut to an extreme close-up of Odia's face. "The county might even charge you with making false allegations. You may think conditions are bad here, but jail is worse. Take my word for it."

Her beady eyes darted from side to side. "I've never been incarcerated myself, of course, but I hear it's no fun. The slammer is no place for old people. You could die in there."

The scene changed to a distorted view of Odia at her desk. It was like watching through someone else's eyeglasses.

"Focus!" Charlie shouted.

"No! She's not so ugly when she's blurred," Ed snapped. "Josie, can you smear the image even more?"

Odia continued, "But you don't have to believe anything I say. You can go on following Colonel Napoleon Armstrong. The Colonel doesn't necessarily have your best interests in mind, though. Why is he stirring up trouble? Who knows? I'm convinced that you are nothing but pawns in his personal vendetta against me. He knows that FRAIL is in financial distress, yet he persists in fighting every single thing I do to try to save your home."

Helen practically skyrocketed out of her seat. "Stop the tape. Stop the tape!"

Josie paused the playback.

"That woman has absolutely no scruples!" Helen shouted. "I won't have it. She can't vilify Bill like that and get away with it." She started up the aisle toward the door. "I'm going over there to give her a jalapeño enema using the biggest—"

"Wait!" Josie moved to intercept her. "Wait. She's not here. She left right after she gave me the disc. Please calm down, Miss Helen." She walked Helen back to her seat.

Wilma moved to the seat beside Helen and patted her shoulder.

Bill stood and faced the rezzies. "Let's remain cool. Remember, we're dealing with a desperate foe who's cornered. It's no surprise she's baring her fangs."

"What are you going to do about it?" Charlie asked.

128

"About what? Odia hasn't done anything so far except run her mouth."

Martin stood. "When will you people face reality? She just told us the agencies won't act on our grievances. What can we do then? I'm not sure who has who cornered."

"It's all propaganda," Bill replied. "We're going to stick to our plan."

Martin sat and sulked.

"Josie," Bill said as he turned and sat, "is there anything more on the disc?"

She resumed play.

The masked maligner's blurry image reappeared. "So along the lines of preventing FRAIL from going bankrupt, I must impose certain minor fee increases."

"Looks like she's sticking to her plan as well," Martin said.

"For starters," Odia said, "laundry services are not cheap. Washing clothes uses lots of water and energy. There will be a 15 percent increase in laundry fees.

"Furthermore I'm closing the coffee shop indefinitely. I'm sure you all know how to make your own coffee.

"Last, since the Colonel forced me to keep the dining room open seven days a week, the cost of every meal plan is going up 25 percent. I have to recover the extra expense somehow."

Various interjections erupted from the audience, many of them not repeatable in mixed company.

The screen faded to black. "Have a Nice Day, Colonel!" appeared in large block letters.

"Hey, Martin," Ed called out as he left his seat. "Come over to my suite. Let's watch *Titanic*. I could use some cheering up."

Others glared at Bill before quietly heading for the exit.

Bill sat motionless. *What just happened?* She had made him the bad guy, and he never saw it coming.

Helen and Josie came over. "Don't let it get you down,"

Helen said. "We knew it would be a difficult fight. We won't underestimate her again."

# # #

The following day Bill reluctantly accompanied Helen to her suite after the morning meal. She had insisted he spend the day with her, although he preferred to be alone.

"Are you sure you won't have some tea?" Helen asked. "You hardly ate anything."

"No. I've decided to go on a hunger strike, like Gandhi."

Helen took his hand. "That may be a bit much, don't you think?"

"It's one thing I can't mess up. The rezzies were counting on me to stop Odia Fangmeister, but I failed. They said so at breakfast."

"Only the fickle ones—those who abandon their team in a losing season."

Bill sighed. There was no single word for what he felt, so he invented one: *embaranger*—a combination of embarrassment and anger.

He couldn't stop thinking of the scene in the dining room this morning. Odia had burst in and gleefully announced that investigators had certified FRAIL to be compliant with applicable codes and regulations.

There was a knock at the door. "Miss Helen, it's Maggie. May I come in?"

Helen got up from the dinette table and let her in.

Maggie smiled at Helen and raced over to hug Bill. "Hi, Grampa. How are you doing?"

He looked up at her but didn't smile. "I'm just patiently waiting to die, sweetie. I've outlived my usefulness."

"Oh, Grampa, don't say such a thing. Is this about the code violations?"

Bill nodded. "It was our last hope, but it's clear there's no way to stop Odia."

"I never saw an inspector. We need to appeal the findings," Helen said.

"No good," he countered. "Anna Janus told me the foundation directors are afraid of Odia. I wouldn't be surprised if the county bureaucrats are scared of her too."

"Or she may have bribed someone to have our complaints quashed," Helen said. "If we can find evidence of that ..."

"It's no use speculating," he said. "Let's face facts. There's no future here for any of us."

Maggie sat next to him and patted his shoulder. "I know it looks grim, but we'll figure something out."

There was another knock. "It must be Philippe," Helen said. "I didn't think you would mind if he came over."

"Whatever," Bill grumbled.

Helen opened the door. "Good morning."

"*Bon jour.* 'Ow is my good friend, zee Colonel?" Philippe used his heaviest French accent. "He is feeling very sorry for himself, *non?*"

The slightest hint of a smile crossed Bill's face. "Well, if it isn't my old friend Pepé Le Pew." Somehow a problem didn't seem as bad as all that after sharing it with Philippe.

"I came over to tell you, *mon ami*, a thing that will cheer you up."

"Has Odia fallen down a mine shaft?" Helen asked.

"Nothing so fortunate," Philippe said. "Colonel Bill, I heard today from Anna Janus. You are acquainted with her?"

"Yes, of course," Bill said.

"She told to me that I should not move out. She promises to remedy the situation with my expired lease within the next thirty days."

"Finally, someone at the Kreakey Foundation has pulled their head out of ... the sand," Helen said.

"That's great," Maggie said. "Are you going to sign it?"

"I told her I will do so only if she does the same for my

friend Colonel Bill."

Maggie gave Bill a surprised look. "Grampa! Has your lease expired too? Why didn't you tell anyone?"

Bill frowned. "This doesn't change anything. It just prolongs our stay at a place we don't like."

"It buys you time," Maggie said.

"It's futile. Here I thought my detailed battle strategy would bring us victory. In the end, though, it only worsened our situation."

"Was Ms. Janus prepared to fix Grampa's lease too?" Maggie asked.

"*Oui*, she assured me she would soon contact the Colonel." Philippe sat in the chair directly opposite Bill. "I have been thinking, my friend. Why do you not allow the rest of us to randomly make the trouble, instead of planning things *avec precision*?"

"Yes ... I like it," Helen said. "Let us take the risks and shoulder some of the burden."

"On top of that we shall also remove from our hands the boxing gloves. The Fangmeister woman, she does not fight per *zee* rules," Philippe said.

Bill was unsure how to interpret this. Was this mutiny, or was it constructive criticism? Either way it went against his need for order and method. It would be like taking a bite of potatoes before having eaten all the steak.

"Suppose what you say is true," he said. "We still don't know what our goal should be. We can't fight without an objective, can we?"

Maggie answered a call on her phone. "Summer, I'm at work. ... Yes, okay. But first say hi to Poppy. He's feeling kind of sad. I'm putting you on speaker."

"Hello, Summer."

"Hi, Poppy. Why are you feeling sad? Is mean old Ms. Fang Monster bothering you again?"

"What gave you that idea?" Bill asked.

"Mommy doesn't like her one bit. I'm glad I don't have

her for a teacher, or I would bring a skunk to school every day until the smell bothered her so much that she ran away and never came back."

"Okay, Summer," Maggie interrupted. "Thank you for the advice. Say good-bye now."

"Bye, Poppy. And don't be sad anymore."

Maggie ended the call. She smiled sheepishly. "She's not getting a skunk."

Bill's eyes lit up. "Summer just gave us our objective."

# # #

The next day Bill was in the FRAIL prayer room, watching Manuel take his time arranging chairs in a semicircle. This room was clearly an afterthought, Bill reckoned, since it shared a wall with the theater and caused a zigzag in the corridor.

"Ees okay, sir?" Manuel asked.

"Perfect. Thank you. You can go now."

Helen came through the door just seconds after Manuel left. "Sounds as though Ed's on his way," she said. "His hearing aids are squealing a symphony in the hall."

Bill took a seat, and Helen sat next to him.

Ed shuffled in a few seconds later. "Whose idea was it to meet in here? Don't you know you shouldn't conspire in a sacred place? There's no telling which god — or gods — might choose to rain down punishment on us."

"Your momma never took you to church, did she?" Helen asked.

"Why would you think that?" Ed responded.

Bill poked him with his cane. "It's just a room. Sit down. If you're really worried, you should stay out of my suite from now on — I have a shelf full of Bibles."

Philippe, Martin, Charlie, and Wilma arrived together and took seats.

"Why are we meeting in here?" Martin asked.

"What is so controversial about this place?" Bill

growled. "It's only a room."

"Easy, Bill," said Helen. "They're just curious. For everyone's information the theater is unavailable all week for repairs or something. And since we're scheming, we didn't want to gather in the activity room where others could eavesdrop."

Ed installed one of his hearing aids. "You know, General — sorry ... Colonel — you've gotten really grumpy ever since half the rezzies quit backing your foiled fight for fairness."

Bill felt his stomach knot and his face grow warm. He counted to ten. He glared at Ed and counted to ten again. Ed could be so insensitive. But, like it or not, Bill had lost supporters.

He terminated the glare and raised an eyebrow. "I am not grumpy. Now zip it."

"*Excusez-moi*," Philippe said, "but the war is not finished. *Non non non.* That is why we prepare ourselves to deliver zee *coup final* to the odious executive."

"After careful consideration Bill has decided on a new objective," Helen said. "We're going to turn the tables. We're not leaving. Odia will be the one to go."

"Hold on a second," Wilma said. "Nobody's gonna fire her. If they was gonna get rid of her, they would have done it already."

"That's right," Bill said, "which is why we've got to drive her crazy, so to speak. Make it so unpleasant that she'll run from the building, screaming all the way."

"None of your plots have worked so far," Ed said.

"I'm aware of that. This time I won't direct your moves. Each of you is free to use whatever tactics you want. Keep the goal in mind and ask for help if you need it. Otherwise you're on your own."

"I need help," Helen said. "We've got to learn about her pet peeves and her fears. I can hack her computer but we also need to bug her office. Who can do that?"

"Hold on," said Charlie. "Surely we're not going to stoop to that? It's unethical and highly illegal."

"The government does it all the time," Ed said.

"Well, it's wrong."

"Is it okay to hack the computer to convey false information?" Martin asked. "For example, tamper with search engine results?"

"Or instead of using a wiretap to snoop on Odia, can we hijack her radio, or the PA system to inject subliminal messages? Surely that's okay, right?" Ed asked.

The group's immediate engagement surprised Bill. He listened to their lengthy debate over moral issues. It gave him confidence that his lieutenants would do the right thing. Why hadn't he encouraged them to act independently from the start?

"I agree it's best to operate ethically, but how can we gather critical information without spying?" Helen asked.

All eyes were on Bill. *Civilians can be so unimaginative.* "Human intelligence," he said. "Go around and talk with people. Maggie, Josie, Manuel, and Lisa probably know things about Odia they don't know they know."

"Bet you can't say that again," Ed muttered.

"What do we do first, Colonel?" Wilma asked.

Bill suppressed his instinct to give a direct answer. Instead he made eye contact one by one with his spirited commandos. "I don't know. What do you think we should do?" Fighting the urge to plan and control every detail was going to be difficult, and would likely give him an ulcer.

Wilma flashed an evil grin that would make even the Grinch cower. "I've got an idea …"

# CHAPTER TEN

Sunlight was gently erasing the last of the starry sky on the first Wednesday of August. Wilma was already in the lobby, waiting for her volunteers to arrive. She had asked her friends at church for help with a little project. Before long a small army had signed up, and the scope had mushroomed.

Charlie walked up behind her. "I can't believe we're doing this. It's a bit of overkill, don't you think?"

"If there's anything that's excessive, it's Fangmeister's behavior. This will serve her right for raising laundry fees so high. I'm gonna show her that we rezzies can take care of our own washing, thank you very much."

A small convoy of pickup trucks turned into the FRAIL driveway just as dawn broke. Wilma went outside to meet them. Charlie followed.

A short, muscular Hispanic man wearing a cowboy hat stepped out of the lead pickup. "Where do you want the pools?"

"What pools would those be?" Wilma asked.

"We have eight-foot-diameter pools for washing and rinsing linens," he said. "Need a large, flat spot for them."

Charlie looked at Wilma and shrugged. "How about next to the patio where Josie set off fireworks?" He pointed to the area in question. "Over there behind the building."

"That might work," the man from the truck said. "Looks like there's a path leading from the parking lot, so we can drive right over there. We'll get them set up in thirty minutes. The water tanker should be here by then."

"Tanker?" Charlie asked.

"We could only spare one, but it holds twenty-six hundred gallons. That should be plenty," the man said.

He got back into his truck and drove to the patio, followed by the other pickups.

Charlie poked Wilma in the ribs. "Do you know what you're doing?"

"I thought it would simply be ladies with washtubs and a water hose. Nobody told me about tankers and pools," she said.

A flatbed truck stopped short with a hiss of its air brakes. A tall man wearing a ponytail climbed down from the cab. He also appeared to be Hispanic. "I brought the poles for the clotheslines. Where do they go?" He practically shouted to be heard over the noise from the diesel engine.

Charlie pointed toward the patio.

"We'll have them up in no time," the man said, and climbed back into his vehicle.

A cacophony of grinding gears caused Wilma to jerk her hands up to her ears. She kept them there until the truck moved on.

"Oh look, Charlie," Wilma said, referring to a minivan coming up the driveway. "It's the women from church."

The van, occupied by at least nine women, stopped, and the driver's side window slid open. "Good morning, Wilma. We're ready to go. I brought my cousin, my neighbor, her sister, and my sister-in-law. Oh, and five more ladies are coming later."

Wilma pointed to the patio. "We're setting up over there."

The van drove off.

"Uh-oh," Charlie said. "Here comes Maggie. Did you tell her about this?"

"Nope. The less she knows, the better off she'll be. We don't want her to get in trouble with Odia."

"It's not like constructing your own laundromat is gonna go unnoticed."

"No, but she can honestly say she wasn't privy to our plans."

Maggie got out of her car and came over. "What's going on over there?"

Charlie looked at his shoes.

Wilma took Maggie's hand and patted it. "Nothing to see here. Have a nice day."

"Oh no," Maggie said. "What are you up to? Please tell me."

Wilma divulged the details of her washday operation.

"Will these people be here all morning?" Maggie asked.

"Until we're done."

"Ms. Fangmeister is going to go nonlinear when she sees this."

"It will be fine, hon."

"I doubt it," Maggie said. "Look, I insist you put a stop to this right now."

Wilma winked at her. "Okay, you've told us off, and we didn't listen. It's not your fault. There was nothing you could do. Sorry, Mags."

Maggie sighed. "I'll have to call Josie and Manuel to come in, for security reasons. We can't have strangers wandering into the building. That means they'll be working a double shift today. They won't like it one bit, Miss Wilma."

Another pickup pulled up, towing a small enclosed trailer. The driver beckoned Maggie over to the cab. Wilma followed close behind.

"Where does this go?" he asked.

"Don't ask me; she's the one in charge," Maggie said and pointed over her shoulder with her thumb.

Wilma advised the driver, then turned around and noticed Maggie heading to the building entrance. *Now where did Charlie go?*

The water tanker and a second minivan filled with women passed Wilma as she walked over to the patio area. The rezzies had commandeered FRAIL's housekeeping carts and were using them to transport laundry. Volunteers were setting up tables on the patio. Mexican music blared from enormous speakers in the bed of a pickup truck.

Helen emerged from the building pushing a cart overloaded with dirty linen. "I see you have plenty of galvanized washtubs, but they're not big enough to wash sheets."

"That's what the pools are for," Wilma said.

"How are we going to keep up with which laundry belongs to who?" Helen asked.

"Charlie was going to take care of that, but I don't know where he ran off to."

Helen smiled and waved at a passing volunteer. "You know, this is a great way to make a point, but I doubt we can do it every week. These people have lives of their own."

"Yes, of course. Isn't it touching, though, that they've come to help us? And in such a big way. It almost brings a tear to my eye."

A volunteer came up to Wilma. "We're ready to start. They're filling up the pools now. We have two portable propane water heaters for them, but we have to use cold water in the *tinas*."

"The what?" Wilma asked.

"The *TEE-nahs*. That's Spanish for washtubs."

"Oh. Thank you for coming. Your support means a lot to us."

"Of course. You have been through so much. We want your nasty landlord to know that you have lots of friends who will fight by your side. Where is she, anyway?"

"She's probably on her way," Helen said.

Wilma spotted Charlie and made a beeline for him. "You're supposed to make sure the laundry doesn't get all mixed up. Where have you been?"

"I had to go fix my choppers," Charlie responded. "The uppers came loose, and it's your fault because you keep leaving your tube of itch cream next to my denture adhesive."

# # #

As she opened her car door, Odia heard trumpet and accordion sounds coming from the back of the building. *Mexican music.* Only country music was worse.

She pressed the Lock button on her key fob. The expected *whoop-whoop* sound was drowned out by the noise of a flatbed truck on its way down the driveway.

*Where did that come from?* Loud music and a big truck. She began to fear that this might not be the uneventful Wednesday morning she was hoping for. *Don't tell me those denture-suckers are up to something again.*

She raced across the parking lot, turned the corner of the building, and stopped. The chaotic scene made no sense. Heavy vehicles. Lots of people. Kiddie pools. A taco truck.

Someone shouted, *"Ay viene la loca!"*

She knew enough Spanish to understand: *"Here comes the crazy woman!"*

The music continued, but all motion stopped. Geezers and unwelcome trespassers stared at her.

Odia crossed her arms and scanned the mob. "Who are you people, and what is going on here?" she hollered over the music.

From the corner of her eye she spied Manuel skulking away from the patio. "Manuel. Manuel!" She stomped over to confront him.

140

"What are these people doing here? What is all this?"

He raised his hands like someone hoping to avoid touching a live wire. "Maggie call me. She say lots of people washing clothes. She want me to do security."

"So … what, then? Does your family have a laundry business?" she shouted.

"What? No. Why you think they my family?"

"Yeah," said a female volunteer who had been listening to the conversation. "Come on, lady, you think all Hispanics are related? You got a problem with Mexicans?" She stuck her chest out and made a fist.

Others were coming over. If they weren't Manuel's kin, they appeared ready to adopt him. And would probably defend him like a brother.

"Never mind," Odia said. "Where's Bill?"

"Right behind you," Bill said.

She spun around. "What's the meaning of this? Get rid of these people—now!"

"I had nothing to do with it."

"You lie. You're the leader of these mummified miscreants. What do you want this time?"

"My lease is not being renewed, and I'm out of the picture now. The residents don't take orders from me. They've gone rogue." He smiled and walked away.

The words zapped her brain like an electric shock. There was no telling what heinous misdeeds could be perpetrated upon her by an army of ungoverned seniors. It was too frightening to accept.

She jumped up and down in an unflattering imitation of a child throwing a tantrum. "I demand to know who organized this!"

Wilma came up to her. "What? No mask? Oh, Ms. Fangmeister, you really should be more careful. Here, cover your face with this." She handed Odia a pair of men's cotton underwear. "It's the best we can do on *shorts* notice—Ha-ha."

Odia flung the briefs to the ground. "That's not funny at all. Did you arrange this frivolous fiesta?"

"I simply invited a few friends over to help with the wash. We can't afford community laundry services anymore. Would you like us to do your laundry?"

"If laundry fees are too expensive for you, then you can't afford to live here. Tell these Mex — tell these friends of yours to go home. And then go find somewhere cheaper to live." Odia felt lightheaded. *This can't be good for my blood pressure.*

"No, I don't think so," Wilma said, then turned and walked away.

Applause broke out. Someone in the crowd yelled, "Viva Wilma!"

"Will somebody turn off that awful music?" Odia shouted. She could hear her heartbeat inside her head. *How do I pull the plug on this pandemonium?*

An idea popped into her head. *Take down the clothesline.* She charged through the group of washer women and stopped abruptly at the clothes-hanging area. A large German shepherd locked eyes with her and snarled.

"Shut up, dog!" Odia commanded.

The canine lunged at her. She backed away.

The dog's owner clutched its leash and struggled to keep it from making a snack of Odia. "Slasher doesn't like people getting near the clean clothes. Especially pale, skinny people." He stepped toward her and the dog took up the slack in the leash.

Odia turned and retreated.

She risked a backward glance. Slasher and his owner were following her. The dog was barking itself hoarse.

She broke into a run and entered the facility via the patio door. Odia leaned hard as she made the turn into the admin corridor. Nearing the lobby, she cleared an errant basket of laundry with an athletic leap and skidded to a stop at the reception desk. "Lisa! I don't have my badge —

unlock my door. Hurry!"

Lisa swiped her own badge in the reader.

Hearing the *clunk* of the lock mechanism, Odia rushed into her office. "Get Ms. Providence over here to take my BP. Now! And get Animal Control to come collect a rabid dog."

She kicked the door shut. Out came the inhaler and the alprazolam. She double-dosed on each, then stretched out on the floor and hyperventilated.

# # #

Three days after "wash day" Martin and Charlie were skulking down the admin corridor, arguing as usual. Both were dressed in light-blue, cotton coveralls.

"You've been watching too many *Mission: Impossible* reruns," Martin said. "We're not trained spies. And we're certainly not electronics experts. Besides, you can't divert people's attention as easily as they do on TV."

Charlie stopped and looked back at Martin. "Come on, keep up."

"I'm trying, but my socks keep falling down. I think they got damaged at Wilma's outdoor laundry. Anyway, we shouldn't be doing this without lots of practice. What if I mess up?"

"Don't be such a pessimist," Charlie said. "You only need to program one new frequency into Odia's police scanner. A few key presses will do it. I can keep Lisa busy for two or three minutes while you do that."

"Why can't we do it at night when everyone's gone home?" Martin asked.

"I told you, we don't have a key to her office. It's got that electronic lock where you need to swipe a badge to get in."

Martin's face advertised worry. "Did you remember to drill a hole in the water cooler?"

"Of course," Charlie said. "Right after Josie clocked out

last night. All I have to do now is pull out the little rubber plug I drove into the puncture. It'll leak like a busted radiator."

"Are you sure I can unlock the office with Lisa's badge?"

"I've seen her do it lots of times. The only thing that could go wrong is if she unexpectedly decided to wear it today. She always leaves it lying next to her desk phone."

They reached the lobby. Charlie went to the water dispenser and waited for Martin to reach Lisa's desk. The plug came out of the huge plastic bottle with no effort. Water trickled down the side of the appliance onto the polished floor. The fast-growing puddle would soon become a slip hazard.

"Lisa!" Charlie waved her over. "Help me take this bottle off. It's leaking."

She ran over to him. "Everyone's in the weekly staff meeting. I'll go get someone —"

"No no no! I'll just put my finger over the hole," said Charlie. "Can you go to the dining room and get some towels, or a mop? Hurry — hurry!" He tried to spur her into action without giving her a chance to think. They needed her out of the foyer.

"I'll be right back," she said and sped off up the corridor.

Charlie looked in the direction of the reception desk just in time to see Martin snatch Lisa's badge and head toward Odia's office.

In just under a minute Lisa returned with a mop and one of the kitchen crew. They made the floor safe while Charlie held back the potential deluge.

"We should empty the bottle before trying to remove it," Charlie advised. "Otherwise we might make a bigger mess."

The fry cook ran off to get a bucket.

"What do you think caused it to leak?" Lisa asked.

"Here, look closely," Charlie said. "There's a pinhole here. Must have been a defective bottle." He removed his finger from the compromised container.

"No! Don't—"

Lisa quickly covered the breach with her finger.

When the cook returned, he and Lisa got to work emptying the bottle. They didn't notice Martin exit Odia's office and return the badge.

"You two seem to have things under control," Charlie said. "Guess I'll go play bingo." He joined Martin, and the pair left for the activity room.

Charlie noticed Martin was sweating profusely. "Was it hot in there?"

Martin pulled out a handkerchief and wiped his face and neck. "No, I just got nervous. I'm glad that's done, but I still don't understand the plan."

"Good golly, Martin. Don't aerospace engineers know anything about electronics? One last time: the frequency you added will let Odia's scanner pick up signals from a walkie-talkie I have in my suite. We'll fake some police radio chatter, but she'll think it's real."

"What if she's not listening?" Martin asked.

"Lisa says she always has the scanner turned on. C'mon. Let's go get ready. We've gotta tap into the building's overhead paging system tomorrow."

# # #

Bill accepted the mug of coffee from Helen and set it down. "How did the scanner reprogramming go yesterday?" he asked. "Charlie and Martin aren't the greatest at subterfuge, you know."

"You promised you wouldn't micromanage us," she said, then scurried back into her kitchen.

She returned seconds later with an Elvis sugar bowl and took a seat across from him.

Bill sweetened his coffee. "I'm a worrier. I can't help it.

That's why I'm uneasy about you hacking Odia's computer. You could get into big trouble."

"Don't worry. Think of it as an elaborate college prank. I'm not going anywhere near her machine. I plan to use *clickbait*."

"Click what?"

Helen chuckled. "Clickbait. Formally known as 'forward referencing narrative strategy.' I'll insert ads in her browser with enticing photos or tantalizing words I think will interest her. She'll click on the ads for more information. The links will take her to bogus sites I've created."

Bill wished he knew as much about computer technology as Helen did. "How will that drive her away from FRAIL? That's our primary objective."

"You said we should prey upon her fears and insecurities. This is a way to validate and even amplify those emotions."

Bill scratched his head. "I don't know if she's that gullible."

"We're not exploiting her credulousness as much as leveraging her curiosity. For example, if you saw the words 'Twenty Ways to Legally Take Revenge on Your Landlord,' wouldn't you click on it?"

"Okay okay. But how do we insert the ads? I still don't understand."

She wondered how much detail to go into. Was he familiar with *adware*? He had probably heard of *phishing*, although she doubted he would support such a strategy.

"Bill, it's a multistep process. I'm sure you don't want me to go into the tedious technical details. But I promise — I won't touch her machine."

"For someone who retired from the computer industry over a decade ago, you seem very confident," he said.

"Just because I left my job doesn't mean I stopped learning."

Bill sipped his coffee. "How long will it take to create the fake web pages? Do you know what you're going to do?"

"We've learned some interesting things from Manuel and the girls lately. Were you aware Odia is not afraid of all germs?"

"Then why does she wear the mask?" Bill asked.

"She only wears it around old people because she believes aging is contagious—caused by catching geriatric microbes from the elderly."

"The woman's loonier than I realized," Bill said.

"And Lisa says Odia's worried that we're out to get her."

He grinned. "There's no doubt about that."

"No, I mean the woman's truly afraid we intend to cause her bodily harm."

"It's hard to decide what fear to prey upon," Bill said. "There are so many."

"I'll target more than one. Give me a few days to get everything set up. Meanwhile, if you want to sleep soundly, don't ask what Charlie and Martin are up to today."

# # #

"Tell me again why we have to go outside," Martin said. "Isn't the paging system at Lisa's desk?"

Charlie entered the five-digit code to unlock the door leading to the patio. "Listen this time, okay? Lisa uses the phone at her desk to make an overhead page, right? But the electronics aren't at her desk; they're in the electrical closet. It's not a difficult concept. Sheesh."

"I wonder why the closet is outside? The building where I worked had them on the inside."

Charlie stopped mid-stride. "You ask more questions than a five-year-old. The answer is, I don't know. Maybe it was near quitting time when they installed the door. In the rush to get done, they probably hung it on the outside by mistake. Hey, where are you going?"

Martin wandered over to a nearby creosote bush. He wrestled with a branch until it broke off. He came back, walking backward and using the branch to erase his footsteps. "We don't want to be followed."

"You're a nut," Charlie said, then resumed walking to the closet door.

"How are we gonna unlock — Oh, I see."

Charlie pointed to the door and gave Martin a smug look. There was a hole where the knob should be. A wooden forklift pallet had been propped up against the door to hold it shut. "Firefighters pried it open the night we had the fire, but Manuel never gets around to fixing it."

Martin dragged the pallet aside.

Charlie entered the tiny closet and paused to give his eyes time to adjust to the dimness. Martin ran right into him.

"Hey, watch it," Charlie said.

"Sorry. I didn't see you. Is there a light switch somewhere?"

"Yeah, it's by the door, but it doesn't work. Give me the flashlight out of the backpack," Charlie ordered.

"Heh-heh. Funny thing — I forgot the backpack."

"You dipstick. Go back and get it. Don't let anybody see you."

Martin hitched up his trousers and hurried off.

Charlie looked around the room. His vision had improved enough to navigate the narrow aisle between racks of telecom and electrical equipment. There was no hint of fire damage beyond a scorch mark on the concrete floor. He identified the modules where he would tap into the paging system.

*Get a move on, Martin.* He couldn't do anything without the tools in the backpack. A dangling coax cable caught his eye. It had been disconnected from something.

*Might as well see what this goes to.* The cable exited the

building near the ceiling. He wondered if it might be the satellite dish feed. He found the satellite TV equipment. Sure enough, nothing was feeding the antenna input.

Martin arrived with the backpack. "Here you go."

"It's about time. Hey, I think I've found the reason our satellite TV won't work."

"Odia said it was damaged by the fire," Martin said.

"She lied. Someone disconnected the dish antenna. I'll just remedy that right now." He screwed the cable into the connector on the receiver. Red blinking lights on the front panel disappeared, replaced by steady green indicators.

"Now get me the paging manual," Charlie said.

Martin dug in the backpack and produced the document. "Where did you get this?"

"Lisa has a file drawer full of instruction and installation manuals. I just helped myself late one night."

"How much work is this going to be?"

"Hardly any. I simply take the audio cable we brought and plug it into the music input jack. Then we drill a hole in that wall over there, which also happens to be my living room wall, and snake the cable through. After that we can sit in my suite and use a microphone to play voices or spooky sound effects through the paging system whenever we want."

Martin cocked his head. "Wait a minute. Won't it be heard all over the building?"

"Nope. The system is divided into nine zones. We're only hijacking the zone for Odia's office. It's separate so she doesn't have to listen to everyone else's pages, or that elevator music we have to endure in the dining room."

Martin switched on the flashlight. He put his finger into the hole in the door and pulled it shut. "The door won't stay closed, Charlie."

"That's why that pallet was resting against it, I guess. You hold it shut while I get to work."

Charlie took the flashlight and the backpack from

Martin and got on with the job.

Twenty minutes later the hole was drilled and the cable was routed. Charlie put the tools back into the knapsack and zipped it up.

"Come on, Martin. Let's go."

Martin opened the door and immediately slammed it shut. "That's not good."

"What?"

"There's a rattler right outside the door."

"You're seeing things."

"You look, then," Martin said.

Charlie nudged the door ajar and peeked out.

The reptile rattled.

"Great horny toads!" Charlie pulled the door closed. "Call Ed. Have him come over and throw rocks at it or something."

Martin phoned Ed and explained the situation. He hung up and scratched his head. "He says he's bringing the judge. Do you know who he's talking about?"

"What? Good heavens. The 'Judge' is a pistol that fires .410-gauge shotgun rounds. Let's get the heck away from the door."

They waited.

The reptile began to rattle continuously.

Charlie put his fingers in his ears.

*Boom! Boom!*

The door opened and bright sunlight silhouetted a man coming into the room. "Let's get out of here before the law comes," Ed said. "Someone might have heard the shots."

"People in the next county heard 'em," Martin said. "My ears are still ringing. Couldn't you have just poked the snake with a broom or something?"

They filed out of the closet, each one stepping carefully over the shredded serpent. Charlie pushed the buckshot-perforated door closed. Martin and Ed shoved the pallet against it.

"Let me have your backpack," Ed said. "I'm gonna hide the gun in there."

Martin handed the pack to him. "Here. It's your bag now. I never saw it before in my life. We're not supposed to have guns on the premises."

"Yeah, well, we're not supposed to do a lot of things, but I do anyway." Ed stashed the pistol in the bag.

The three outlaws started back to the patio door.

Bill appeared in the doorway. "What was that noise?"

"Nothing to worry about," Charlie said.

"Ed shot a rattlesnake," Martin volunteered.

"Great. Why don't you get on the PA system and tell the whole building?" Ed said.

"Where's the gun?" Bill asked.

Ed held up the bag. "In here."

"Give it to me." Bill took the backpack. "And nobody saw or heard anything. Let's get inside."

# # #

Charlie, Ed, Philippe, and Martin were having lunch in the dining room. They were discussing yesterday's modifications to the PA system.

"Did you test it?" Ed asked.

Charlie shook his head. "Don't need to test it. I know I did it right."

"Still seems like you should have blasted some KISS songs through it last night, to be sure."

"Why KISS? Nobody listens to those guys anymore," Martin said.

Ed put down his fork. "Are you kidding? They'll be revered forever. They're legendary." He motioned for the dining room server to come to the table. "Connie, help us settle a dispute. Are you familiar with the rock band KISS?"

"Those guys with the crazy makeup? Yeah, everybody's heard of them. They still play, but I don't think all of them are the original members."

151

"See? I told you guys they're still popular. Even a youngster like Connie knows who they are." Ed held out his water glass for Connie to refill.

"I agree," Charlie said. "Otherwise they wouldn't be included in the songs for that rock 'n' roll video game."

"You mean *Guitar Frenzy?*" Martin asked.

"Yeah."

"I have a friend whose grandson has the game," Philippe said. "It is *très amusant.* Most of the bands are from the '70s and '80s."

"Is it hard to play?" Charlie asked.

"Not at all," Philippe said. "The guitars, they are not real. They have color-coded buttons you press according to prompts on the screen. If you follow closely, you gain the points. If you make a mistake, it diminishes your score."

Martin laid his fork down and pushed aside his plate. "I hear you can also attach simulated drums to it."

Ed squeezed a lemon wedge over his glass. "Say, Philippe, do you think your friend would let us borrow the game and all the accessories?"

"I did not know you were interested in the video games," Philippe said.

"No, I'm not. But I just had an idea ..."

152

# CHAPTER ELEVEN

One week later Odia pulled into her reserved parking space at FRAIL and shut off the motor. Still safely locked in the vehicle, she took a good look around.

Not a resident in sight. *Where are they?* It had been almost two weeks since the laundry protest. The geezers were overdue for another chaotic caper.

She took a deep breath. Perhaps they had run out of energy, or ideas.

*No, they're out there.* She could feel them watching. Biding their time. Snickering at her.

The butterflies in her stomach abandoned their fluttering and moved on to outright flapping like pterodactyls. What horrible devastation were those pernicious pensioners waiting to unleash?

Maybe something would explode as soon as she stepped out of the car. She was terrified of loud noises, like fireworks, motorcycles, and airplane toilets flushing.

"Ack!" She clutched her chest at the unexpected ringing of her phone. Lisa was calling.

Odia didn't give her a chance to speak, but instead blurted out, "I'm outside my private entrance. Open it for me and wait. Hurry!"

After a few seconds Lisa appeared at the door.

Odia grabbed her backpack, leapt from the car, and ran past Lisa into the building. "Lock the door! Lock the door! And get me some water."

She reached into her drawer for the alprazolam, hands shaking uncontrollably.

Lisa returned with a bottle of water. "Is something wrong?"

Odia swallowed two tablets. "What are the gerries doing?"

"I'm sorry?" Lisa said.

"The old people. Where are they? What are they up to?"

Lisa backed away from her. "There's nothing unusual going on, if that's what you mean. Are you okay? Should I have Maggie stop by and take your blood pressure?"

"I don't want her to touch me. Let's go over the work assignments for the next two weeks. I'll feel better once my mind gets focused on paperwork.

Fifteen minutes later the crash of a cymbal outside the office shattered the quiet and startled Odia. A racket of drums and squealing guitars caused dust to fall from the ceiling. "That's coming from the foyer."

She pushed Lisa aside and rushed to the vestibule. In the center of the lobby three geezers dressed in tight pants, sporting full face paint and long hair, were playing what appeared to be toy guitars. Another was banging on a miniature electronic drum set. They were lip-syncing to "Rock and Roll All Nite." A large portable speaker blasted the music loud enough to rattle the windows.

Nearly a dozen residents had gathered to watch the tribute to KISS. Some were singing along while others had their hands in the air and were flicking lighters.

"I thought you said there was nothing amiss!" Odia shouted to Lisa, who had followed her out of the office.

"Honestly, they weren't here when I went to let you in."

"This music isn't even from their generation. Get Maggie to make them stop. I'm going back to my office.

Find me some earplugs."

Thirty minutes later the concert showed no signs of ending. Odia wondered where the old-timers got their energy. And why didn't they choose a more age-appropriate band? Something like Harry and the Hemorrhoids, perhaps.

She buzzed Lisa. "Get Maggie in here."

The earplugs muffled the higher-pitched sounds, but the drums were as intense as ever. If they didn't stop soon, she feared a migraine would come on. *Where's Maggie?*

Five minutes later Odia's door opened and Maggie poked her head in. "I knocked, but you probably couldn't hear me!" she yelled. The geezers had just started playing "Calling Dr. Love."

"Get in here and shut that door." Odia took out her earplugs. "Why haven't you stopped that rumpus?"

"I tried. They want you to reopen the coffee shop. They say they'll do this every Monday until you do."

Odia crossed her arms. "I'll evict them before I agree to any demands."

"So … what then? Are we all going to leave at the end of the day with ringing ears?"

"You might, but I won't," Odia replied. "I'm heading home right now. I've got a pounding headache."

# # #

Odia opened the blinds and looked outside The sun had sunk behind the building to the west of her apartment. It was the day following the geezers' air guitar spectacle. *Should I call?*

She pondered her options for a minute before snatching up her phone and dialing.

"Library Fugitive Helpline," said the voice on the line. "This is Prunella."

"I have some books that I lost in the second grade. You've got to help me."

155

"Yes, of course. First, may I ask how you heard about us?" Prunella spoke with a pleasant Southern accent.

"I saw your banner ad on the Vigilante Interest Group of International Librarians website."

"Oh yes, VIGIL. They worry a lot of people."

Odia wiggled her mouse to prevent the screen saver from coming on. "I'm looking at the page with the headline, 'Overdue Book Fugitives Face Wrath of Library Police.'"

"Mm-hmm. We get lots of calls about that one. How long have the books been missing?"

"They were due in January of 1967," Odia replied.

"Oh. Oh my. My oh my. Which library would that have been?"

Odia shivered. "It was a public library but I'm not saying where. Why do you want to know?"

"Well, from time to time a few libraries grant amnesty. However, I don't think anyone has ever been merciful to a bibliothecal outlaw who's been on the lam for over thirty-five years."

"Would it be safe to assume that if they haven't found me by now — "

"Gracious, no," Prunella interrupted. "It's only a matter of time. They haven't forgotten, I can tell you that. In fact it might not be the library enforcers that find you. It would surprise me if a bounty hunter wasn't on your trail."

"What?" Odia broke out in a sweat. "Would they do that?"

"Hon, although your fines only amount to about a thousand dollars per book, civil and criminal penalties apply after five years. You probably owe fifty thousand dollars, at least. That's worth it to a fugitive hunter."

"The website had an article," Odia said, "where a woman described her ordeal once the library cops finally caught up with her. Is that a true story?"

"Yes," Prunella said. "It really happened. And it's eerie that once she was sentenced to prison, nobody ever heard from her again. They don't explain that in the article."

"What do I do? Should I try to pay the fifty thousand?"

"I think it's too late for that. My advice is don't get pulled over—"

"Yes, there was a photo on the website where the library cops had a roadside checkpoint to nab people with overdue books," Odia blurted out.

"Mm-hmm. Obviously you want to stay out of any libraries. Oh, and whatever you do, don't get on the TV news. You might also want to change jobs every six months. If I were you, I would quit my job tomorrow."

Odia felt weak, and her entire body trembled. "I've got to go."

"I'm sorry, hon. I wish you the best of luck. Bye now."

Odia dropped the phone. She ran across the living room, closed the blinds, and listened at the door for a moment.

She turned out all the lights and stood silently in the dark for several minutes.

*What am I going to do?* She crouched, sat on the floor, and pulled her knees up to her chest. She wished she had her police radio scanner with her.

# # #

At breakfast the next morning Bill chose a remote table in the FRAIL dining room. He waved off Helen, who hovered over him as he took his seat. "I'm fine," he said. "The knees are a little stiff today, that's all."

"Just trying to be helpful," she said, and sat across from him.

The server appeared. "Good morning, Colonel and Miss Helen. Coffee?"

"Of course," said Bill. "Thank you."

"Two coffees coming up," she said, and departed.

Helen grinned. "Guess what happened yesterday."

"You saw Elvis—and he's alive."

She rolled her eyes. "Be serious. You-know-who called my fake helpline."

"I sure hope you don't get in trouble if they trace that phone number to you," Bill said.

The server brought two empty mugs and a coffee carafe to the table. "Cream and sugar are on the table, and they're free. But we charge for the coffee. Do you know how far we'd get if we didn't charge for coffee?" She paused for a moment and smiled. "Not too far."

Bill laughed. "I never get tired of that. Gomer would say it on *The Andy Griffith Show*, only he was talking about free air and water at the filling station."

"I loved that show. Breakfast will be out in a minute." She smiled again and left.

Helen poured coffee into their mugs. "The prepaid cell phone is untraceable. Nobody asked for a name or anything. And I paid cash, so you can stop worrying. I'll throw it out right after we eat."

"Are you sure Odia didn't recognize your voice?"

"I really doubt it since I used a Southern accent. Besides, she was so stressed out about getting arrested for overdue books, I'm positive she doesn't suspect a thing."

Bill sipped his coffee. "What now?"

"I've got to take down the web page so she can't share it with anyone. I need to cover my tracks."

"Could someone tie any of this to you?"

"Not without a lot of effort. The chances are very low 'cause I'm good at what I do." She winked at him.

The server delivered their meal and Bill said grace.

"What about your other fake pages?" he asked.

"She hasn't been to any yet. I'll see her IP address in the logs when she visits."

Bill put his fork down. "I don't know. It seems kind of mean to toy with her sanity."

"I've got no sympathy for her," Helen said. "She's got it coming."

# # #

Bill usually spent Monday evenings watching classic old movies with Philippe. The Colonel left his suite and navigated the quiet residential corridor. *It's been an entire week since the Guitar Frenzy concert.* The way things had been going lately, that was a long time to go without some form of excitement.

He arrived at Philippe's suite and knocked.

The door opened, and a worried-looking Philippe appeared. "Come inside quickly, *s'il vous plaît.*"

Bill handed him the DVD of *This Property Is Condemned.* "Did I come at a bad time? We can watch the movie later."

"Alas, *mon ami,* Natalie Wood shall have to wait. You must help me to find Orson."

"Who is Orson?" Bill asked.

"He is my ferret, who has escaped."

Bill laughed. "Are you serious? You actually got a ferret?"

"I did, indeed, and named him after the French word for the bear cub—*ourson.* His face has the appearance of a little bear."

"When did you last see him?"

"Last night, when I kissed him good night and put him into his crate."

Bill raised an eyebrow. "I didn't think ferrets wanted to be kissed."

"*Oui.* Orson is very affectionate, and also most clever. It would appear he unlatched the cage door during the night."

"Well, he can't go far. He's got to be in here."

Philippe wrung his hands. "I fear not. I have been calling out, but he does not come."

Bill gave him a sidelong glance. "You're pulling my leg."

"*Non non.* I am in earnest. Ferrets may be trained in that

manner."

"We'd better track him down before someone else finds him. Pets are not allowed — you know that."

"I care not," Philippe said. "What can they do — decline to renew my lease? They have already done that, yet you see that I am still here."

Bill pulled out his cell phone. "I'm going to ask the girls to watch out for him."

Philippe gasped. "Can we trust them to be discreet?"

"Don't worry. They won't tell Odia, but we had better find your ferret before Ed does. He's liable to shoot the little fella."

# # #

*Did I dream it?* Odia lay still on the couch in her apartment and listened intently. She had come home from work with another headache and stretched out for a few minutes. Correction — a few hours. The vivid blue display of her digital clock pierced the darkness like the sign for a strip club. It was 11:31.

There it was again. A clucking sound. It was no dream. *What is that?* It didn't sound exactly like a chicken. Anyway, what would a chicken be doing in the apartment?

Her headache was gone, but she feared it would come back if she turned on the lights. *There it is again.* Was it coming closer or was she imagining things?

"Ack!" She felt something pounce on the sofa. She leapt off. A warm, furry object brushed against her ankles. She flipped the light switch. Three hundred watts of recessed lighting assaulted her eyeballs. Her headache returned.

Odia looked around.

A throw pillow had been torn open and its stuffing scattered. A ribbon of bathroom tissue extended from the bathroom to the kitchen, entangling furniture legs along the way.

*Chicken? No. Dog? Don't have one. Cat? They don't cluck.*

What kind of animal intruder was she facing?

She went back to the couch for her shoes. They weren't there. Puzzled, she searched the area beneath and behind it. No shoes. *Where did I leave them?*

The clucking started again and a blur of black-and-gray fur raced past her. A hairy rocket leapt onto the couch, then flew toward the window like a superhero.

The ferret hung from the drapes by its front claws. Its lower body dangled like a pendulum, the clucking punctuated by intermittent, joyful squeals.

"How in the world did you get in here?" she asked the mischievous mammal. *You probably came from next door.* Odia's twenty-something neighbor worked at an animal clinic. She was known to bring home exotic pets for overnight observation — in violation of her lease.

The pounding in Odia's head wore her out. She should be livid at having a hyperactive hairball tear up her home, but had no energy left for anger.

"You stay put. I'll be right back," she said to the chatty climber.

The curtain rod was sagging and the uninvited acrobat seemed intent on bringing it down, drapes and all.

She went next door, still barefoot. Light shone through the kitchen window. *Amanda must be up late.* Odia knocked.

The door opened.

"I want you to come and collect your ferret," Odia demanded.

"Hello, Ms. Fangmeister," Amanda said. "I'm fine, thanks for asking. So nice to see you. Now what ferret would we be talking about?"

"Your ferret is loose in my apartment. It's worse than a tornado."

Amanda gave her a withering look. "I haven't got any ferrets. It must be someone else's."

Odia glared at her.

"Would you like me to come over and catch it for you?"

161

Odia nodded. "Let's go. We're wasting time."

"Wait a sec. Let me get a cage."

Amanda went into her kitchen and promptly returned with bacon bits and a pet carrier. The women exited and Amanda closed her door.

Odia opened the door to her own apartment and practically shoved Amanda inside. "Hurry — before my home is reduced to rubble."

"Shh. And be still," Amanda ordered. She sat on the floor and held the bacon bits in her open palm.

"It isn't on the drapes anymore," Odia said. "Should we chase it down?"

"It'll come to me. Now keep quiet please."

Within seconds the ferret ran up to Amanda and made friends with her. She gave it some bacon bits and played with it until she could scruff it. She read the tiny engraved nameplate on its collar. "It says Orson. This must be somebody's pet."

"Well it's not mine. Take it away. I don't know anything about caring for one."

Amanda placed Orson into the carrier. "Can I look around? I'm curious how he got in here."

"Sure, and tell me if you find my shoes," Odia replied as she picked up after Orson's escapades.

Amanda's search of Odia's tiny residence took less than five minutes. "Here you go."

"My shoes?"

"No. Here's how he snuck in." Amanda held up Odia's backpack and pointed out the ferret-sized hole in its side.

"But that's my workbag. There's no way I carried him home without knowing."

Amanda smiled. "Ferrets can be very sound sleepers. Owners often panic and think their pet has died because they can't wake it."

Odia was still too exhausted to get angry, but was determined to discover which geezer had stuffed Orson

162

into her backpack. They would pay dearly.

"I think I know who owns him. You keep the animal tonight, and I'll collect him in the morning. Now if you don't mind, I've got to take something for my migraine."

Amanda collected her captive and headed for the door. "Oh, by the way — Orson probably hid your shoes. They do that. Look under the bed or behind the furniture. Good night."

# # #

"Thank you for seeing me on short notice, Dr. Sessions." Odia placed the back of her hand against her forehead. "I've had a terrible week. I don't know where to start. It's been awful."

"Why don't you tell me about the most recent trouble," the therapist suggested.

"Last night a ferret stole my shoes, pulled down my drapes, and scattered toilet paper all over my apartment."

"Is this a pet?"

"No. Of course not. I brought it home from work."

"From the retirement facility?" the doctor asked.

"Yes."

"I didn't know you kept ferrets there. Why did you bring it home? Was it sick?"

Odia thumped the arms of the recliner with her fists. "We don't keep ferrets, and I didn't bring it home on purpose. It was a stowaway."

"Did you harm the creature in any way?" asked the therapist.

"No, of course not. I took it back to FRAIL early this morning. My receptionist is trying to locate its owner."

"It sounds like the ferret created quite the mayhem. How could you have minimized it?"

*Here she goes.* The implication that she created her own problems irritated Odia. She wasn't stupid. She was the victim of others' malicious bullying.

163

"What? Like put up a sign that says 'No Tearing Up the House While I'm Asleep'? If I had known the ferret was there, I would have locked it up or something. Sheesh."

Dr. Sessions wrote something in her notebook. "What else happened this week?"

"I heard voices."

The doctor sat up straight and her eyes opened as wide as an owl's. "Go on."

"Oh, don't worry. They weren't sinister voices. They were people singing—'They're coming to take me away, ha-ha.'"

"Were these voices in your head?"

"No, in my office. I mean, I actually heard them, but they were very faint."

The doctor wrote in her notebook. "Did anyone else hear them?"

"Are you kidding me? You know people are determined to have me committed. Why would I give them an opportunity to accuse me of being crazy? I kept it to myself and sang along sometimes—when nobody was looking, of course."

The doctor wrote some more in her notebook. "Remind me who is trying to have you committed."

"It's in your notes. Right now, though, I'm most worried about the library cops."

"Ah, yes. It's been awhile since they've bothered you. Are they back?"

"They're getting more aggressive. There's probably a library bounty hunter after me. I might have to go off-grid."

The doctor scribbled something in her notebook. "Who told you about this bounty hunter, and why do you think the information is credible?"

"She was from the Library Fugitive Helpline. I found their ad when I was looking at the library vigilante web page."

"How did you find *that*?" the doctor asked.

"I linked to it from the RCMP website."

"The Royal Canadian Mounted Police?"

Odia rolled her eyes. "No, silly. Retirement Community Mutiny Prevention. They've got information for administrators and staff, to help us recognize and squash resident uprisings before it's too late."

The doctor turned the page of her notebook and wrote some more. "How common is it for residents to rise up and rebel?"

"There have been several mutinies this year alone. Usually the administrators just get fired, but sometimes they're tortured and killed."

"Did it say that on the website?" Dr. Sessions asked.

"Yes."

"That sounds serious. You've had trouble with the residents before, but you never mentioned they would harm you."

"I'm convinced they want to. They sicced a German shepherd on me the day the Mexicans had a laundry fiesta out in the parking lot."

The doctor made a lengthy entry in her notebook. "Why do you continue to work there if you're afraid of being injured?"

"I don't let the residents get close to me. But they'll soon move out, or get evicted, and then I can make PIEDRA a reality."

"You haven't changed your mind about that?"

"No."

"And you're not deterred by the evidence that suggests PIEDRA is an unrealistic expectation?"

"I'm going to make it happen—one way or another. Heaven help anyone who tries to thwart me."

The doctor wrote in her notebook and looked at her watch. "Our time is up. I'll send a report to Dr. Mannicks. She may want to adjust your medication next time you see her."

Bill was the first to see the flier posted outside the dining room. "Uh-oh, Philippe. Looks like Odia is holding your ferret hostage."

Philippe buried his face in his hands. "*Quel désastre!*"

"At least you know where he is. The notice says to contact Odia to claim it. Come on, I'll go with you. Let's see how much she wants for ransom."

Philippe put his hand on his forehead. "Colonel Bill, it does not say whether Orson is alive. Perhaps he is not. Oh, I am so upset."

"Calm yourself. Let's go find out."

They encountered Maggie as they passed the activity room.

"Hi, Grampa," she said.

"Mags, Odia has Philippe's ferret."

"Yes, I know. I was on my way to tell you. It hid in her backpack and she unknowingly took it home last night. Don't worry, Mr. Pelletier, he's okay. I have him in the PCA office, only I'm not allowed to release him until you've seen Ms. Fangmeister."

Philippe's countenance brightened. "Then you think she will let me keep it?"

"I can't be sure, but why would she bring it in unless she wanted to return it?" she asked.

Bill's eyes narrowed. "That woman always has an angle. I don't trust her." He put his hand on Maggie's shoulder. "Sweetheart, if she does return the ferret, would you keep it at your house for a while?"

"Summer would love that," she said.

He looked at Philippe. "Would that be okay with you?"

"But of course," Philippe said. "Miss Providence, do not concern yourself with the expense. I shall pay gladly the cost of his keep."

"Oh, wait—we have a kitten. Won't they fight?"

"We shall introduce them to each other and see. Ferrets often get along *très bien* with the cats and the dogs," he replied.

They resumed their journey to the office. As they neared the reception desk, Maggie veered off to resume her duties.

Bill smiled at Lisa. "We're here to see Lord Vader."

She laughed. "Let me see if she's back from her doctor's appointment. What should I say this is about?"

"Ferrets," he replied.

She silently mouthed the word "Ah" as she picked up the phone and buzzed Odia. "Someone's come about the ferret, Ms. Fangmeister."

Odia's door swung open before Lisa had put down the handset. The aggravated administrator emerged, struggling to tie on her surgical mask. "Whose is it?" she demanded.

"The creature, Orson, he belongs to me. May I recover him please?" Philippe asked.

"On one condition—that you reimburse me for damage to my apartment. And you must leave a nonrefundable pet deposit. On top of that there will be a monthly pet fee of a hundred and fifty dollars. And I shall need proof that Oscar has all his shots."

"Orson," Bill said.

Odia glared at him. "What?"

"His name is Orson. And, no, Mr. Pelletier will not pay such an outrageous monthly fee. We've read the landlord-tenant laws, and we know you can't charge that much."

She frowned. "What? So you're his lawyer now? This is none of your business."

"We residents always stick together. May we have Orson now?"

"If you fail to pay the fee, I'll have you evicted."

Bill moved into her personal space. "First, pet fees were never written into his lease. Second, we can have the ferret declared an emotional support animal. Finally, your threats of eviction don't scare us anymore, so give it a rest."

167

He inched even closer. "Philippe will pay for damages up to the amount of your insurance deductible, and will leave a *refundable* pet deposit. Let's say a hundred dollars. No fees. Nothing else. Agreed?"

She backed away. "Yes yes, okay. But if it ever gets loose again, I will personally take it by the tail and turn it in to Animal Control."

Philippe cleared his throat and grinned at Odia. "Perhaps you should obtain for yourself the emotional support animal. It would improve your disposition. May I suggest to you a Gila monster?"

# # #

The middle of the following day the desert baked under typical late-August heat. Ed had been outside for nearly an hour. His task had taken longer than he estimated, but now he was done. He had been lucky not to be missed, and even more fortunate not to be seen. The only thing between him and the windows of the administrative wing was a low hedge of Texas sage. His back ached from crouching behind the shrubs for so long.

He dialed Charlie. "Hey, I'm finished. Lisa should be leaving for lunch shortly, like she does every Tuesday. As soon as she does—" The sound of a car door closing caught his attention. "Oh, there she goes. Send Martin and Philippe to the lobby now and make sure they have their props. Helen had better play a convincing police dispatcher on the walkie-talkie."

Ed turned on his own two-way radio. "Okay, I've set the frequency on my handheld so I can listen in. Go ahead and start chatting it up. I just hope Odia's listening to her scanner. I'm hanging up now."

He watched Lisa drive off. *This ought to be good.*

# # #

Odia froze. She thought she heard the word "library" come

over the scanner. She sat on the edge of her seat, waiting for any more radio traffic that warranted her attention.

Silence.

She relaxed a bit and continued processing the mountain of tiresome paperwork that filled her in-box. The paperless office had not yet arrived at FRAIL.

"Base to Library Five," said a female voice over the scanner.

"Five, go ahead," replied a male.

"Two-Adam-21 and Library Four report they are in position."

"Ten-four. Our ETA is two minutes. Be advised that units are authorized to use force if subject resists."

Odia broke out in a sweat. *Library cops! … But where?* She hurried over to the window, but then backed away without opening the blinds. If they were after her, they would be watching the building.

More radio calls: "Library Five is ten-ninety-seven at the old folks' home. Negative on subject BMW. It's not our day."

Odia knew the radio codes. Ten-ninety-seven meant they were on scene. *They're right outside!* Her heart raced. She grabbed her inhaler, tore off her mask, and snarfed.

*Don't panic.* Maybe her evasive strategy would pay off. The cops knew she owned a BMW, but ever since learning about the bounty hunter, she had been driving a rental. Soon they would decide she wasn't here and go away.

"Library Five to Library Four."

"Go ahead."

"Let's call it off. Subject appears to be GOA."

Odia's paranoia would not let her relax. Even though they radioed that she was *gone on arrival*, an officer might stay behind to watch for her return. She wished she knew for sure. *Why didn't I listen to Josie and install surveillance cameras?* There was only one way to be certain. She had to risk peeking into the lobby.

### # # #

Martin nudged Philippe. "Okay, look menacing." The two stood near the unoccupied reception desk, in clear view of Odia's office door. Both wore black tactical vests borrowed from a friend at a private security firm. They also wore black ski masks, black shirts, and black trousers. They looked the part of fugitive hunters—as long as one overlooked their poor posture and lack of weapons.

Odia's door cracked open, then immediately slammed shut.

Philippe pressed the transmit button on his walkie-talkie. "Ed, do it now."

### # # #

Ed waited around the corner from Odia's private entrance. He wished he had remembered to bring his sunglasses. When Philippe's broadcast came over the walkie-talkie, he pressed the trigger on the propane torch he had borrowed from Manuel's storage shed. The tool hissed, and a jet of blue flame poofed into life, resistant to the desert breeze that would have extinguished an ordinary lighter. He lit the fast-burning fuse that led to the entire cache of Josie's leftover fireworks he had taken from the same shed.

Odia burst out of her private door and fumbled frantically with her car keys.

*Bang-bang-bang-bang-bang!* A rapid-fire salvo of loud reports erupted from behind the hedge just a few yards from Odia's rented vehicle.

Odia flung herself facedown on the pavement, inches from her car door. She covered her head with her hands and repeatedly screamed, "Don't shoot me!"

Ed radioed, "One on the ground," and fled the scene.

### # # #

The shooting had stopped, but Odia didn't dare stand. She

took a mental inventory of her situation. *No pain.* How could the library cops have missed her after firing so many rounds, and why did they stop? *Probably reloading.*

She lay motionless and counted to fifty, expecting to be handcuffed and hauled off to the belated book borrowers' brig. When no one approached, she continued counting to one hundred. *Do they think I'm dead?*

Annoyed at the lack of attention, Odia shouted, "Hey! I'm not hurt. Are you gonna arrest me or what?"

*Nothing.* She lifted her head and looked around. "You can come out. I'm unarmed," she yelled, then waited for a response.

"Oh, this is ridiculous," Odia grumbled as she stood. *Where is everybody?* There were no officers, no SWAT vans, no helicopters. An eerie silence and the distinct odor of spent fireworks surrounded her.

*Fireworks?* Her blood pressure, which had dropped below the "sudden death" line while she was sprawled on the ground, spiked again. *I've been duped by those malicious mossbacks!*

The car alarm emitted a brief *chirp-chirp* as Odia pressed the Unlock button on the fob. "I'm going to make them sorry they did this to me," she muttered as she gunned the engine and barreled down the driveway. Gravel flew as she veered onto the shoulder while fumbling with her phone.

"Lisa? Fangmeister here. Shut up and listen. First thing tomorrow I want you to post the following notice all over the facility ..."

# CHAPTER TWELVE

Maggie raced her car up the FRAIL driveway. She was late for work. *Oh good.* Odia's car was not there yet, but a small group of rezzies was standing in Odia's reserved parking space.

*That's odd.* Maggie parked and walked over to the gathering. She noticed Ed was trying to conceal something behind his back, but to no avail. "What are we doing with the eggs?"

Charlie stepped forward. "Er ... we're hiding them. Then we're gonna have an egg hunt."

"Easter eggs are not usually fresh and white. Try again."

Ed gently shoved Charlie aside. "We're waiting for the dragon lady. You can go on inside. There's nothing to see here."

She pointed to the main entrance. "That's right, because you're all going inside this instant."

The group shuffled toward the front doors — except for Ed, who stood his ground.

Maggie crossed her arms and leaned back. "Do you want to tell me what this is about?"

"Lisa posted a notice from Fangmonster this morning." He pulled a crumpled yellow sheet of paper from his back pocket and handed it to Maggie. "It says that on-site laundry service is now discontinued, satellite TV is suspended, and dining room hours are shortened."

Maggie unfolded the bill, read it, and sighed.

Ed gently took the paper from her hands and stuffed it back into his pocket. "And she's changed the Wi-Fi password. None of us can get onto the Internet now."

She couldn't blame Odia for taking punitive measures — not after the rezzies scared her so badly with the simulated police raid yesterday.

"Ed, you'll just make things worse if you throw eggs at her car."

"Oh, we wasn't gonna egg her car. We was gonna egg *her*." Ed often had lapses of proper grammar when he became irate.

"Look, I'll talk with my grampa and see what he plans to do. Meanwhile please go inside and don't rile the rezzies. We don't want to escalate things. And I'll take the eggs, thank you."

He ceded the carton of eggs before turning and stomping into the building.

Maggie was retrieving her purse from her car when a pickup truck pulled into the adjacent space. A man in overalls got out.

"Are you Odia Fang … Fangmeester?" he asked.

"Good heavens no." She shut her door.

"Could you get her for me?"

"I don't think she's here yet. And it's pronounced Fang-*MICE*-ter."

He adjusted his cap. "I'm from AA Industrial Gates. She left a voice mail over the weekend saying she wants to gate off the lobby from some other part of the building. Do you know what she's talking about? I need to take measurements."

"No, I have no idea." *Oh no.* Maggie could guess what Odia was up to: she wanted to keep the rezzies away from

173

the lobby and admin areas. World War III would start as soon as they figured out the gate's purpose. It wouldn't surprise her if the rezzies blew up the building in retaliation.

"I suspect" — Maggie went out on a limb — "that it was probably a prank call. She hasn't said anything to me about gates." She felt guilty about lying, but surely a fib to avert a retiree riot was allowed.

"Oh," said the man. "But she asked for an estimate. Maybe I could just measure the — "

"No. That's not necessary. It's all a misunderstanding. Sorry. Bye now." She turned abruptly and strode into the building. Maybe "Fangmeester" would forget about it.

# # #

Odia waited all morning for Maggie's call. She was still sore about the malicious library cop episode two days ago, and was eager to empty the place of elderly evildoers, if only for a day.

Finally, it came. Odia jumped right to the point. "Ms. Providence, are all the inmates loaded onto the shuttle?"

"Yes, Ms. Fangmeister. I'm taking fourteen residents to the Indian gaming resort. That's everybody, because 104 and 207 are away with family this week. Looks like it's just you and Lisa in the building this morning. It's Friday, you know, and Manuel doesn't come in until four."

Odia lowered her mask. "I don't see why I should have to pay you a day's wages to accompany a bunch of senile spenders to the casino. Can't you put them on the bus and let them fend for themselves?"

She waited several seconds but got no response. *Did the call get dropped?* "Ms. Providence?"

"I can hear you. It would cost you the same if I stayed behind and picked my nose all day."

"No, I don't want that. Go with them and keep them out until they go broke."

Odia hung up without waiting for a reply. It was hard to understand why the geezers would want to spend all day having fun. Old people should stay home and knit or something. You weren't supposed to enjoy yourself while waiting for the sand to run out of the hourglass, were you?

She went to the window and watched the shuttle drive off. Now she was free to carry out a little plan she had cooked up. But first she had to confirm one thing. She buzzed Lisa over the intercom.

"Yes, Ms. Fangmeister?"

"Is anyone in the lobby?"

"No, ma'am," Lisa replied.

"Will you check?"

"I'm looking at the lobby right now. Nobody's here."

"What I mean," Odia said, "is go and check behind the plants and under the furniture. Also look outside."

She wasn't taking any chances. A few irresponsible instigators might have sneaked off of the shuttle before it left, and she had vowed never again to be ambushed by the aged.

Her eyelid twitched as she waited. Anxiety stalked her like a hungry lion. *Hurry, Lisa.* How long did it take to hunt for hidden hoodlums?

"All clear, Ms. Fangmeister. I even made sure that the plants were nothing more than decorative foliage."

Odia opened her door and leaned out of the office, methodically scanning every corner of the lobby. She eased the rest of her body out and inspected the admin area.

Satisfied, she pulled her mask up over her nose and marched off toward suite 106, reaching Philippe's door in less than a minute. She glanced up and down the corridor, slid her exclusive administrator's master key into the lock, and let herself in.

The apartment was darker than she expected. Even with the blinds drawn, there should be some natural light filtering in. She toggled the light switch. Nothing happened.

She would have to get Manuel to check it.

Odia felt her way around and tried to switch on the kitchen light. Nothing. *How odd.* The electricity had to be on because she could hear the refrigerator running.

She backtracked to the window and tugged at the mini-blind cord. The blinds flipped open, but no light came through. "Arrgh!"

Odia grabbed a handful of mini-blinds and swung them aside. *So that's it.* The entire window had been neatly covered with cardboard and duct tape. She wondered if Philippe was a vampire but quickly dismissed the notion. Who had ever seen a French vampire? She imagined a pale, fanged zombie wearing a beret.

Too bad she hadn't brought along a flashlight, or her phone, for illumination. She would have to find the ferret's cage using what little light spilled in from the corridor.

It didn't take long to search the small living room and find the pet carrier. Odia listened carefully but heard no sound from the animal within. *Must be asleep.* She reached in her pocket for a baggie of bacon bits and laid a trail from the cage to the apartment door. Then she went back and gingerly unlatched the carrier's wire door. "The minute you step foot outside this suite, you foul-smelling furball, it's off to the pound," she said out loud.

Odia backed out of the suite, pulling the door almost shut. She left enough of an opening for a determined ferret to escape into the corridor.

She turned away from the door. "Ack!" she uttered and backed into the wall.

Bill was capturing every movement with a camcorder. Philippe peered over his shoulder.

"*Excusez-moi,* we did not mean to interrupt your breaking and entering. I came back only for my wallet," Philippe said.

"There was a noise, and I came in to investigate," Odia said. "That's not the same as burglary. I'm the landlord, after all."

"Investigating in the dark?" Bill asked. "Snacking on bacon bits?"

"I was afraid Oswin had gotten out of his cage. He might eat something unhealthy for him," she said.

"Orson. His name is Orson," Philippe corrected, "and it pains me to tell you that the creature is away on holiday."

"I don't believe you."

"Please to see for yourself."

"There's no light," Odia said.

"Oh," Philippe said. "We will just screw in the light bulb, *non*?" He went to the living room lamp and twisted its bulb until it lit. He repeated this with the lamp over the dining table.

She stomped over to the pet carrier and looked inside. "It's a stuffed toy ferret!"

"*Oui.* You are right. Orson put it there to discourage the cage burglars. Perhaps I should position a stuffed Philippe in my suite for a similar purpose."

Odia's twitch returned and her eyes narrowed. "Get your wallet and go gamble. I hope you lose it all."

Philippe patted his pockets and frowned. "Alas, I am such the forgetful person. ... *Regard*, I had my wallet the entire time! I was looking in the wrong pocket."

"This video is going to the tenants union," Bill said.

Odia's beady eyes widened. "No! You can't."

"I'll tell you what, then," Bill said. "You forget about nonrefundable deposits and monthly pet fees, and I'll keep this incident to myself. Deal?"

Anger and embarrassment raged inside her. She glared at Bill. How did he manage to stay one step ahead of her all the time?

"Yes yes, all right." She pulled the door shut and locked it. "I hate you," she added.

"Should I be sad?" Bill asked.

"No, you should be worried. You don't know what I

might think of next."

# # #

After dinner that evening Bill unlocked his suite and went in. "Come on in, Ed, and shut the door behind you."

Ed followed him into the living room and sat on the couch. "I wanted to talk with you about this during dinner, but everyone was busy discussing today's trip to the casino. Besides, the fewer people that know what I'm thinking, the better."

"Don't keep me in suspense all evening. Get on with it," Bill urged as he got comfortable in his recliner.

"I discovered the identity of the burglar who smashed through the door this summer," Ed said.

Bill raised an eyebrow. "How did you do that?"

"Remember how I said he had green hair, like the Hulk, but nobody believed me? People questioned why a burglar would have green hair. 'Nobody has green hair,' they said."

"Yes yes, get on with it," Bill said.

"Remember last week when I snuck into Manuel's shed to get fireworks to scare the vinegar out of Odia? Well, guess what I found? No, don't guess—I'll tell you. Empty cans of green hair spray, like people use at Halloween."

"But Manuel has short hair, and I thought the person you saw that night had long hair."

"Well, he could've had a wig," Ed said.

"That's disturbing," Bill muttered, then frowned. "Manuel doesn't have any reason to do anything destructive. Either he's getting back at Odia for something or—"

"Wait until I tell you the rest," Ed interrupted. "I'm pretty sure he set the fire in the electrical closet."

"That's a serious accusation," Bill said. "You'd better be able to back that up. Otherwise keep it to yourself."

"I can—and then again, I can't. On the night in question I saw him make several trips between his shed and the

178

closet."

"You can't see the electrical closet from your window," Bill said, "so how do you know that's where he went? Besides, it was dark. Can you be sure it was Manuel?"

"He started just before dark. I was on the patio about to enjoy a cigar when I heard the squeaky door of his shed. I hid between the tall bougainvillea bush and the corner of the building. I watched him the whole time. On the last two trips he was carrying his propane plumber's torch."

"But you didn't personally witness him start the fire, did you? He could have been working on the pipes or something."

Ed took a throw pillow and used it to thump the couch. "Darn it, Colonel! Whose side are you on, anyway?"

"Take it easy there, Ed. It's just hard to imagine Manuel doing a thing like that when it would put our lives at risk — even if Odia put him up to it. He's got more sense, don't you think?"

Ed shook his head. "We don't know anything about his past. Maybe Odia coerced him — you know, as in blackmail. Anyway, I don't think he intended to hurt anyone."

"How can you say that? According to you, he tried to burn down the building."

"No, he didn't. I was talking with Josie the day after the fire. She's friends with one of the firemen." Ed grinned. "Do you know how a fireman — "

Bill raised a hand. "Don't go there. Finish the story."

"Oh. Well, this guy says it looked like the work of either a really stupid arsonist or someone who took great pains to prevent the fire from spreading. Like they only wanted to trigger the alarm but not cause damage."

"I hadn't heard that," Bill said, "even after all the attention the detectives gave Maggie. She was under suspicion for a while, you know."

"What should we do about it?"

"Nothing," Bill said as he got out of his chair. "You've

179

got very little hard evidence. I'm sure you're right, but we should leave it to the cops to sort out."

"I don't think they're interested in us. I'll bet the case file is at the bottom of the unsolved crimes pile. Maybe they'll do something if we give them new information."

"Why didn't you tell the cops about Manuel's movements when they investigated the fire?" Bill asked. "It might have spared Maggie a lot of worry."

"Nobody asked me—not the cops, not Josie, nobody. Besides, I didn't put two and two together that evening. It wasn't until I found the green hair spray that it dawned on me there might be a conspiracy afoot."

"And what good would it do if you come forward now? Since nobody got hurt, I suggest you keep quiet and don't cause trouble for Manuel."

"You may be right, Colonel, but all the same, I'm gonna keep my eye on him. Just in case."

# # #

Early the following morning Bill and Philippe entered the coffee shop at Plumbett Aviation. Even smaller than the one at FRAIL, it nevertheless sufficed for the infrequent visits from private pilots flying into the tiny rural airport for fuel or repairs. Bill removed his sunglasses and scanned the unoccupied room that smelled more of lubricating oil than coffee.

"Hello, Mr. Armstrong," Anna Janus called out from the adjoining office area. She hurried over to shake hands. "You must be Mr. Pelletier," she said to Philippe. "We can sit in this booth. Nobody's expected to land for a few hours, so we'll have the place all to ourselves."

"Madame Janus," Philippe said, "I am pleased to meet you, and may I say also it was a pleasure to meet your daughter. She was a most pleasant driver."

Janus smiled. "Oh, she drives very well, but she isn't always on time. She underestimates distances. Anyway, I thought it would be better to send her to collect you, rather than be impersonal and order a cab."

Bill cleared his throat. "Ms. Janus, when you called to arrange this conspiratorial convocation—"

Janus interrupted with feigned surprise. "Conspiratorial?"

"That's what I said," Bill continued. "Why couldn't we meet at FRAIL? And why did you send your daughter to pick us up rather than doing it yourself?"

"Patience, Colonel," Philippe said. "I presume that Madame Janus has the reasons most logical for *ses méthodes clandestines.*"

"Well, now is the time to explain them," Bill snapped. "I have had just about all the inconvenience I can take from Odia, from Detective Marshall, and from you, Ms. Janus. It seems all I do is meet with people, but nothing improves."

Janus produced a large manila envelope and pulled out two sets of documents. "These are lease agreements, good for five years—with no fee increases, and no need to change suites. One for you, Mr. Armstrong, and one for Mr. Pelletier."

Philippe quickly scanned the pages of his copy. "Madame Janus, I do not wish to appear ungrateful, but could we add a clause to allow me to possess the comfort ferret?"

Janus laughed. "You want to keep a ferret? Sure, we can add that."

Bill tapped Philippe on the shoulder. "Not so fast. I'm sure there's a catch." He looked at Janus and raised an eyebrow.

She sat back. "No, there are no strings attached. It's true that I do want something, but it's a completely separate topic from the leases."

"That may be," Bill said, "but I'm not signing up for a five-year sentence with that maniac running FRAIL."

"*Oui.* I, too, wish to be rid of *la femme schizophrène*,"

Philippe added.

Janus nodded. "You and your fellow residents are very close to doing that. I may be able to help you finish the job. And that's why we're meeting out here instead of at FRAIL. I wonder if I could ask you to increase the pressure on Odia."

Bill frowned. "We're running out of ideas. What's the point?"

"I want you to win. And from here on, I'll make sure the deck is no longer stacked against you," Janus said.

The words reverberated in Bill's head like a sonic boom. The residents hadn't failed because of poor leadership. They had been doomed from the start.

"Why not simply remove Odia and be done with it?" Bill asked.

"Not right away. I need her there, for the time being."

Bill shook his head. "We want her out. We've had enough of her."

Janus grinned. "The board insists on documenting performance issues before removing her, to avoid claims of wrongful termination. We plan to order Odia to fill every vacant suite within an impossibly short period. You will suddenly find her eager to attract residents rather than repel them." She lowered her voice and added, "I'm sure you can imagine a whole host of roadblocks that might cause her to fail."

"Right now I'm having trouble imagining why you're so intent on siding with the residents," Bill said, looking Janus straight in the eye.

"I have many reasons," she said, "but the top one is that my parents are ready to move to a senior living community. I would prefer they continue to live nearby. Unfortunately FRAIL is the only game in town, and I won't let them anywhere near Odia. If we don't get rid of her, my folks may choose to play golf alongside gators rather than do yoga among the yucca."

182

"Won't Ms. Fangmeister be bent out of shape about our leases being renewed?" Bill asked.

"On the contrary. That will be two fewer vacancies to fill."

Philippe smiled. "Somehow, Madame Janus, I do not believe Mademoiselle Fangmeister will see it as a blessing."

She looked at her watch. "I hate to seem pushy, but I need your answer right away. So if you're game, you can sign the new leases. My daughter will drive you home."

"*Attends une second*," said Philippe. "One second please. Can we put in the ferret approval, *s'il vous plaît?*"

Janus took his contract and handwrote a provision allowing him to keep any comfort animal he wanted. "There we are. Thank you both for meeting with me. Enjoy the rest of your Saturday."

# # #

The Monday morning sun was taking its time to rise above the horizon. Odia stepped out of her car and looked around. The tubular-steel driveway gate at the county fairgrounds was chained and locked. A tattered and faded banner advertised an event that was only a memory now.

She wouldn't have to feel silly much longer. Janus promised to be on time.

A white Range Rover pulled up behind her car. Anna Janus emerged from the highly polished vehicle. "Have you been waiting long?"

"Not long. What a magnificent SUV. I've always wanted a Range Rover."

Janus opened the padlock and undid the chain that bound the gate to a fixed metal post. It swung open on its own accord. "Drive all the way to the pond. Wait for me there."

The horseshoe-shaped pond was as big as two high-school football fields placed side by side. Odia exited her vehicle and stood in the shade of a ramada. The color of the stagnant water reminded her of pea soup. She watched Janus drive up and park.

"I chained up the gate again," Janus said as she approached. "We're all alone and nobody can eavesdrop on our conversation."

"Did we have to meet next to this cesspool? There's no telling what virulent pathogens are proliferating in there."

Janus sat at the picnic table. "Don't worry. If you agree to do what I ask, then I promise not to throw you in. How's that?"

Odia couldn't tell if Janus was serious, because her eyes were hidden behind dark sunglasses. "Something tells me it might not be the worst possible outcome for me. What do you want?"

"I can see you're not one for pleasantries," Janus said.

"Tact is for weenies."

"Then I'll get straight to the point. Your friend Cozen is under criminal investigation. You did not hear that from me."

Odia took a seat opposite Janus and used her hand to shield her eyes from the bright sun. "He's no friend of mine."

"Then you won't be tipping him off?"

"I didn't say that." Odia adjusted her position to use Janus's head as a sun blocker. "Are you suggesting that I keep quiet about it?"

"Why did he put you in charge of FRAIL? Why are you running it into the ground?" Janus slid along the bench a few inches to the left.

The sun was back in Odia's eyes. "I have no idea what you're talking about."

Janus shook her head. "I was subpoenaed by a federal grand jury. Based on the questions they asked, it wasn't hard to figure out your part in his scheme."

The intense glare caused Odia's eyes to water. She went around the table and sat beside Janus. "I have done nothing illegal. And even if I have, you can't prove anything."

"I'm not accusing you. Cozen is the criminal. Would you like him to get what he deserves?"

Odia relaxed a tiny bit. Revenge on Cozen was something she could get excited about. She would love to see him indicted and convicted. It would serve him right for going back on his promise to fund PIEDRA. Too bad he couldn't be hanged.

"I argued with him," Odia said. "I told him we needed to invest in the facility and make it the top retirement community in the state. But he wanted FRAIL to fail so he could steal the endowment money. He pressured me to find a way to throw out those poor and helpless old people."

"You're not fooling anyone. You detest the residents and you know it."

Had Cozen betrayed her secret contempt for the ancient fossils? What else had he told Janus about her? *What makes her think I'm the one who wants to evict them?* It would probably be unwise to argue with someone as sharp as Janus. "Doesn't everybody dislike old people? They're cranky and they *smell* like mentholated heat rub."

Janus removed her sunglasses. "I take it you're unhappy running FRAIL."

Odia nodded her head vigorously. "Not only am I not happy, I'm terrified of showing up for work each day. Those ornery old-timers are trying to give me a nervous breakdown. They should be arrested for assault, or malicious mischief, or aggravated hazing."

"Why don't you resign and do what you really want?"

This was it: the chance to salvage her dream. Her heart raced like a speedboat, and she broke out in goose bumps. "There *is* something I vowed to do a long time ago ..."

Odia meticulously laid out her concept for PIEDRA, conveniently omitting the fact that Cozen had promised to fund it with misdirected endowment dollars.

Janus stood. "That's a great idea. If I were chairman of

Kreakey, I would make that a top priority."

Janus's lack of opposition worried Odia. Was she leading her into a trap?

She reasoned that Janus was too principled to stoop to conniving. She could be ambitious without being unethical. "With Cozen out of the way, you would be the chairwoman."

Janus brushed away a fly. "It's more complicated than that. Cozen's mismanagement is ruining Kreakey's public image. If that doesn't change, our wealthy donors will withdraw financial support. Poof. No more Kreakey Foundation. No chance for PIEDRA."

Odia pondered her next move. Could she work with Janus? The board member had a squeaky-clean reputation. It would be nearly impossible to manipulate her. Cozen, on the other hand, had figurative skeletons in every closet, and possibly a few literal ones buried in his backyard.

"I may be able to get information that would strengthen the case against Cozen," Odia said. "Are you interested?"

Janus's sunglasses went back on. "Don't tell me. If you have something, take it to the grand jury."

*Drat.* Surely the woman wasn't completely incorruptible. "Did you invite me out here to come to an arrangement or not?"

Janus leaned on the table. "No. I don't make sneaky, clandestine pacts."

"Then what is it you want? My time is valuable."

"I'm only interested in the foundation's well-being, and *you* are getting in my way. You need to run FRAIL as if your livelihood depended on its success."

"I told you, Cozen put me up to it," Odia said.

"Then I'll fix it so he won't interfere anymore," Janus replied.

Odia stood. "I've been betrayed and bullied enough. I think I'll just quit."

"Then the police would learn a few things about *you.*"

Odia flinched. "You've got nothing on me."

Janus stiffened. "I have Detective Marshall on speed-dial. Shall I make an appointment?"

The woman might be bluffing. Had she uncovered something? What had Cozen told her? *How does she know Detective Marshall? Does she think I'm involved in the fires?*

"Suppose I cooperate. Will you keep quiet? Will you fund PIEDRA?"

"First things first," said Janus. "No further contact with Cozen. Fix everything wrong with FRAIL—facilities and amenities. Fill the place to capacity. And most importantly, *no negative publicity* of any kind. I mean it."

"But that's—"

Janus lowered her sunglasses and glared at her. "I'm giving you thirty days. It's all or nothing. If you succeed, I'll support PIEDRA when I become the head of Kreakey. If you fail, you'll be wearing an orange jumpsuit."

# CHAPTER THIRTEEN

Arriving for work the next day, Maggie noticed the fire truck as soon as she entered the FRAIL driveway. *Oh no. What now?* She hoped the incident was minor.

Police vehicles occupied her usual parking space and the four adjacent ones. She couldn't see any firefighters or deputies, and no hose lines had been laid.

Maggie exited her car and ran toward the main entrance. She yanked open the lobby door and rushed to Lisa's desk. "What's going on?"

Lisa stood and shook her head. "There's no emergency. The rezzies are offering free coffee and donuts to first responders in the coffee shop."

Maggie raised an eyebrow. "But Odia closed the coffee shop."

Lisa smiled. "Someone must have forgotten to tell them."

Maggie set off to assess the situation. There was nothing to stop the strong-willed seniors from commandeering the shop for their purposes, since it wasn't physically walled-off from the corridor. All they needed to do was turn on the lights and make coffee.

Residents and public safety professionals filled the seating area and overflowed into the hallway. Lively conversation and colorful decorations created a party atmosphere. *Where did they get all those helium balloons?*

She saw Helen behind the counter and squeezed her way over. "Was this your idea, Miss Helen?"

"No, dear. Someone else's." Helen put a filter into one of the coffee makers. "Would you like a donut?"

"Um, no. Thanks. Where did the donuts come from?" Maggie asked.

"Donated by the Bad Breakfast diner in town. The coffee and the balloons too."

"I don't suppose anyone got permission from Odia to host this event?" Maggie asked.

"Why would we? We live here. We pay rent and fees. 'We don't need no stinking permission,' as Ed would say."

Maggie frowned and ran her fingers through her hair. "I wish you would warn me about these protests so I can wear my Kevlar scrubs. I always end up getting my rear chewed for not preventing your geriatric antics."

Helen waved her hands. "Oh, hon. You don't need bulletproof scrub pants. This isn't a protest. We're doing something nice for the police and firefighters. They come here so often, you know."

"Yes, but Fang the Ferocious is going to foam at the mouth because you've hijacked the coffee shop, and I suspect that none of your visitors have been signed in. Our security protocol is for your protection."

Helen put her hands on her hips. "They're cops, for goodness' sake, not Washington lobbyists. Not to worry, I'll explain to Odia how you tried to stop us."

"I'm not sure she'll even come in the building once she sees the police cars in the parking lot. She might—"

"Ms. Providence!" There was no mistaking Odia's splenetic squawk. "Did the downtown donut shop burn to the ground? Why are Barney Fife and his friends hanging out in my facility?"

Maggie's jaw dropped. *Did Odia really say that in front of the deputies?*

# # #

Odia scanned the crowded coffee shop. Peace officers and residents alike were giving her threatening looks. The room was as quiet as a soundproof booth filled with mimes.

She felt a tap on her shoulder and spun around.

"Eeek!" The unexpected sight of a geezer wearing a firefighter's breathing mask and holding an ax startled her. "You scared the devil out of me!"

The senior removed the breathing mask. "I doubt that. You're one and the same."

Laughter burst out across the room, easing the tension. Conversations resumed.

She recognized the prankster as Ed. "Are you responsible for" — she swept her arm over the scene — "this intrusion?" She turned away from him and addressed two deputies who were watching her tantrum. "I want this man arrested for burglary and theft."

"We're on break," said one of the officers.

Ed handed the ax to a firefighter and returned his attention to Odia. "I can't stand around here all day arguing with you. I've got to return my library books. Do you have any? I can save you a trip."

Odia felt the rage boiling up within. "Where did that ax go?"

Maggie stepped between the two adversaries, facing Odia. "They're not doing it to annoy you," she said. "It's a community service project."

"Oh, sure," Odia sneered, "and there are no alien corpses in Area 51. How gullible do you think I am? Get this mayhem under control, Ms. Providence!" she shouted over her shoulder as she accelerated toward her office.

# # #

Two days later FRAIL's staff meeting was the usual frenetic

Fangmeister bloviation. Maggie felt like a draftee in a third-world army platoon led by a psychotic drill sergeant. Odia frequently shouted at and upbraided staff members. At least she didn't make them do push-ups.

When the meeting ended, Maggie gathered up her belongings and headed out to do today's BP checks. Helen was at the top of her list—she always had coffee or tea brewing, and Bill was there most mornings.

Maggie had only gotten as far as the reception desk when Odia popped out of her office. "Ms. Providence, you must remember that staff meeting discussions are not to be repeated, understand? Especially not to the residents."

"Yes, Ms. Fangmeister, I know. Is it all right if I tell Josie? She wasn't there because of a final exam. Would you agree that she should learn of your plans?"

"Did I approve the absence?"

"Yes, of course you did," Maggie said, truthfully.

"Well then, it stands to reason that you may discuss it with her. Have you done your blood pressure checks yet? We need to make sure everyone's healthy."

Her last comment threw Maggie off guard. "I'm on my way, Ms. Fangmeister." She rushed to put some distance between herself and trouble before Odia could say more. It took less than a minute to reach Helen's suite. The door was ajar. Maggie knocked. "Miss Helen, it's Maggie."

Helen responded from within. "Come in, hon."

Maggie entered. "Oh, Grampa, I'm glad you're here." She gave Bill a hug. "I'll do the BP checks in just a second," she said, then texted Josie, asking her to call.

Helen placed a cup of coffee in Maggie's hand and gave her a side hug. "Sit down, hon. Today was staff meeting day, wasn't it? It shows. What did y'all talk about?"

Maggie smiled. "Now, Miss Helen, I'm not allowed to say. We have rules about that."

Bill feigned a look of surprise. "Helen, you should know better than to press sweet Maggie for confidential information." He grinned. "She'll tell me later."

Maggie's phone rang.

"Hi, Josie," she answered. The two exchanged greetings, and Josie filled Maggie in on her scholastic ordeal.

"I'll bet you're glad it's over," Maggie said.

"Yes, I am. What did I miss this morning?"

*Bingo.* Maggie could not contain her smile. "You missed staff meeting. Odia said I should fill you in on the discussion." Ordinarily she would take a privileged conversation into the corridor, but she didn't this time.

"Apparently the board is pressuring Odia to fill our facility to capacity. She's planning an open house for prospective residents. She also intends to bring in a film crew to shoot a promotional video. It's all supposed to happen two weeks from now. She's really afraid of it all going wrong, so you mustn't say a thing to the rezzies."

"Did she share any details about the video?" Josie asked.

"A few, but I can't talk right now, if you know what I mean."

Maggie ended the call and gave her grandfather a sly look. "Oops. You weren't supposed to hear that."

"I didn't hear anything," Bill said. He glanced at Helen. "Did you?"

Helen grinned wickedly. "Nope."

# # #

Nearly two weeks later Hamish Macphisted strode into the FRAIL lobby radiating confidence and enthusiasm. This was his first solo assignment for BudgetCom, a local producer of marketing videos.

A tall, older man wearing Air Force coveralls was standing at the reception desk. A gray-haired woman sporting an "Elvis Lives" T-shirt stood next to him. She was speaking with the gorgeous receptionist.

"Good morning. My name is Hamish. I'm from

BudgetCom. I understand you want to make a promotional video."

The receptionist gave him a thorough look-over. "I'm Lisa. You say you're from the video place?"

"My, you're a young one," said the gray-haired woman. "How long have you been with them?"

Hamish blushed. "I'm only an intern. To be honest, this is my first big project. I'm just nineteen."

Lisa handed him a pen. "You'll have to sign in, and you must be escorted at all times. The administrator won't be in today, but she let me know you were coming. Let me see who I can get to accompany you."

"I would be happy to show him around," the older woman said. "Do you have a list of things you want to film, and people you wish to interview?"

"I've never been in a place like this before," Hamish said, "but I'm supposed to tell the story of retired life here. Action shots of the residents having fun would be a good start."

"Oh, look no further. I'm Helen, and this is Bill. We'll help you."

"Absolutely," Bill said, winking at Helen. "I'll go tell the others to get ready for their close-ups. Why don't we film the residents going to breakfast?"

"Great idea," she said, then placed her hand on Hamish's shoulder. "Let's get your equipment."

They unloaded the camera, tripod, and lights from his car and brought them into the building. Helen pointed out the entrance to the dining room. "Set up in the corridor and catch people on their way in. They should be arriving any minute now, so hurry."

Hamish rushed to position his camera and light the hallway.

A parade of eleven residents struggled to reach the dining room. Eight were using walkers, canes, or crutches. Two had their arms in slings, and one had his head fully wrapped in gauze. All, even the bandaged one, wore surgical masks.

"Here they come," Helen said. "Start filming. Quick."

Hamish fiddled with the camera, panning and zooming to capture the disabled diners. He turned to Helen. "Aren't they going into the dining room?"

"Once it opens. There's always a rush to be near the front of the line — to get in before they run out of food."

He hadn't realized that old folks had to compete for food at retirement homes. If this was true of all facilities, it was puzzling why people would accept such an arrangement. Perhaps he should ask.

"Helen, do you think I could interview a few of the residents after breakfast?" he asked.

"You can set up in the prayer room." She showed him where it was. "I'll round up people for you to talk to. Don't wander off," she said, then departed.

It took him fifteen minutes to move the equipment and set up anew. The makeshift chapel was tiny, but it would do fine for interviews.

The door opened. "I've got some interviewees for you," the man in the doorway said.

"Oh, great," said Hamish. "Uh, it was Bill, wasn't it?"

"That's right." Bill entered and held the door open. "Ed, come on in."

Hamish's mouth hung wide open as a rock star impersonator — in full costume and black-and-white face paint — shuffled in and sat before the camera. "Are you —"

"No, of course not," the rocker interrupted. "I'm Dr. Ed Cutter." He offered Hamish a bag of sunflower seeds. "You want some? I was too late for breakfast, so these will have to hold me until lunchtime."

"Uh, no. Thanks. Do you always dress this way, with a wig and a big star around your eye?"

"Have we started the interview? Don't you have to put makeup on me, or something?"

Hamish began to have second thoughts about doing interviews. Maybe he would do this one, just to be polite, then interview Helen. She seemed to be normal.

"No makeup needed," Hamish said. "We're recording now. Let's begin the interview."

"Wait a sec," Ed said. "I don't have my guitar." He went to the door and cracked it open. "Charlie, give me my guitar, will ya?"

Ed came back to the camera, followed by a second old-timer impersonating another member of the same band.

"You didn't tell me we was gonna need guitars," Charlie said.

Hamish worried he was losing control. "Gentlemen, it's not necess—"

"We're being interviewed on video," Ed said. "It's a visual medium. You gotta have your guitar. Otherwise how will people know you're a rock star?"

"No, really," said Hamish, "you don't—"

"But people won't actually see it," Charlie said. "They only do headshots in interviews. You don't even need to wear your boots."

Hamish raised both hands. "Really, it's not—"

Ed kicked off his boots. "Well, in that case, I don't need these"—he stood and began to unbutton his black leather pants—"if they're not going to be on camera."

The argument continued. Ed's boxers remained safely hidden, but only because his rock star pants were too tight to pull off without lying down. Ultimately Ed walked out of the room, sans boots, and Charlie followed. Hamish could hear the two arguing all the way down the corridor.

Bill returned. The friendly face comforted Hamish. He was relieved to speak with a sane person. "I don't think that worked out too well."

"Not to worry," Bill said. "Why don't you come to my suite? You can interview a PCA and show viewers the inside of a luxury apartment."

"What's a PCA?"

"Personal care assistant. The PCAs are the angels who look after us to make sure we're healthy and safe. We love them."

They retired to Bill's suite. Hamish set up his equipment.

Bill's phone rang. "Hi, Maggie," he answered. "Come right in when you get here."

"Is this a luxury apartment?" Hamish asked. "It's very small."

"Yes, but it has its own bathroom. That's why they charge so much, I suppose."

Something nagged at Hamish. Things didn't seem ... believable. He began to worry that his colleagues at BudgetCom had set him up.

The door opened. He turned just in time to behold a very attractive young woman in scrubs. Her smile captivated him. He suddenly wished he was a bit older than nineteen.

"Hi. I'm Maggie," she said, and offered her hand.

"Hello. Nice to meet you," Hamish said, accepting the handshake.

"And you are?" she asked.

"Huh? Oh." He blushed and released her hand. "I'm Hamish."

"Maggie and I are very close," Bill said. "She's the best PCA there is."

She gave Bill a big hug. "Oh, you're so sweet," she said, and kissed him on the cheek.

Hamish wondered *how* close they were. Was there a little mischief going on? Who knew about it? Was it something that he should report?

"Are you ready for us to move to the couch?" Bill asked.

"The couch? Uh, oh, sure," Hamish said.

Maggie waited for Bill to settle in then sat beside him. She took his hand in hers.

Hamish zoomed and panned until their hand-holding was out of the frame, then began recording. "Okay, let's start."

An announcement over the PA system interrupted the interview. "Attention," a woman's voice said. "Anyone finding a set of dentures is requested to turn them in without first trying them on. That is all."

"We're going to have to do the question over," Hamish said. "That was so loud, I'm sure it drowned out your answer."

They re-taped the question and covered two more. Hamish was asking a new question when a second announcement blared from the PA speaker. This time it was a male voice. "Attention. Today's golf cart races are canceled due to circumstances beyond our control. It seems the golf course people came over and took back their carts. That is all."

Hamish had suffered enough. "I think that will do. Thank you." He turned off the camera and started stowing his equipment.

Bill got up from the couch. "Don't you want to stay for lunch?"

"No."

"How about filming our Elvis trivia game in the activity room?"

"No."

"Well, thank you for coming to visit us. We look forward to seeing your final version. Maggie will escort you to the lobby."

Hamish picked up his gear and followed Maggie. He had wasted an entire morning, and for what? He doubted that any of the video was usable, unless it was destined for an episode of *The Twilight Zone*.

# # #

The following morning Odia buzzed Lisa over the intercom.

"Yes, Ms. Fangmeister?"

"Find yesterday's email from BudgetCom and dial me into the conference call they scheduled."

Lisa entered the office. "Do you want to use your headset or the speakerphone?"

"Put it on speaker," said Odia.

Lisa dialed and made sure the call went through. "Will there be anything else?"

Odia waved her away. Lisa exited and shut the door.

"Is anyone on?" Odia's inquiry was met with silence.

A few seconds passed. The speaker emitted a brief tone. "Anna Janus is here," came from the low-fidelity speaker.

"Fangmeister," announced Odia. "The BudgetCom folks are not online yet."

"Did they tell you why they wanted to chat?" Janus asked. "Surely they haven't had time to create a sample video, have they? They filmed only yesterday,"

"I'll bet they want to upsell. You know, get us to buy better background music or special effects. Or maybe they need another week to complete the editing."

Another tone sounded. "Hello? This is Rhonda Howard at BudgetCom. Who else is on the line, please?"

Odia introduced herself and Janus.

"I called to inform you," Howard began, "that we've decided to let you out of your contract. We will, of course, refund your deposit."

"What are you saying?" Odia asked.

"We spent all morning yesterday at your facility, but unfortunately came back with completely unusable footage."

"Absolutely not!" Odia barked. "You can't throw in the towel just like that. Send over another crew. You're under contract. I'll take you to court."

"No we won't," Janus interjected. "At least not until we hear the details."

"It's obvious," Odia said. "They're amateurs and

chiselers. No! Worse — they're amateur chiselers, thinking they can get us to pay more by coming back for additional filming. Well, we're on to their scheme."

"Let the woman explain," Janus said.

"Thank you. In a nutshell we can't produce a quality promotional video by your deadline," Howard said. "At the risk of offending you, I'll be blunt. After reviewing the video clips, we don't believe FRAIL is the safe and caring community you wish to portray."

"No! You lie," Odia blurted. "I'm told that you sent over a squeaky-voiced teen. He was destined to fail. He probably had an attitude."

"Is that true, Ms. Howard?" Janus asked.

"We assigned a young but talented and well-trained intern. He used professional equipment. He tells me that the residents were the ones with attitude."

"I understand," Janus said, "and I will personally come by to collect the footage. We will use it to start an investigation. Ms. Fangmeister will release you from your obligation. If you like, keep the deposit and send a bill for yesterday's expenses directly to me in care of the Kreakey Foundation."

"You can't do that," Odia argued, forgetting that BudgetCom was still on the line. "We need a completed video to attract new residents. There's no time to find another production company."

"You're right about one thing," Janus said. "Time is running out for you. Maybe you should go door to door and hand out discount coupons to prospective tenants."

# # #

Three days later Odia emerged from her office and marched into the lobby. She resented having to work on a Saturday morning. Nevertheless today's carefully planned open house required her full attention, if it was to succeed in attracting new residents.

*Why did Janus insist on filling all the suites with brittle-boned boarders?* Subsidizing luxurious living for old codgers was an egregious waste of funds, in Odia's opinion. *Let them move into their children's basements.* The foundation could put its money to better uses.

Lisa, Maggie, Josie, and Manuel stood there, lined up like soldiers awaiting inspection. Paying extra wages to prepare for and supervise the event ran counter to Odia's frugal nature. *Janus had better appreciate this.* Woe be unto her if she didn't follow through on her promise to fund the PIEDRA project.

Odia faced the staff and put her hands on her hips. "Well? Why are all of you standing around instead of preparing to receive visitors?"

Maggie saluted. "Ms. Fangmeister, we've gone through every item on your checklist. The place is ready to go."

Odia glared at her. "You can dispense with the sarcastic tribute, Ms. Providence."

Lisa held out a surgical mask.

"I won't be wearing one today," Odia said. "Janus insisted on it, so I had my doctor give me a bagful of antibiotic samples. I'll just have to hope they protect me."

Josie raised her hand. "Are you doing guided tours?"

"No. Visitors arrive, sign in, and get a brochure. I need each of you to keep them moving along. Answer questions, but don't let them dawdle. Above all, keep them away from our residents. I don't want potential clients scared off."

"What's Manuel going to do?" Maggie asked.

"Thank you for reminding me." Odia reached into her backpack and pulled out a black T-shirt with "SECURITY" printed in yellow, block letters. "Here, Manuel. Stay in the lobby and look protective."

Lisa's desk phone signaled an incoming call. She hurried over to answer. Maggie and Josie headed over to the staff break room.

Odia paced.

Lisa hung up. "Ms. Fangmeister, that was someone trying to find the facility. They're not sure where to turn off the road."

Odia stopped pacing. "That's why old people shouldn't be allowed to drive. Their poor vision makes them a menace on the highway. For goodness' sake, there's a monument sign at the end of the driveway with eighteen-inch-tall lettering."

Lisa shrugged.

A thought occurred to Odia. "Manuel!"

Manuel and Odia raced outside and looked down the driveway.

She jumped up and down in frustration. "Remove those tarps covering the sign. Pronto!"

"Okay," he said, then hitched up his pants and ambled down the driveway.

She went back inside and made a beeline for the dining room. She burst in on the collection of residents having breakfast. "There will be a reward for information on who covered up the driveway signage."

No one so much as looked up from their plate.

"I'm warning all of you: if I catch anyone defacing property, I'll have them arrested for vandalism—and I'll do it too."

No reaction.

*Fine.* They could ignore her at their own peril. She lurched out of the dining room and wandered the corridor like a zombie in a B-movie. Any troublemakers would be preyed upon and made undead. On second thought maybe a facility of immortal instigators wasn't a good idea.

# # #

Odia had been patrolling the corridors of FRAIL for ten minutes when Lisa called to tell her that a visitor with questions was waiting at reception.

It was a short walk to the lobby, where Lisa introduced

Odia to a tall, well-dressed man who looked too young for FRAIL.

"I'm not here for myself," the man said. "I'm checking to see if this place might be suitable for my parents."

"What's your question?" Odia asked.

"I was wondering why you think you need to charge visitors for parking."

"We don't."

"There's an older gentleman outside wearing a lime-green safety vest and a surgical mask. He collected five dollars from me as soon as I got out of my car."

"Lisa will refund your money. It's a mistake." She dialed Josie. "Ms. Ditzski, you've got an inmate charging people to park. Make him stop."

An elderly couple walked up to Odia. "Excuse me. Are you in charge?" the man asked.

"I'm the administrator," Odia replied.

"I'd like to know what caused the health department to rope off your coffee shop," he said.

"Has it been closed long?" the woman asked.

"What? No. I closed it because the residents did not use it enough to justify its expense," Odia said.

The couple looked at each other. "But there's caution tape all over," the man said, "and big red signs saying it's in violation of health codes." He showed her a photo he had taken with his phone.

She scanned the lobby for Manuel and spotted him inspecting the contents of a female visitor's purse. "Manuel! You're not the TSA. Get over to the coffee shop and take down the tape and the signs. *Arriba!*"

Odia turned back to the couple. "One of our residents is playing a practical joke, it would appear."

A gray-haired man with a long ponytail joined the conversation. "I heard your explanation for the coffee shop. I'm surprised they haven't shut down your entire facility." He turned to the couple. "Did you notice the bags of trash just sitting in the hallway?"

Odia felt the panic and frustration that came upon her whenever she lost control of a situation. "What? That's not—"

The man with the ponytail turned his phone screen so the couple could see it. "I just took this picture five minutes ago. I talked to a resident who told me that sometimes the trash stays out two days or more. Eventually they give up and take it to the dumpster themselves."

"That's an outright lie," Odia said. She turned and raced down the corridor. "Manuel! Manuel!"

She encountered Maggie in front of the activity room.

"Manuel's taking down the yellow tape around the coffee shop. Can I help you?" Maggie asked.

"Why is there trash in the hallway? Get rid of it. Get rid of it!"

"Josie's got it nearly cleared up. I was busy trying to explain to a guest that the dining room doesn't serve hot dogs and tapioca pudding for lunch every day."

"Who said they did?"

"There was a menu posted on the door. Obviously a fake one."

Odia's eye twitched. The open house had devolved into a chaotic nightmare.

The PA system crackled to life. "Attention," a gravelly voice said. "This is a reminder that the pest control guy will spray for bedbugs again tomorrow. Be sure he sprays your apartment if you're still seeing them."

Odia ran back to reception at full speed. "Lisa!"

She skidded to a halt at the desk. "Who's been on the PA?"

"That announcement didn't come from here," Lisa said. "The same thing happened when that video guy was here."

Odia thumped the desk with her open hand. "Don't tell me those reprobates have learned how to activate the system remotely. Call Sonic Paging right away and ask them how to disable it. Hurry — hurry!"

She turned away and noticed an older couple making their way to the front doors. The man was tall and thin. He wore a faded brown sweater with missing buttons. Odia grabbed a promotional brochure and intercepted them. "Thank you for visiting. I'm the administrator." She offered the leaflet. "This has our contact information, rates, and amenities."

The man declined the flier. "You're delusional if you think anybody would ever want to live here. Someone told me the satellite TV is always on the blink. I also heard that you don't have laundry services. That sign tells it all."

"What sign?"

"The one right behind you."

Odia whirled around and caught sight of a black sign affixed to an easel. The words "Days Since Last Clash With Management" were printed in bold white letters. Beneath that statement, styled after numbering on a scoreboard, was a large, yellow double zero. Odia snatched the notice from the easel, stomped into her office, and buzzed Lisa. "Open house is over. Have Maggie and Josie round up all the visitors and kick them out. I'm going home."

# # #

Monday morning, Odia entered her office through her private entrance and slammed the door. The weekend's disastrous open house irritated her like a poppy seed wedged between her molars. All the alprazolam in the world could not alleviate her exasperation with those ancient antagonists.

*Keep your eye on the prize.* A weaker competitor would have given up hope when faced with a sure loss in the bottom of the ninth. She would not despair, though. All she needed was a pair of back-to-back home runs. Just sign up two tenants before the end of the week. It could happen. She would make it so.

First things first. She buzzed Lisa. "Get Manuel in here."

"He doesn't come in today until 3:30, Ms. Fangmeister."

"The kitchen staff called him to unclog a sink. He'd better be over there."

Odia wrote three goals on an index card:

1. *Lease the two empty suites*
2. *How do I punish the tenants?*
3. *Make Janus fund PIEDRA*

She stared at the list. The first would be done today if all went according to plan. The second was underway and would present no problem at all. She had hatched a plan for the third, back when Cozen chaired the board. Although Janus was now acting chairman, Odia was confident the plan was still sound.

Lisa's voice came over the intercom: "Manuel is here, Ms. Fangmeister."

"Let him in." Odia needed him for item two.

The door opened and Manuel entered with shoulders hunched. He removed his ball cap, held it with both hands, and locked his gaze onto his shoes.

"You're not in trouble, so stop with the sad puppy act," Odia growled. "I want you to paint the hallways — black with vertical yellow stripes."

"You want me to find somebody? I have a cousin — "

"No *familia*. You're going to do it, starting today."

He ran his hand over his freshly buzz-cut hair. "I think I will need to buy an airless esprayer. It will save time."

"Did you say sprayer?"

"Airless esprayer," he enunciated carefully. "Ees like a pump. You put the hose in the paint" — he used his hands to illustrate — "and the motor push paint to espray gun."

Odia struggled to envision the machine. "Do you mean those big tanks with the noisy air compressor?"

Manuel shook his head. "No, *Jefe*. These ones are small. No tank. They not loud."

"Oh." She wondered if this might be the answer to a

problem that had been nagging at her for months. "Can you use one to spray other liquids?"

He gave her a puzzled look. "You mean something else different from paint?"

She nodded.

He nodded.

"I can't hear the rocks in your head. Are you saying yes?" Odia asked.

"*Si.*"

Odia reached in her drawer and extracted a blank purchase order. She filled in the name of the local hardware store and signed at the bottom of the form.

"Here. Go buy the paint and two of those airless sprayers. One for you, and one for me."

"You are going to help me?" he asked, wide-eyed with disbelief.

"Don't be silly. When you get back, bring a sprayer to my office. Do it now. *Pronto.*" She kicked off her shoes, slipped on a pair of hiking boots, and began lacing them.

"You going four-wheeling?" Manuel asked as he turned to leave.

"None of your business." She picked up the phone and buzzed Lisa. "Hold my calls for the rest of the day."

# CHAPTER FOURTEEN

The opening to Jackrabbit Cave was not easy to spot. There were no signs or improved trails to guide one to it. Odia had been to the small, underground limestone cavern only once before. That was years ago when she belonged to the "find meaning through expensive hobbies" crowd. Here, Odia had experienced her first—and last—caving expedition. Climbing over sharp rocks in the dark had utterly failed to inspire her.

Today's trip to Jackrabbit was for a different reason altogether. The cave was the perfect out-of-the-way place to host a secret meeting. That is, if she could find it. She stood on the imaginary line from the highway milepost to the unmistakable rocky peak in the distance. *It should be here.* Perhaps she had not gone far enough.

"Fangmeister!" called a voice from off to her right.

Odia glimpsed Cozen, less than twenty yards away, dressed in jeans and a maroon T-shirt.

She trekked over to him. The cavern entrance—a narrow, horizontal slit on the face of exposed caprock—was visible directly behind him. "How long have you been here? Where did you park your car?"

"I came in the hard way, in a four-wheel-drive," Cozen said. "I should also tell you I'm not alone. An associate of mine is watching the cave. If I don't leave first, he will be most unkind to you."

"Let's go in and get out of the sun."

"I'm not crawling on my belly to squeeze through that gopher hole," Cozen complained.

Odia thrust a flashlight at him. "Don't be difficult. You can stand comfortably once you get past the narrow opening."

He got down on hands and knees and backed into the darkness. "You and your paranoid, obsessive-compulsive, neurotic eccentricities. Okay, I'm in."

She followed, headfirst.

They stood side by side, like two kids holding flashlights in a cool, dusty closet.

"What is this deal you want to make with me?" Cozen asked.

"Are you aware there's a grand jury looking into your dealings?"

"It's supposed to be a secret," he said.

"Ah. So you *do* know."

He waved his free hand. "They've got nothing on me— or at least nothing that will stick."

"I've got something they would like to have—an audio recording from the laundromat."

He backed away. "You contemptible … weasel."

"I'll give you the tape if you agree to lease two units at FRAIL."

"Why should I do that?" he asked.

She reached into her back pocket. "You might want to read this transcript of the tape."

Cozen read the front of the page, then shined the flashlight beam in her eyes. "The Wicked Witch of the West was a saint compared to you."

She nudged his flashlight aside. "Surely you have clients whose trusts would never notice modest outlays for apartment rent."

208

"I thought you wanted to close the place down."

"That didn't work. Try to keep up," she said.

"Won't phantom tenants arouse curiosity?" he asked.

"If anyone asks—which I doubt—I'll say they're retired spies. You know, very stealthy."

Cozen sighed and pointed his flashlight at the ground. "When do you want this done?"

"I need signed leases and deposits by tomorrow afternoon."

"When do I get the tape?"

"It's already at a secret drop zone. When I get the forms, I'll text you the location."

He pointed the light into the cavern depths, dimly highlighting crumbling stalagmites on the floor. "Okay. But let's be clear—I'm not helping you anymore after this."

"You're either fearless, or foolish," she said. "Here you are, under investigation, and still you're willing to breach your fiduciary duty to your clients."

"It's no big deal. And anyway, I won't get caught. Now let's get out of this dungeon. You first."

Odia's eyes narrowed. "Nice try, Brutus. Not with your henchman waiting outside. By all means, you lead."

# # #

There were only two other customers at the Road Sign Diner on Tuesday morning. Bill poured creamer into his cup. "I wonder if all of these road signs are reproductions. I'd hate to think the restaurant owner was pilfering real ones."

Helen smiled. "It's interesting décor, for sure, but I miss the coffee shop at FRAIL. The cappuccino was really good, and it was cheaper than this place."

Bill nodded. "Yup. And you didn't need to ride a cab to get there."

"It was vicious of Odia to remove all the appliances from the shop after we served the police and fire crews," she said.

"If only we had thought to hide the coffee makers before she could take them out."

Helen took a sip. "Well then. Let's hear about this call you had with Janus."

Bill reached for the sugar packets. "She surprised me by discussing her plans openly over the phone. She used to be so careful at first, not wanting to meet at FRAIL, for example."

"That's because she trusts you a lot more these days, and she may also feel she's got Odia and the Kreakey board right where she wants them."

"I wouldn't know about that," Bill said. "Janus plays her cards close to the vest. We know she's trying to sack Odia, but she's also up to something else. I suspect she wants to dethrone the board chair as well."

The waitress brought over a carafe of fresh coffee, set it on the table, and took their breakfast orders. "Holler if you need anything. Your plates will be right out," she said.

Helen topped off both of their cups. "Out with it. Tell me what she said."

Bill grinned. "She said to holler if we need anything."

Helen gave him a scornful look. "Silly, I mean what did Janus say?"

"Janus asked if I knew of any rezzies who wanted to leave, but were afraid to break their lease."

"Why would she want to know? She's not the administrator," Helen said.

"She didn't explain her reasons, but she did say she would waive the usual penalties for those who want to leave before the end of September."

Helen shook her head. "I thought she was on our side. She sounds like Odia — wanting to kick people out."

"No, I don't think that's it. She made it clear she doesn't want to pressure anyone. If I had to guess, I'd say she's looking for a quick way to cut revenue and make Odia's life difficult."

"Oh, I get it," Helen said, her pensive look changing to one of recognition. "She's not satisfied with thwarting Odia's recruitment efforts—she wants to go a step further and un-recruit rezzies."

"Bingo." Bill pushed his cup to the side in preparation for delivery of his meal.

Helen gazed into the distance. "Let's see ... I know Emily Crankshaft has been looking into assisted living. She might be ready."

"And what about Buddy Krebs?" Bill said. "He spends more time in hospitals and rehab than he does at FRAIL. He needs even more help to get around than Emily does."

"We can't tell Janus about them unless they agree."

Bill took a paper napkin and wiped a few stray drops of coffee from the table. "I agree. We would have to talk with them first."

"What do we say?—'Hey, are you ready to go into a nursing home?'"

"I think we should tell the rezzies about the offer, as a group," he said. "Whoever wants to can contact Janus directly. We shouldn't be in the middle of it."

"What else did you two talk about?" Helen asked.

"We kicked around some ideas for adding a little drama to move-out day—assuming anyone decides to leave. Trouble is, September thirtieth is only three weeks away, so we've got to get a move on, pardon the pun."

"You'll have to fill me in on the plan," Helen said. "In the interim I'll be creating some drama of my own if our breakfast doesn't appear very soon."

# # #

The user's guide for Odia's airless paint sprayer turned out to be as useless as an inflatable dartboard. The first fifteen pages exclusively contained warnings against using the device for certain tasks, including spraying paint. The

211

manual included an exploded view of the gadget, which might have been helpful except that the illustration was labeled in Chinese. The last four pages enumerated specific items and usage conditions not covered under warranty.

She threw the booklet into the wastebasket and sat on the edge of her desk. Sprayer parts were scattered on the floor. She would have to find Manuel and ask him to demonstrate its setup and operation. Then she would chastise him for not having started on the hallway repainting.

Someone was calling her mobile phone. *Oh, good.* It was Janus. She couldn't wait to tell her about having leased the empty suites.

"Fangmeister here," Odia said.

"I'm giving the board a status update today," Janus said, "and I need to know how things are progressing on your end. Let's start with the facility repairs."

"We've started repainting, and I've ordered the upgraded hallway light fixtures."

"I'm glad to hear that. How was your open house?"

Was Janus asking out of curiosity, or did she already know what had happened? It might be best to evade the question.

"Let's focus on results," Odia said. "You'll be thrilled to learn that I have, here in front of me, signed leases for the two vacant suites."

"Did they pay the fees and deposits?"

"Absolutely."

"Did these new tenants attend the open house?" Janus asked.

"I couldn't say."

"Why not? Weren't you there?"

Odia felt a momentary pang of anxiety, but quickly rallied. "I'm no good at remembering names and faces."

"When do they move in?" Janus asked.

"It's complicated. I'll let you know later."

"Is anybody moving out soon? That would count against you."

"Nobody's going anywhere."

"How can you be sure?" Janus pressed.

"We're all one big, happy family here at FRAIL."

"That's a load of meadow muffins," Janus said.

Odia internally debated raising the subject of PIEDRA funding. On the one hand she had complied with her end of the deal. On the other hand, until Janus was chairman of the board, she would be unable to commit Kreakey Foundation funds to new causes.

"I've done my part," Odia said. "Do you intend to keep your promise?" *It can't hurt to ask.*

"Do you mean funding your paranoid junkie junket?

"Paranoia Intervention Education and Drug Rehab Assistance—PIEDRA," Odia said.

"Goodness knows you need it. I said I'd find the funds when I became chairman."

Odia seized the opportunity to flatter her. "It's a cinch. As soon Cozen is indicted, he'll have to step down. Then the board will crown you—the best-qualified and the most visionary among the directors."

"May I give you some advice?"

Odia rolled her eyes. The flattery must have gone to Janus's head. "Yes, please do."

"Stay on top of things. A single vacancy, or just one item of bad publicity, and our deal is off."

# # #

A week later, in FRAIL's theater, Bill counted noses. *Fifteen rezzies.* That was everyone, not including himself.

He scanned the crowd methodically, row by row, face by face. "Today is the last of September, and that means it's move-out day. Thank you for getting up early and coming to say good-bye to Emily and Buddy. I am confident that I speak for all when I say that we will miss them."

213

The rezzies applauded.

"Now let's review today's agenda. A fleet of twelve-foot moving trucks will show up in less than fifteen minutes. Of course, only two are needed—one for Emily and one for Buddy. The others are decoys meant to panic Odia."

Applause broke out again.

"A crew from Conglomerated Moving will take care of loading Emily's and Buddy's goods. The other company will simply scatter boxes and blankets around the facility to make it appear that the rest of us are also shipping out."

Charlie raised his hand. "Who is paying for the fake movers?"

"That's a fair question," Bill said. "Anna Janus is covering all costs out of her own pocket, and that includes expenses for Emily and Buddy. The whole thing was her idea."

"What's her angle? I mean, why would she do that?" Charlie asked.

"The best I can figure is Janus wants to help us eject Odia," Bill replied.

Charlie furrowed his brow. "Why doesn't she just throw her out?"

"It's not that easy. This entire mess is like a soap opera and a spy novel all rolled into one."

Helen stood. "Listen, everyone, please don't impede the movers. I suggest we have breakfast in the dining room and stay there until the excitement is over.

"Won't Odia catch on?" Martin asked. "After all, none of us have given notice, and the fake movers can only fool around for so long."

"Remember," Bill said, "this is simply one part of a complex scheme. If I understand Janus's plan, Odia won't have time to figure things out before she's confronted with something even more urgent."

"She's gonna blow a gasket," Ed said, "and we'll get blamed for cooking this up. Then she'll probably retaliate by installing pay toilets in our suites. Anna Janus had better claim responsibility."

"Don't worry, she will," Bill said. "She's coming over this morning."

"Did she tell you why?" Ed asked.

Bill ignored the question and glanced at his watch. "Oh, look. It's time for breakfast. Save me a seat. I'll be there shortly."

He left the theater and strolled over to Lisa's desk. From there he could see the parking lot through the front windows. *Here we go.* The first of the moving trucks was pulling up.

"Good morning, Lisa."

Lisa had just arrived and was busy stowing her purse. "Hello, Mr. Armstrong. Is there something I can help you with?"

"Has Ms. Fangmeister come in yet?"

"Mmm-hmm. I saw her car in the lot. Did you want to speak with her?"

"No, but I think she might want to know that the moving trucks have arrived."

# # #

There were two sharp knocks on Odia's reinforced office door before it swung open.

Lisa appeared. The panic on her face was disconcerting. "You've got to see this. Moving trucks. Lots of them. It's practically a convoy."

Odia sprang from her chair and ran to confront the invading army.

The driver of the lead vehicle climbed down from the cab just as Odia arrived. He hitched up his pants and spit. "You Emily Crankshaft?"

"Do I look like someone with one foot in the grave? Can't you see I'm not an overripe retiree? I'm the administrator, and I demand to know why you're here."

215

"We're movers. See the gigantic letters on the truck?" Odia placed her hands on her hips and tried to appear menacing. "Don't get all snarky with me. I want you to get in your truck—"

A TV news van sped up the driveway and screeched to a stop alongside the second moving truck. Faye Kanooze climbed down from the passenger side.

"You!" Odia pointed at Faye. "Get off this property right now."

"Can you confirm the rumor that FRAIL is closing its doors for good?"

"Where did you hear that? It's a lie, but I'm not allowed to speak to the media, so go away."

The camera operator walked up, stationed herself near Faye, and handed the reporter a microphone.

Faye took the mic and looked into the lens. "This caravan of moving trucks behind me could be all that remains of a once-lively retirement community. Residents here appear to be moving out en masse, perhaps protesting the allegedly intolerable living conditions. Or could it be that they have been evicted wholesale? The administrator—"

Odia jerked the microphone out of Faye's hand. "Lies! Lies! Nobody's leaving. We're not closing."

Maggie emerged from the building and walked over to the scene.

"Ms. Providence," Odia said, "get rid of these scandalmongers. Call the sheriff if you have to."

Maggie shook her head and placed a hand on Odia's shoulder. "Lisa says Anna Janus is on the way with your permanent unpaid-leave package. Her helicopter should be here anytime now."

Odia gasped, ran to the middle of the parking lot, and scanned the sky. "Ahhhhhhh! This can't be happening."

The *thump-thump-thump* of the approaching chopper grew louder by the second. She ran inside, reached behind a

216

large decorative planter, and produced a chain and padlock. Fighting adrenaline-induced jitters, she looped the chain through the push bars of the lobby doors and clicked the lock shut.

"Lisa, don't answer the phone," Odia said as she flew past the reception desk. Sweat trickled down her face, and her heart galloped.

She propped open her office door. With shaking hands she opened the bottom drawer of a file cabinet and retrieved a heavy box covered in caution labels. *I didn't want to do this, but they've gone too far.*

# # #

The chopper landed in a cloud of dust, just east of the patio. Janus exited the helicopter, followed by her companion. The pilot stayed behind and shut down the engine.

Janus noticed Maggie on the patio, waving her arms. "Has it all gone south already?" Janus asked.

"Odia's padlocked the lobby doors, but we can get in this way," Maggie replied. She led them to the patio door and entered the access code on the keypad. The door automatically swung open, and they entered.

They reached the residential wing hallway, only steps away from where it intersected the admin corridor.

Lisa turned the corner at full speed and nearly ran head-on into Maggie. "Odia's hiding out in her office. I think she's snapped. Her eyes are bulging and she may be foaming at the mouth."

"Calm down," Maggie said, putting her arm around Lisa. "It'll be okay. This is Ms. Janus."

"We've spoken over the phone," Lisa answered.

"Hello, Lisa," said Janus's companion. "Remember me?"

It took a few seconds for Lisa to recognize him. "Roger! You've grown a beard." She hugged him. "Are you coming back?"

"Yes, he is," Janus said. "He will be reinstated as administrator as soon as we've dislodged the present regime."

They rounded the corner. Rezzies crowded the admin corridor. Maggie cleared a path by easing individuals aside and suggesting they seek shelter in their suites.

"Roger, maybe you should stay here for now," Janus said.

Janus acknowledged Bill and another male rezzie standing at the end of the corridor where it emptied into the lobby. Beyond them a wild-eyed Odia Fangmeister stood in front of the reception desk, holding an object that resembled a garden hose spray gun. It was attached to a long hose that wound its way into the office area. To Janus's horror Odia was wearing safety goggles, chemical-resistant gloves, a surgical mask, and an x-ray protection apron.

Janus turned to Maggie and lowered her voice. "Call the sheriff—just in case. Have Lisa meet them outside where Odia can't see." She returned her attention to the mad scientist at reception.

"Anna Janus!" Odia said. "Do you know what I'm holding?"

"Looks like you're ready to wash someone's car."

Odia gave a maniacal laugh. "The end of this hose sits in a bucket of highly radioactive liquid. All I have to do is squeeze the handle, and I'll make this facility permanently uninhabitable—unless I get my way."

"Is this about Pedro again?"

Odia stomped her feet. "PIEDRA! PIEDRA!"

"Well, you didn't keep your side of the bargain. You failed."

"The game was rigged. I was set up to fail and—" Odia pointed to something behind Janus. "Get those reporters out of here. Now! Or I'll hose them down."

Janus turned and glared at the news crew. "You promised to stay out of sight. Please back off." She focused on Odia again. "Do you mind if I ask you where you got this allegedly radioactive material?"

"What difference does it make?" Odia said.

"You could be bluffing, for all we know."

Odia backed up a few steps. Using her free hand, she reached for the open box she had set on Lisa's desk, grasped a flap, and hurled the empty carton across the lobby. "There. It's the package that the concentrate came in."

Janus stepped forward and picked up the box. Aside from the main label identifying its contents, every square centimeter of the parcel was hidden beneath warning stickers.

"Ms. Janus," whispered Bill from behind her. "Charlie was a nuclear physicist. No kidding. Let him look at the package."

Without taking her gaze off Odia, she handed the carton to Bill. "What does he think?"

Charlie stepped forward and took possession of the box.

"What are you doing over there?" shouted Odia.

"We're verifying the authenticity of your threat. You don't mind, do you?" Janus said.

"With a bunch of senescent stooges? What do they know?"

Charlie shook his head. "It's dangerous all right. Radioactive iodine-131. We'll be okay as long as she doesn't spray it."

Janus turned to Odia. "You appear to be telling the truth."

"Hey, Fangmeister!" Charlie shouted. "How much liquid do you have?"

"More than enough. Now don't interrupt. I'm talking to Janus."

"Tell us what you want, Odia, so we can end this standoff," Janus ordered.

"Close this place down and spend the endowment

money on PIEDRA."

"That's legally impossible. It's also unethical and unjust."

"Cozen was willing to do it!" Odia snapped.

Janus sighed. "Cozen was indicted today. That should tell you something."

"Serves him right. Look, he explained it to me. We can use our variance powers. It would be completely legal."

"I don't have the authority to agree to your demands."

"Then you need to figure out how to get it. Otherwise I'll turn this place into Chernobyl."

Janus scowled at her. "Would it be all right if I made a phone call?"

"You'd better not call the cops. Come over here and use Lisa's phone."

Bill placed his hand firmly on Janus's shoulder. "Stay put."

"Odia, I won't let you take her hostage," he bellowed.

"You keep out of this," Odia warned. "Your meddling is what got us to this point."

Charlie shoved Janus aside and half shuffled, half marched straight toward Odia.

"What are you doing?" Odia shouted. "Stay back. Stay back."

A chorus of shouts called out for Charlie to abandon his spontaneous assault.

"I'm putting an end to this pointless posturing," he growled and continued his advance. "Put down that sprayer, you nasty nudnik."

Odia squeezed the sprayer lever with both hands, dousing him with a jet of malignant moisture.

Charlie kept going despite the soaking.

"Ms. Fangmeister, STOP!" Maggie screamed.

Odia aimed the stream at walls, windows, ceiling, and floor, shouting, "I warned you! Never cross Odia Fangmeister."

Charlie lunged for the spray nozzle but she swung it out of reach. She stopped spraying, pushed him against the reception desk, then aimed the nozzle at Janus and charged at her.

Two steps into her assault Odia lost her footing on the wet floor and went down like a beginning ice skater.

# # #

Charlie saw Odia hit the floor face-first. She had let go of the spray nozzle during her tumble. He had to get it before she did.

The hose ran right beside him. *How lucky.* He reached down and gave it a good yank.

Momentarily stunned by her sudden contact with the ground, Odia recovered and attempted to stand.

Charlie swung the hose like a baseball bat. The heavy metal nozzle whooshed along an arc and connected with the side of Odia's head, causing her to collapse faster than an unstuffed rag doll.

"Charlie!" Maggie shouted. "Move away from her. Go sit in Lisa's chair. Help is coming."

A deputy wearing a hazmat suit was running down the corridor toward the lobby. Two fire trucks were coming up the driveway.

Charlie sat down. "I'm all right."

"Why did you do that, Charlie?" Maggie asked. "You're contaminated now."

"No, I'm not. Honest, there's no danger."

The suited officer knelt down and checked Odia for signs of life. "She's gonna have a whopper of a headache when she comes to."

Two deputies without protective garments strung crime scene tape across the hall. "Nobody is to enter the lobby," one of them commanded.

"Really, it's safe," Charlie said. "Iodine-131 has a half-life of only eight days. The label on the box says it's over three months old. Ninety-nine percent of the isotope would have decayed by now."

A pair of firefighters in hazmat suits ducked under the yellow tape. One used bolt cutters to undo the chains on the doors. The other took readings with a Geiger counter. "There's no danger," he reported.

Paramedics entered through the main entrance and hovered around Odia, who was beginning to regain consciousness.

"Charlie Newcomb!" Wilma shouted from behind the crime tape. "They told me what you done. Is you tryin' to make me a widow? I can't leave you alone for twenty minutes—"

Bill put his arm around her. "It's okay, Wilma. You're married to a real hero."

Cheers broke out in the corridor, which had filled with rubbernecking rezzies.

"I'm no hero," Charlie said. "I simply had enough of that mangy malefactor."

# CHAPTER FIFTEEN

The Monday after Odia's meltdown Anna Janus led an emergency meeting of the Kreakey Foundation board of directors, minus Morris Cozen. She had just completed recounting the drama of the prior week.

"Have the police picked up Morris?" asked Sam Antone, the longest-tenured director on the board.

"Cozen must have anticipated his indictment, because he is nowhere to be found," Janus replied. "Detective Marshall asked me to enlist your cooperation. If any of you know where Cozen might be hiding, please contact the police."

"How are things at FRAIL?" Sam inquired. "Has Roger righted the ship?"

"As far as operations go, the facility is running smoothly, and the residents are glad to have him back in charge. On the other hand it will take a while to straighten out the bookkeeping fiasco that Odia left behind."

Sam walked to the head of the conference table and stood beside Janus. "Well, that's the first thing you need to do as Kreakey's new chair … er … chairwoman? Chairperson? I don't know what to call you."

Janus smiled. "Chairman will be fine. I'd like to thank the board for their faith in my abilities."

Sam reached out and shook her hand. The other directors applauded briefly. "The other challenge you face, Ms. Janus, is restoring the reputation of the foundation. Our donors are none too pleased with what has happened."

"I'm sure we can win back their support," she said with confidence.

# # #

Bill knocked on Philippe's door. "Hurry up," the Colonel said. "I haven't got all day."

Philippe emerged at once. "Pardon, Colonel Bill, but I was turning on the *musique classique* for Orson so he will not be bored while I am away."

"It's a town hall meeting. You'll be gone less than an hour."

"General, wait for me!" Ed shouted from several doors down.

"Oh no," Bill mumbled.

The three turned into the admin corridor and Ed broke the silence. "I wonder if they're serving snacks now that Roger is in charge again. I hope it's not tapioca pudding, though."

"You'll eat whatever they've got and you'll like it," Bill snapped.

"I'm just saying Roger's been back over a week already, and he's had plenty of time to stock up on pistachio ice cream," Ed said.

"Monsieur le Doctor," Philippe said, "if you want so much to have the *crème glacée*, then why do you not buy it yourself?"

"Why don't you leave me alone," Ed replied, "and go watch Jerry Lewis or something?"

Roger was standing at the doors to the dining room, smiling and greeting residents as they entered. "Colonel Armstrong, how wonderful to see you. Have I told you

224

lately that I'm so glad to have your granddaughter on staff? Everybody loves Maggie."

Then Roger turned to Philippe. "I heard your lease allows you to keep a comfort ferret. We'll have a welcoming party next week so you can introduce him to everyone." Roger patted Philippe on the shoulder and reached past him to shake Ed's hand. "Ed Cutter, you're looking well. I've signed you up to play air guitar at talent night. Be sure to put on your rock star wig and face paint."

"Let's go in," Bill ordered before Ed could protest.

Crepe paper streamers and helium balloon centerpieces created a bright and cheery mood. Wilma came up to the table as Bill and his buddies were taking their seats.

"It's been a long time since we've seen this place decorated," she said.

"It looks great. Did you do all this?" Bill asked.

"Helen helped me with the balloons, and Josie dragged in a ladder and hung the streamers."

"Why didn't Manuel do that?" Ed asked. "Lazy bum."

"He's gone," Wilma said. "Didn't show up for work this week, and nobody can get ahold of him. Josie says Roger is looking for a replacement."

Ed snorted. "Did anybody call the jail?"

"Enough of that," Bill said in a stern tone. "Wilma, tell Charlie I'm going to the air museum next week, and he's welcome to come along."

"I'll tell him. Oh, look, here come the snacks. See y'all."

Bill stared in horror as a server approached with a tray of blue gelatin parfaits in stemmed glass bowls. *You've got to be kidding me.*

Ed laughed. "You'll eat it and you'll like it. Isn't that what you said?"

"So I did. Let's hear what Roger has to say."

Roger fiddled with his lapel mic and grinned. "Did ya miss me?"

The rezzies cheered and clapped, undiminished, until

Roger signaled them to stop.

"I'm glad to be back at FRAIL, the friendliest independent living community in the Southwest. Let me begin this town hall gathering by addressing a concern several of you shared with me. A hazardous spill cleanup outfit checked the lobby right after our unfortunate incident. Rest assured, there is no danger. In fact one of the technicians told me a bunch of bananas is more radioactive than the foyer—no kidding—because they have potassium isotopes, or something. I see Charlie Newcomb nodding his head over there."

Ed stood and said, "Speaking of Charlie, he deserves recognition for conking our psychotic sociopath on the skull. Stand up, Charlie."

Charlie rose from his seat. The intensity of acclamation and table-pounding was far greater than what Roger had received earlier.

Roger resumed, "While we're on the subject of Ms. Fang—"

His audience booed and hissed, drowning him out.

After a brief pause the reinstated administrator continued, "All I was going to say is that an acquaintance of mine at the newspaper tells me Odia is being held without bail while awaiting trial. She will likely be charged with aggravated assault, and as an accomplice to arson and fraud, all of which are felonies. She may also undergo psychiatric evaluation. I'm sorry you had to suffer because of her actions."

"I feel sorry for her shrink," Ed blurted.

Roger continued, "Now some good news: the coffee shop will reopen next week."

Shouts of approval and clapping filled the room.

"Free coffee and donuts for the first month," he added.

More clapping and whistling followed.

He listed several more perks and improvements, then stopped and waited for the crowd to quiet down once more.

"Finally, I have been assured by the Kreakey Foundation that everyone's lease will be automatically extended by one full year with no fee increases."

Roger nodded to Josie, who was patiently waiting at the back of the dining room. She flipped a switch on the karaoke machine and Kool & The Gang's "Celebration" began to play.

Philippe leaned toward Bill. "Well, Colonel, it looks like your campaign to *expulser* le Fang has turned out better than expected, *non*?"

"It surely has," Bill replied, "but don't give me credit. The real progress came when I stopped trying to plan every little detail."

"What will we do now that we do not have zee chaos to fight?"

Bill rubbed his chin. *That's a great question.* "I suppose we should take advantage of being retired and go on a long trip to recover from our adventures."

# EPILOGUE

Odia sat in the tiny conference room at the Timor Remedium Inpatient Program residential treatment facility. *I'm not getting anywhere.* Six months had passed since the standoff in FRAIL's lobby. In that time she had been charged with multiple felonies and struggled to eventually find a defense lawyer who would take her case. She was sent to TRIP in exchange for pleading to lesser charges and promising her lawyer to hire someone else next time.

A three-hour drive from FRAIL, in the capital city, TRIP was housed in a converted 1930s-era residence. Odia blamed the traffic noise by day and streetlights at night for her frequent migraines. *I hate this place.*

A tall, thin woman stepped into the room. "You are Odia?"

"Who the heck are you?" Odia asked, fixating on the woman's bright-red hair, which was pulled tightly into a bun.

"I am Clinical Director Böser Traum," the woman said with a marked German accent.

Odia's eyes narrowed. "That's not your real name. That means bad dream."

"Perhaps I am," said Traum.

"What happened to Smiley, the previous director?"

Odia asked in a panic.

"He did not verk out. You deal viss me now. You may not like me but I don't care." Traum crossed her arms. "Why do you persist with these meetings? It is highly irregular."

"Because someone must do something about the wretched conditions here," Odia growled. "For one thing, where is your security? People haven't given up trying to get me just because I'm in a nuthouse."

"Yah. Der previous director warned me about you. After two months of therapy still you think someone means to harm you? That will not do. I believe you are faking to prolong your stay."

"You don't understand," Odia complained.

"*Nein*. It is you who does not understand."

Odia sprang from her chair. "Oh no? What good are the therapists, the group sessions, the tests, and the meds?"

"This is leading-edge treatment," Traum said. "You don't like it?"

"No, I don't," Odia replied. "It's all talk and drugs. I want to get off of the meds. Look, I have novel ideas for treating anxiety. You should listen to me."

"So you know more about psychology than we do? I have ideas too. I can remove you from group therapy and send you to community service at das Regional Recreation Center, where you vill read stories to the senior citizens."

Odia gasped and turned pale. "Are you trying to do me in? I can't go near geriatric germ-carriers. That's inhumane treatment. I'll report you, if I'm not killed first by an unhinged old-timer."

"Furthermore," Traum continued, "Helga will take you to get a library card so you can check out books."

Odia stomped her feet. "No! Don't do that. You know I'm a library fugitive."

"*Das ist unsinn*. Utter nonsense."

"This is stupid. There's no good reason for keeping me

here," Odia grumbled.

Traum put her hands on her hips. "Nobody is holding you. Perhaps Frau Fangmeister would feel safer in prison? That may be arranged with a phone call."

Odia glared at her. "You sound like you *want* me to leave."

"It would certainly make life easier on everyone here, for sure," Traum said, then turned and left the room.

Odia stared out the window for several minutes, pondering the situation.

*I'll do it.* She got up, shut the door, and locked it. *Why does everybody treat me so badly?*

Odia walked up to the dry-erase board, pulled the cap off the red marker, and began writing:

*I've been abducted. See, I told you they were out to get me and they finally did. It's no good looking for me – you'll never find me. But I'll find those who got in my way – especially Faye Kanooze and Bill. They had better watch their backs.*

She dragged the conference table against the door, slid open the window, removed the screen, and climbed out. Then she ran across the parking lot and followed the sidewalk to the nearest arterial street, just a block away. She checked her pockets for cash and scraped up a little over five dollars. *I wonder how far this will get me on the city bus?*

<<<<>>>

How did you like *GeriAntics*?

Thank you for purchasing this book

If it made you laugh, we would appreciate it if you would tell others about it. We also encourage you to post a review.

# About the Authors

Carlos and Crystal married in 1989. They have now been married longer than they were single.

Carlos retired from the high-tech industry after thirty-one years. He is a railfan and enjoys operating his model railroad when he isn't riding or photographing real trains.

Crystal is also retired, after writing computer programs for eighteen years. She's been a hard core figure skating fan ever since she watched Dorothy Hamill win her gold medal in the 1976 Winter Olympics.

They have been inspired over the years by the wit, wisdom, and determination of senior citizens. *GeriAntics* attempts to capture the humorous side of leveraging those assets.

Made in the USA
Monee, IL
03 December 2019